Steampunk Sleuths

Want more thrilling anthologies from Black Beacon Books?

The Black Beacon Books of Mystery
The Black Beacon Book of Ghosts
The Black Beacon Book of Horror
The Black Beacon Book of Pirates
Tales from the Ruins
A Hint of Hitchcock
Murder and Machinery
Shelter from the Storm
Lighthouses
Subtropical Suspense

www.blackbeaconbooks.com

STEAMPUNK SLEUTHS

Edited by
CAMERON TROST

**BLACK
BEACON
BOOKS**

Steampunk Sleuths
Published by Black Beacon Books
Edited by Cameron Trost
Cover art by Greg Chapman
Copyright © Black Beacon Books, 2025

Tears of the Dragon © S.B. Watson
Murder in Whitby © Karen Bayly
The Untimely Death of Clockmaster Tollsmead © Cameron Trost
The Copper Train © Diana Parrilla
The Strange Case of Private Ornshaw and the Martian Detective © David Turnbull

Black Beacon Books
blackbeaconbooks.com

ISBN: 9780975611814

You were probably thinking we couldn't get any more imaginative when it comes to anthology themes here at Black Beacon Books—and yet here we are. After *Subtropical Suspense*, *Lighthouses*, *Shelter from the Storm*, *Murder and Machinery*, *A Hint of Hitchcock*, and *Tales from the Ruins*, it's time for *Steampunk Sleuths*. This latest publication brings you five novellas that will get the gears of your mind turning. We've added a twist to the traditional detective story by asking our talented authors to set their puzzles in a steampunk or clockpunk world. The result? As captivating as you would expect—a locked-room mystery with an ingenious murder weapon, pirates roaming the skies in airships, a case to crack in a Japan that could have been, *The World of the Worlds* revisited, and strange happenings in Whitby.

Steampunk Sleuths takes the most intriguing elements of the mystery tale and lets them shine in a speculative setting, like gaslight on a foggy night. Clockwork crime and mechanical murder. Steam-powered puzzles and airborne adventure. Forget Poirot's "little grey cells"—you'll be needing "little brass cogs" for this anthology.

The game's afoot, by Jove!

- Cameron Trost, editor

Black Beacon Books would like to thank our patrons, whose passion for great fiction and independent publishing helped make this anthology happen.

If you'd like to join the team and reap the benefits, subscribe on our Patreon page at: *patreon.com/blackbeaconbooks*

The five patronage tiers are
Shipwreck Survivor, Moonlight Smuggler, Sea Witch, Assistant Keeper, and *Lighthouse Keeper.*

TEARS OF THE DRAGON
S. B. Watson

In the hills of Katsuragi,
I walk foot-dragging in the morning mist,
And weep to walk alone;
My husband lies in Fukakusa,
And will never hunt again.
I will hide as a quail in dewy fields,
And dream in grass-pillowed sleep,
Alone with my grief.
Will he come for me then,
And raise his bow to pierce my heart,
As he did so long ago?

Envoy

In Katsuragi I am aimless with grief,
Alone upon my grass-pillow bed,
I travel in my dreams,
To my husband in Fukakusa.

- Anonymous poet, from *The Man'yōshū*

The distant lights of the daimyo's procession wound slowly beneath the trees. Although the morning sky had begun to brighten the eastern horizon, the valley defile that wound below the vaulted city of Tengokuyama was still draped in shadow. From the third-floor balcony of the Yuyami Teahouse, Aoyama Ohatsu watched the indistinct lights beneath the trees, their shifting illumination rising through the boughs, until they disappeared into the mountain haze.

The night had been full, the hanamachi of Tengokuyama vibrant with song, dance, exhibitions of skill and craft, poetry, and of course, feasting and drinking. It was the night prior to the daimyo's departure for Edo. Under the law of sankin-kōtai, all daimyo were required to alternate yearly between their castles and the imperial capital. It followed, then, the night before they left, the hanamachi—"flower towns"—would overflow with the patronage of the samurai attending their lord on his journey.

A summer-sweet wind gusted along the old wooden balcony where Ohatsu stood. It was soft and cool against her cheeks, playing refreshingly through the elaborate folds of her hair. After an entire night of poetry, musical performance, and repartee, Ohatsu could feel the ragged looseness of her Shimada hairstyle, the untucked imbalance of her tightly girdled kimono, and, most unpleasant of all, the dried sweat beneath her arms. For all that, she accepted the breeze with a thankful sigh, and turned to re-enter the empty chambers of the teahouse behind her.

For geisha of Tengokuyama, the night before the daimyo-gyōretsu was always full. Grace and beauty were expected to be implacable, and wit and conversation limitless. It was a taxing performance in the best of years. For Ohatsu, however, and all the geisha of Yuyami Okiya, this night had proved especially difficult for one other reason—one of their geisha was missing.

Alone in the teahouse room, Ohatsu took a moment to tighten the folds of her kimono, and tried in vain to re-brace her elaborate hairstyle, before giving up and venturing into the mazelike building.

Soft voices murmured through paper-thin shoji walls as she moved swiftly down narrow wood-braced corridors. The tatami mats beneath her wooden geta sandals softly pillowed her weight as she navigated the twisting hallways. Occasional gas-globes flickered with a mesmerizing rhythm against the walls. The brassy notes of a shamisen, played by expert hands, reached her as she descended a delicate stair to the second story and opened a sliding door to the outside.

A wooden skybridge arched away from the teahouse, curving over another such bridge, a story lower, towards the multi-storied Yuyami Okiya, her geisha house's living quarters.

The sun had broken the horizon now, warm shafts of golden light cutting across the bridge and nestling through the hanamachi's interconnected web of buildings. Ohatsu walked across the bridge as quickly as propriety would allow, enjoying the warmth even as the lower wing of her hair began to slip. Below, the other bridge stretched from a garden walkway along the city's fortified wall to a raised courtyard in the center of the hanamachi. From there, bridges flowered out to other buildings, built around, within, and through each other with dizzying complexity. Taverns, inns, other geisha teahouses, and elegant brothels, were all laced by delicate bridges of woven wood and brass. In the morning light, gas-globes flickered throughout the hanamachi like wandering fireflies.

Ohatsu hurried across the bridge. Beautiful as the morning was, she wasn't eager to meet anybody in her disheveled state.

At the okiya, she took a private passage—normally reserved for servants—that wound along the backside of the building, to her own chambers where she threw open the shutters to the sun.

It had been eighteen days since Ryuzoji Ai had been seen. Ohatsu had heard tales of maiko becoming lost in the nestlike neighborhoods of the hanamachi, and once a kamuro—a young courtesan in training—had been found wandering on the other side of the city itself, dazed and disoriented. But in either case, no longer than a day had elapsed before the confused girl was found.

And those missing girls had been young. Inexperienced. Not the most senior geisha of a house.

The sunlight caught small particles of dust in the air, falling on the three-panel changing screen standing on the floor. A narrow, black table stood before it. A few lacquered-wood chests sat against the wall. Two sleeping mats lay on the floor. Ohatsu took a deep breath and knelt before the table, looking at the room that she and

Ryuzoji Ai, her oneesan, had shared.

For her whole life, Ai had been there. As babies, they were given to the Okiya. As children they played along the old hallways and rooms. As girls they practiced dance and poetry. As women, they learned grace and wit. And in all things, Ai, the older of the two, had excelled. She graduated from maiko to geisha first. And in the entire hanamachi, Ai was the only geisha honored to become Hitodama—the trusted position of a wandering performer, allowed to leave the city limits.

And now, she was missing.

The wooden shoji-door rustled as it slid across the lintel. Slowly, Ohatsu's maiko—a young girl named Kiku—stepped into the room, her bright furisode kimono shimmering in the sunlight.

'Oneesan,' Kiku said, her eyes large, 'are you only returning now?'

Ohatsu smiled. 'You shouldn't see me like this, Kiku.' She sighed and lifted her sleeved arms, the kimono drooping.

'Let me help you,' Kiku said, stepping closer.

Ohatsu stood and, with Kiku's assistance, loosened the large obi belt holding the kimono in place, resituated the kimono folds, and then held her arms out as Kiku retied the obi.

'How did you know I was back?' Ohatsu asked, as Kiku folded the obi tightly at Ohatsu's back.

'You took the private passage?' Kiku asked.

'Of course. I didn't want to be seen!'

'The boards creak. It's right above my chambers. You are the only one, Oneesan, who ever uses that passage. So...' Kiku tightened the tuck and stepped away. 'Better?'

Ohatsu turned to the lacquered black table, peering at her reflection in a polished brass mirror. 'Now help me with the hair.'

'You're going somewhere? After spending the whole night—'

'There's someone I need to see,' Ohatsu said.

'Who?' Kiku asked, beginning to gather the loose curls of hair into tighter folds.

'Ukifune.'

The Funeiricho Brothel was high in the hanamachi, sprawling across the tops of three buildings. Narrow bridges made of spindly wood crisscrossed the buildings—in the rising sun, the brass highlights on the bridges sparkled like spun gold.

The windows and shoji-doors of Ukifune's apartments had been thrown open with the sun, and a cool breeze drafted through the open space. From the windows, Ohatsu could see her okiya, across the hanamachi, perched by the battlements of Tengokuyama.

In a rustle of garments, Ukifune stepped from behind a long folding screen, her silk brocaded outer kimono draped across one arm, and walked past Ohatsu to a set of ornate tansu cabinets. She laid the kimono over the cabinet door, and began to undo her under kimonos, casting a sideways eye at Ohatsu.

'Your hair is slipping,' Ukifune said, the suggestion of a smile curling the corner of her mouth.

Ohatsu shifted uneasily in her place by the windows.

Ukifune was tall, with long, graceful lines. A famous poet had once likened her to a willow, bending in the snow. Watching as Ukifune slipped out of kimono after kimono, her long arms fair and smooth, the skin of her chest and shoulders shining in the morning light, each movement, casual though they were, seductive in their measured simplicity, Ohatsu felt suddenly shabby in her muted geisha attire.

'I'm sorry to call on you so early,' Ohatsu said, reaching up and again feeling her sagging hair, 'but you were the last person to see Ai—you knew her as Mitsuhana—and, well, I wanted to ask…'

'I see,' Ukifune said, as she draped the last kimono over the cabinet. Only a simple under kimono remained covering her nakedness. 'You think I can tell you more than I already told the magistrate?' She turned, and began slowly pulling the long brass hairpins from her hair, still tied with black silken ribbons, the symbol of the Hitodama.

Ohatsu shook her head slightly. 'No,' she said. 'I just wanted to know, for myself.' In the large, open room her voice sounded very small.

Ukifune's brows rose, and she seemed to consider a moment before placing the last pin on the cabinet and lowering her hair. 'The business of Hitodama is confidential.'

13

'I know, but—'

'In the whole hanamachi, there were only the two of us—of course, not counting those geisha or courtesans who have retired. Now there is one. Myself. You understand what you ask of me?'

Ohatsu was silent.

Ukifune crossed the room and lowered herself to a long futon, leaning against a wooden pillow. 'Is Tenkoguyama not enough for you? Are you asking me for your oneesan? Or are you prying for her position? Either way, you ask for treason,' Ukifune said. Her voice was suddenly sharp. 'Tengokuyama is a holy city, and its people are holy residents, held separate by their lord. The outside world, girl, is corrupt. To ask about it, then, is to corrupt yourself. Do you think being Hitodama is a blessing? It's a burden.'

Ohatsu sank to her knees and bowed her head. 'Please,' she said. 'I don't ask as a geisha of Yuyami Okiya. I ask you as Aoyama Ohatsu, a girl who has lost her sister, and desperately wants her back. I don't care about…any of that.'

'You're speaking treason.'

'Then report me,' Ohatsu said, raising her head and looking up at Ukifune. 'I don't care. I'm only saying what I must.'

Ukifune was motionless on the futon, dark eyes locked on Ohatsu, a gentle snarl on her small, perfect mouth.

After a succession of silent moments, Ukifune spoke. 'We descended through the Dragon's Gate,' she said. 'Ai, myself, and a small group of serving girls. At Yokidani's gatehouse, we met a reception from Nikkō, as is customary. They took us up Boiler Street to the hanamachi. There, we separated, Ai going to the teahouse, myself to the brothel…'

Yokidani, Boiler Street, Nikkō… Ohatsu leaned forward. Sweat began to prickle her hairline. Ukifune spoke of secrets. Secrets which, although rumored in the drinking houses and alleys of Tengokuyama, were as foreign to Ohatsu as the mysteries beyond the morning horizon.

'After that,' Ukifune continued, 'I saw her rarely. Twice we attended parties in the hanamachi, and once…' the courtesan paused, as though considering how much to say, 'and once we were both in the Hanging Garden. After our stay in Yokidani, our groups rejoined for the trip to the gatehouse. Ai was not with us.'

14

Ohatsu opened her mouth to speak, but Ukifune cut her off. 'I asked, I really did,' she said. 'Her servants were there. They simply said, one evening, she never returned from the Hanging Garden. So, we all ascended, again by the Dragon Gate, and I returned to Funeiricho.'

'She just…disappeared?'

Ukifune shrugged, her shoulders slipping from the loose kimono. 'A few days after our return, the magistrate came and asked me the same questions. I told him what I just told you.'

Ohatsu rose, the morning sun blinding her. 'Thank you,' she said, turning to leave.

'Wait,' Ukifune said, still bathed in the shadows of the room. 'You've just elicited an act of treason, Ohatsu.'

'What else can I do?'

For a moment, Ukifune was silent, then Ohatsu heard her sigh, long and deeply. 'Look,' Ukifune said, 'officers of the magistrate have searched here, *and below*, for your oneesan. Neither have found her. You won't either, unless…'

Ohatsu took a step, closer, lowering her head from the sun's glare. 'Unless…what?'

Ukifune's gaze shifted, for the first time since they'd spoken, and drifted uneasily. 'Funeiricho,' she said, 'is well stocked, no?'

Ohatsu frowned. 'What do you mean?'

'Rice, fish, saki, fruit, fresh flowers, the finest silks from Sakhalin… See those flowers, there?' Ukifune pointed to a display of peonies in a crystal vase. 'I request them special.'

'I don't understand.'

'The Dragon Gate is but one way, Ohatsu, below the city. Our servants, for example, regularly travel below, at the Fisher's Gate, for supplies.'

Recognition dawned slowly on Ohatsu. 'Are you suggesting…'

'As Hitodama, I of course have the power to deputize anyone I require, any servant I require, for provisioning…'

The breeze blew against Ohatsu, bringing with it the tang of pine trees from beyond the city's walls, as well as a peculiar odor she'd never been able to identify—something sharp and tannic.

'Why?' Ohatsu asked.

Ukifune smiled, and pulled the black ribbon from her hair. 'I had

15

an oneesan once, too.'

The private chambers of Naohana, the okasan of Ohatsu's geisha house, were dim and cool as Ohatsu kneeled and watched the serving girl carefully pour tea for her and her house-mother.

Naohana was gaunt beneath her robes, the style of her hair respectable and muted—her only adornment twin red and black ribbons, her obi plain. But her eyes were soft as she responded to Ohatsu, and her voice gentle. 'You have asked every day,' she said, 'and every day I have answered with all I know. Today will be no different, Ohatsu.'

'Naohana-san,' Ohatsu said, lowering her head, 'I've committed a sin.'

She heard the older woman sigh, and felt Naohana's small hand grip her shoulder.

'Sit up,' Naohana said. 'The only sin you've committed is loving your oneesan too much.' Naohana shook her head. 'I'm worried that I already know what you're planning... Ohatsu, I can't condone—'

'What else can I do?' Ohatsu said. 'Ai is everything to me.'

Naohana took the teacup and gently sipped the still liquid. 'Ohatsu, the honor of your daimyo should be everything to you.'

'I know, but—'

Naohana shook her head sharply. 'I can't stop you from doing what you choose, child.' She shrugged. 'I also can't allow what I fear you will ask of me. However, I can't forbid it either, if your questions remain unspoken.'

Ohatsu looked up. Naohana evaded her gaze, smiling softly.

'Give me three days,' Ohatsu said.

Naohana laughed. 'You overworked yourself, child, last night. You're exhausted, and in no state to perform. I am of course forced to postpone your appointments...'

Ohatsu reached out and took the older woman's hands in her own. 'Thank you.'

'The truth is your right,' Naohana said. 'Seek it if you must. Just be warned, child, sometimes—'

A distant crash broke the serenity of Naohana's chambers. Both women turned towards the sound—a hissing clockwork of movement. Harsh voices carried through the paper screens. Soft steps swished close in the passage beyond the room, followed by a rhythmic stamping. The hissing clank grew louder.

Naohana and Ohatsu sprang to their feet as a partition slid aside and two maiko stumbled in, dropping to the floor immediately and lowering their heads to the ground.

The towering figure of a samurai loomed in the doorway. Dark armor glistened wetly in the dimness of the room. Tatami-mesh hoses snaked beneath the armor, twisting with the man's movement. Glints of brass steam-reservoirs glimmered beneath the joins of his suit, hammered into a scale pattern. His sloped helmet shadowed his face. Armored tatami hoses rose along his neck like ruptured veins, disappearing into the helmet.

At his side, a long katana trailed in its wooden saya like the tail of a dragon.

Naohana and Ohatsu dropped to the floor, lowering their heads.

'Get up, woman,' Tanaka Hatsutaro growled, stepping into the room, the armor rustling like mechanical leaves. 'The missing geisha… Have you found her yet?'

Naohana struggled back to her feet, murmuring obsequiously, 'No, my lord Tanaka-sama.'

'Take me to her rooms, then. Now.'

Naohana moved quickly across the chamber. Ohatsu remained where she knelt, face against the tatami. Hatsutaro walked slowly past her, his scale-armored boots crinkling the reeds as he stepped, leaving a wet residue, as though his armor itself sweated under its weight.

A partition slid open. Ohatsu waited until the thunderous footsteps receded before sitting up, shaking.

The sun was well risen when Ohatsu stepped into her chambers.

The folding screen was shredded, strewn across the room in tattered pieces. The futon mats had been cut open, the cabinets

17

rifled, every drawer opened. Clothes, kanzashi hair adornments, ribbons, kimonos, all thrown about the room in disarray. The black-lacquered desk sat askew on the floor, one leg partially broken, the drawers shattered before it. Papers littered the room. Spilled ink splattered the wall.

Hatsutaro had searched with a rapist's hand.

Ohatsu's knees gave out. She stumbled to the mats before the table, her hand striking one of the drawers and breaking the fragile wood.

Why was this happening? Just *what* had Ai done? As was his imperial right, Hatsutaro hadn't explained anything. Merely came, pushed his way in, destroyed what remained of Ohatsu's sense of peace, and left. She picked up the broken pieces of the drawer, trying to put them back together, as though their reconstruction would mean something, a welling building in her breast.

Then, just as the first tears were about to fall, Ohatsu stopped, and frowned.

Leaning forward, she gathered the drawer pieces together, and laid them out. She lifted them to the table.

The drawer that she held didn't extend all the way to the back of the table.

Carefully, Ohatsu peered into the empty recess. Nothing. She put her hand inside, and felt along the seasoned wood.

Something clicked, and a drawer she had never seen before fell out onto the floor.

Hands shaking, she picked it up.

There was a folded patch of fur cloth, banded by thin twine. She lifted it out. Beneath that, papers, covered in Ai's unmistakably measured writing. And tucked into the corner, a small, brass device.

Ohatsu lifted the mechanism from the drawer and held it up to the light.

It was a small box, delicately machined, fitting easily into the palm of her hand and only a few finger-widths tall. The sides were thick, made of polished wood; the edges were rounded off and covered by corner guards of tarnished brass. On one of the sides an arrow was etched. In the center, a peculiar mechanism seemed suspended like a faceless dial—hundreds of narrow, brassy rods, all pointing inward, like weird teeth, apparently hinged within the

18

frame.

Ohatsu stood and stepped towards the window for a better look.

The box snapped and clacked in her hand. She startled, almost dropping the thing.

The teeth had changed.

Ohatsu moved to the window, holding the arrow pointing forward, and every few steps a tooth from the arrow-wall levered down into the box. She stepped to the side, and a few teeth on the corresponding wall snapped down, while a few teeth from the opposite direction snapped up.

Frowning, she put the contraption back in the drawer and looked at the papers.

Nothing but Ai's poetry. Ohatsu read.

'I stand and wait,
Rain falling on my kimono
Like the patient tears of a dragon.'

Stumbling, Ohatsu shuffled along in the line of servants moving toward the Fisher's Gate in Tengokuyama's Merchant Quarter. Her wooden sandals caught on the polished cobbles of the street. Her hair was bundled upon her head in a simple bun, and she wore the plain robes of a commoner, robes Ukifune had given her.

The instructions were clear. 'Your name will be added to the servants' roster,' Ukifune had said. 'At the gate, don't say anything. Just wait, with your head down. You will be carrying a basket with provisions. You can hide your supplies there, at the bottom.'

The basket felt coarse and brittle in her hands, the woven fiber biting into her smooth skin.

'Won't your servants wonder who I am?' she had asked.

'My servants stopped wondering about my whims long ago.'

The sun hung high above her.

'The afternoon is a strange time for a journey to set out,' Ohatsu had said, when Ukifune gave her the time the servants were to leave. 'Why in the middle of the day?'

To which Ukifune gave a veiled look. 'In Yokidani, there is no night or day.'

The gate towered above Ohatsu, tall stone foundations jutting up from the dirt-and-cobble street, heavy wooden ramparts fixed above them.

The procession stopped.

Ohatsu was faint with tiredness. She hadn't slept in a day and a half. But this wasn't the time to drowse. A guard took the documentation from the head servant, read it briefly, glanced down the line, his gaze passing Ohatsu without a second thought, and turned to the gate.

Orders were called. A frenzied whirring churned the air, as hidden flywheels spun to slow the mechanism that raised the massive door. The passage yawned like a gaping mouth, gaslit dimness flickering inside. The servants silently trudged forward.

Ohatsu turned and took one last look at the sprawling city atop the mountain before she was engulfed by the darkness of the gatehouse. The gate mechanisms thrummed the air around her, and the door closed, sealing her inside.

Chapter Two

The gatehouse was a long building with low, intricate roof rafters, similar to the storehouses Ohatsu had occasionally visited on okiya business. Although dimmer than outside, it was by no means dark—gas-globes burned brightly, nestled among the sweeping roof beams, casting warm, yellow light across the sprawling enclosure.

Ohatsu shuffled along in the line of Ukifune's servants, her heart beating quickly. For the moment, the heavy beckoning of sleep was put behind her, replaced by a strange anxiety. She had never been inside any of the gatehouses—she had never been outside the city. Her eyes roamed the building as she walked, devouring everything she saw.

A maze of aisles filled the building, winding back and forth towards a central, rectangular enclosure where a large gated platform—perfectly circular—rose from the ground. Narrow guard stations stood like tall, thin houses, amid the bristling labyrinth of fences, flickering gas-globes hanging from their roof-eaves. The aisles were wide—easily wide enough to pass a small cart or wagon —and Ohatsu saw many different pathways through the maze, towards the enclosure, no doubt to help organize a great flow of people.

Today, however, Ohatsu's group seemed to be the only travelers there. Most of the guard stations were empty, and only a few held sleepy attendants that watched with barely concealed boredom as they entered the aisles.

Ohatsu followed the path the head servant took through the maze, cutting through side-gates to directly approach the central enclosure. The air was strangely moist, sodden with an aroma of cattle, poultry, fresh-cut wood, spices, and other foreign smells Ohatsu didn't recognize, including the tannic scent she'd noted earlier. Leaning forward, she wiped the sweat on her brow against her coarse sleeve as she walked.

When they reached the center of the building, approaching the great, circular platform, an elderly attendant stepped from the cramped darkness of a guard shack that was slightly larger than the rest. He was a narrow man, in a thick, tattered kimono. Brass-rimmed glasses shimmered on his face as he spoke quietly to their leader, a scrolled piece of paper unfurled in his hands, eyes skimming across their ranks.

Again, the man's gaze passed Ohatsu without comment. She lowered her eyes to the ground. After a moment, the man nodded and returned to his station. Another attendant unlatched the gate to the circular platform and the procession filed inside, climbing a gently sloped ramp of well-trodden wood.

The platform was built of heavy oak, thick rings of iron recessed into the planks for securing large loads. Great chains stretched up from the edges of the platform to large, spiked wheels, their axles pinioned through the heavy rafter beams. From these wheels the chains ran through the rafters into strange iron boxes suspended below the roof, where they were coiled in enormous spools.

One by one, the servants climbed to the platform and sat. Ohatsu followed suit and squatted, sitting on her heels.

Calls broke out across the gatehouse. Above them, the iron-boxed contraptions began to hum and hiss, and the spiked wheels

21

ground to life. The platform lurched downward, and jolted to a stop. One of the servant women screamed softly, quickly stifling her cries. The other servants grinned. The sudden movement had thrown Ohatsu's heart into her throat. She hunkered lower, bracing her hands against the wood.

Again, the wheels groaned to life, more measured this time, and the platform began to lower down a stone-walled pipe. Wet vapor curled up the sides, wisping along the planks. The same pungent odor Ohatsu noticed earlier stung her nose.

'What is—' she began to ask, but her voice trailed away as the platform suddenly broke into open air.

Stretching away hundreds of feet below her was a city. Nests of flickering light, tucked in sprawling wooden complexes, covered the cavern floor like brittle moss, bristling along the steep rock walls. For as far as Ohatsu could see, the jagged cityscape crawled back into the heart of the mountain, following the wending basin of a subterranean valley. At the bottom of the valley, a languid, yellow river flowed in turbid roils. Among the puzzle of buildings there was movement—the indistinct wraiths of people, milling across boardwalk streets and lining rickety balconies.

Turning, she followed the play of the valley downward with her eyes. The city continued along the rocks, creeping along the sickly course of the strange stream to a vast opening in the cavern. Ohatsu's breath caught in her throat—outside, trees bristled. Hundreds of pines, standing tall, their boughs interlaced. For her whole life, she had looked down at those trees, from the fortified city above. Never had she seen them from the side... Tengokuyama parks had small quercetums of oak and stands of stunted black pine, but nothing approaching the sprawling majesty of the forests below.

As she gazed, the platform continued to lower until the vast cavern mouth loomed above her and the city rose on either side. Tall scaffolded buildings glimmered from the light of a thousand lanterns. Vapors and smoke drifted across the streets, filling the cavern's air like misty clouds.

Ohatsu crept to the edge of the platform and peered down, towards the gatehouse below. This one was open, built without a roof. The chains that stretched down from the platform to stabilize its journey were disappearing into dark recesses in the gatehouse floor.

The platform lowered into the gatehouse with a grinding thud, slamming to a halt inside a circular depression. Attendants opened the gate. The servants rose, retrieving their baskets. Ohatsu scrambled to her feet and followed them out, her legs trembling softly. The servants walked quickly, following a familiar path through the fence-maze and out of the gatehouse, into a vapor-swept city street.

'What *is* this?' Ohatsu asked, to no one in particular.

'It's Yokidani,' a servant girl beside her said, a snobbish smirk on her pert face. 'The City of Steam.'

In Yokidani's streets, all sense of scale was lost. Jumbles of buildings, built in elaborate complexity of vapor-blasted wood, arched above Ohatsu, every structure endlessly connected to the next, towering over the roads and alleyways. Gasps of noxious yellow mist drifted through the streets, settling through the hives of buildings like smoke curling through kindling. Everywhere was the glitter of old-fashioned lanterns, the rattle of cart-chains, the calling of voices, the braying of donkeys, clutter of chickens and geese, punctuated music, laughter, and voices arguing in dialects Ohatsu had never heard.

The ground beneath them alternated between slick rockface and wooden planks as they wound their way through the city, climbing further into the sleepless night of the cavern. They crossed the stream Ohatsu had seen from above, then later crossed it again, on narrow plank bridges. The yellow water seemed smoky and thick, flowing with unnatural slowness, and reeking with that mysterious pungent odor.

'What is that smell?' Ohatsu asked the servant girl.

'Sulfur.'

Above them, the cavern ceiling was bathed in darkness, except for pockets of gleaming light. Platforms hung up there, and Ohatsu could just make out the sloped-armor outlines of men-at-arms, suspended in guard stations above the city.

'Finally,' the servant girl muttered as they exited an alley onto a long, wide plank-road. 'Nikkō Hanamachi.'

The flower town sat at the edge of the city, nestled into the wall of the cavern. Tall buildings spired up into the gloom, glittering like enormous lanterns. A mossy stone wall wound around the miniature neighborhood.

The city thinned abruptly nearing the hanamachi. Beyond it, the cavern continued, following the turgid stream, into the heart of the mountain. Ohatsu looked further up the incline. Slick plains of stone swept into darkness. Soft lights glowed in the distance, in muted phosphorescent colors. Here and there, nettled clumps of brassy light broke the gloom.

'What's out there?' Ohatsu asked, hesitating beneath the open gate of the hanamachi.

The servant girl merely smiled. 'The boilers,' she said, slipping into the hanamachi and disappearing into the shadows of a nearby building.

Asa Ochaya—the teahouse of Nikkō Hanamachi—was a long, low building, twisting like the coils of a snake around consecutive private gardens. When Ohatsu handed her introductory papers from Ukifune to the teahouse's kenin—a thin, mousy girl with a sharp face—the girl frowned and looked Ohatsu up and down.

'The kitchens are that way,' the girl finally said, blandly. 'Tell them Yome sent you.'

Ohatsu bowed, and walked quickly away.

For the next three hours, Ohatsu carried tea—and other delicacies—back and forth between the gardens, watching the Nikkō geisha and courtesans entertain their patrons. Most of the guests of the teahouse seemed to be of the merchant class—middle-aged men in loose robes with rough, weather-beaten faces, along with their servants and attendants. The women, also, were rougher, less veiled in their conversation, coarser in their music, more openly sensual. Yet, the practice of the arts was still there. Ohatsu watched from her servant's vantage, unseen, as geisha led their patrons into endless paths of conversation, playfully cornering the dull minds of the merchants before releasing them, drawing them into a web of poetry and culture. She watched as wandering hands were gently deflected —something geisha in *her* okiya would never have permitted at all —and saw courtesans slip away with the more earthy men, and some women, to shoji-wreathed pergolas, glimmering with lantern light. She brought hot towels and refreshments to the love beds, where courtesans lay in languid knots with their benefactors.

Contraceptive sea-sponges were required by the courtesans, prior to their acts of lovemaking. Ohatsu delivered them and watched with lurid fascination as they inserted the sponges into themselves. She delivered special teas as well—herbal concoctions to prevent pregnancy—to the courtesans in their private resting chambers, and blushed at the explicit anecdotes and crude jokes they shared among themselves, away from the ears of their customers.

It was a rougher world than the only one Ohatsu knew. And yet, even in the steam-snarled depths of Yokidani, a semblance of order prevailed, the geisha leaving sex to the courtesans, the arts of culture and seduction remaining ever delineated.

Yome was always present, her mousy figure hovering along the edges of the servants, watching, always watching as Ohatsu struggled to perform her duties innocuously.

Finally, as Ohatsu carried a small tray of contraceptive teas down a lantern-lit back hallway, Yome appeared from a side chamber and beckoned.

'What are you doing here?' Yome hissed, sliding the door closed behind her.

Ohatsu shrugged. 'You read my papers. I'm—'

Yome shook her head vigorously, stepping closer and taking the tray from Ohatsu. 'You're no servant,' she said. 'You're geisha.'

Ohatsu stammered—an experience new, and altogether unpleasant. 'No, I'm—not at all, I work for—'

'You've balled your hair, you've scrubbed off that silly makeup, and put on servant's clothes... But you can't hide the walk you spent your whole life learning. I'll ask one more time. Who are you, and why are you here?'

Ohatsu bowed her head. 'My name is Kome. I've come from Ukifune's household, to—'

Yome moved in a flutter of motion, pressing close into Ohatsu, the short kaiken blade glinting from its wooden sheath. Ohatsu startled, moving back, but Yome caught her, pressing the blade up, holding the keen edge against her throat.

Their faces were inches apart, Yome's dark brown eyes tracking back and forth to Ohatsu's. 'I don't appreciate spies trying to infiltrate my service,' she whispered, loose strands of hair falling across her face. 'Especially bad ones. There's nothing you can say now, girl, but the truth. Speak. Or my blade will speak for you.'

'My name is Aoyama Ohatsu. I am a geisha of Yuyami Okiya, in Tengokuyama, and I'm searching for my sister.'

Yome's eyes narrowed. The knife edge bit into Ohatsu's neck. She felt a sudden, stinging warmth, that trickled down to her clavicle. 'What's your sister's name?' Yome asked.

'Ryuzoji Ai. But you probably knew her as Mitsuhana.'

Yome's slender body was tense, coiled like a spring against Ohatsu's.

'Please,' Ohatsu said, closing her eyes and lifting her hands in a sign of acceptance.

Slowly, Yome relaxed, and withdrew the sharp edge from Ohatsu's throat. Taking a sudden breath, she stepped away, wiping the blade of the kaiken on a cloth from the tea tray, and sheathed it in its wooden saya. 'I knew her,' Yome said.

Ohatsu took a step forward, but her knees buckled beneath her, and she fell to the tatami floor.

'Sorry,' Yome said, looking down at her, 'but you've walked into something, Ohatsu, you might not walk back out of.'

'What do you mean?'

Yome stepped closer and kneeled, bringing her face closer to Ohatsu. 'You're in a den of spies, Ohatsu. And we're all more than ready to kill.'

The paper screen slid aside and Ohatsu followed Yome into the unlit chamber, a small porcelain oil lamp guttering in Yome's hand. The room flickered in the orange light as Yome moved from corner to corner, carefully lighting a series of candles, each prick of light brightening the cramped chamber.

A matted futon lay crumpled in one corner, beside a takamakura pillow—a tall, cushioned prop on which a geisha could rest her head without damaging the ornate tresses of her hair. Kimonos lay in scattered disarray across tansu cabinets, a spare obi was draped over a brass mirror. A low desk in one corner held a few ink-stained pages upon which poetry had been practiced, in scratchy blotches.

Yome turned to Ohatsu and smiled. The serenity on the narrow, shrewish face, standing in the middle of the messy chamber, sent a chill down Ohatsu's spine. 'Clearly,' Yome said, 'the girl using Ai's room now is not as…kept…as your oneesan.'

Ohatsu crossed to one of the tansu cabinets and shifted a wrinkled kimono, draped across it, to the floor. Kneeling, she opened the cabinet door and looked briefly through the folded clothes inside. 'And Ai really stayed here, not at the okiya?' she asked.

'Usually,' Yome said. 'She apparently found the environment of the geisha house…less favorable.'

Ohatsu turned on her knees and looked at the next tansu. Behind it, a stack of cloth sat folded. Upon the cloth were forty or fifty tight rolls of fibrous paper—tampons, and the cloth to bind them in place, enough for two or three days. Ohatsu pointed, and turned to Yome. 'Your current girl is in her moon cycle?'

Yome peered behind the cabinet and frowned. 'I don't think so,' she said. 'However, I believe Ai was, when she came last.'

Ohatsu rose to her feet.

Was this what it meant to be Hitodama? Was this the honor Tengokuyama afforded the select few, allowed to leave the city? A small room, overseen by a shrewish kenin. A vulgar teahouse full of common whores in brocaded silk. A cramped cell for the illustrious Hitodama, where even her unused menstrual cloths weren't collected after her stay.

'How long was Ai here, last?'

Yome pulled a small scroll from the sleeve of her kimono and held it beneath a flickering candle. 'Her last stay…was three days.'

Ohatsu watched Yome's face as the woman continued scanning the document, even after she finished speaking.

27

'And that is all you can tell me of my oneesan?'

Yome furled the scroll and secreted it back within her sleeve. 'That is all that is documented.'

Ohatsu raised an eyebrow. 'Then what *isn't* documented?'

Yome thought for a moment, then turned and left the chamber. 'Follow me,' she said. 'And blow the candles out as you come.'

Ohatsu stood with Yome in the shadows of a long walkway, peering through tall, mossy garden stones set within a yard of perfectly raked sand. The men's laughter from the party across the garden carried like rolling thunder. They were tall, with dark skin, almost sunburnt. Bare heads gleamed in the lantern light. They had long beards that bristled down their leather-studded chests. Leather-and-fur vambraces and greaves wrapped their arms and legs.

They looked like savages, kami from hell, nostrils flaring fire and smoke, eyes red with lust for murder.

And surrounding them were elegant willows of women. A geisha, playing the shamisen, the staccato notes breaking the stillness of the garden fountain. Another geisha quietly inscribing poetry on a long scroll, under the barbarous gaze of a towering savage. A courtesan, her outer kimonos removed, dancing a dance meant to represent trees and wind, but with the folds of her kimono loosened, allowing brief glimpses of the lily-white skin of her chest.

'What are they?' Ohatsu asked.

'Ainu,' Yome said.

'What?'

'Ainu. Or Emishi. Hairy savages, from the land of Ezo to the north, and Sakhalin above that.'

'And what does this have to do with Ai?' Ohatsu asked.

'Spies, and counterspies, girl. Those savages are barely ruled in the north by Daimyo Matsumae Takahiro. And yet, Ohatsu, their emissaries come, every month, to the tip of the Land of the Gods, here, and meet with *our* lord in his castle above.' Yome's eyes absently roamed upwards, towards the distant cavern ceiling above them.

Ohatsu shook her head. 'Yome, I have lived my whole life in Tengokuyama. I know nothing of the world but how it looks in the sunrise from the city walls. If you expect me to realize something from what you've said, you will have to excuse my ignorance. Explain it clearer. Please.'

Yome sighed, and pulled Ohatsu further into the shadows.

Good. The lie had worked.

'Your daimyo, Iwamura Tadanori, has tried for an entire year to enter a treaty with the Emishi. In the northern islands, in Ezo, there are thirty-*thousand* savage warriors, living in fishers' huts by the sea. If Iwamura could harness that power, he could *take* Ezo from Matsumae, and he could wrestle this city from the Tokugawa Clan in Edo.'

Ohatsu blinked a few times and shook her head. 'I'm worried I still don't understand, Yome. What you say would be impossible...'

Yome turned and spat angrily into the stone garden. Ohatsu felt the blood drain from her fingertips, and yet she still held the dumb look of confusion on her face—she had chosen this line of questioning, now she must stay with it, come what may.

'No, it would be simple,' Yome said. 'Simple as stepping on the neck of an unwanted infant.' The little woman stamped her foot on the tatami mat. 'But only with the help of the Ainu.'

'And these...creatures...they come every month? To bargain, with Iwamura-sama?'

'To bargain, and enjoy his hospitality. His finest courtesans and geisha.'

'Ai?'

Yome grinned, her snaggle-canines lending her mousy face a startling, vulpine intensity. 'Ai was the favorite of one Emishi in particular. A great, hairy monster, with a name to match—Kuuklekle. Every month, after the official discussions, Ai would write poetry and play music for him, late into the night.'

Ohatsu turned and looked out into the garden, struggling to keep her face in icy composure. 'And these treaty meetings,' she said, 'took place here? In a dingy, mosquito-infested brothel, masquerading as a teahouse?'

Yome was silent. 'No,' she finally said. 'Not with Iwamura's men. *Those* conferences are held above, in the Hanging Garden.'

29

'The Hanging Garden?' Ukifune had mentioned the same place.

'It's a great hanamachi. Very private,' Yome said. 'Built downwards, from the very rocks, beneath Iwamura's castle in Tengokuyama. The Ainu delegation lodges there, during the monthly council—they never stop here, or anywhere, in the city.'

'And Ai attended these…meetings?'

Yome nodded. 'As did all Hitodama.'

The two women moved silently along the uneven stones of the cavern, following the noxious stream, the lights of Nikkō Hanamachi—and Yokidani—glimmering behind them like an eternal fire. In the distance ahead, a phosphorescent glow shimmered like the reflection of light on water, broken only by the strange, spiky lights dotting the cavern depths.

When they reached a wide bridge that spanned the roiling stream, Yome turned.

'This is as far as I go,' she said.

Ohatsu looked out into the darkness, strangely populated by the mysterious lights.

'You said the…body…is out there?'

'Yes.'

'But you're not sure if it's Ai?'

Yome shook her head. 'My girl didn't stop to look.'

Ohatsu turned and locked the gaze of Yome. 'Why was your girl out there, in the first place?'

Yome smiled. 'Spying.'

Despite herself, Ohatsu smiled. 'I suppose I have no other choice but to trust you.' Again, she turned and peered at the distant lights. 'Yome, what's out there? The girl I came with said…'

'The boilers,' Yome said. 'You see, that's what Yokidani does, Ohatsu. We are the City of Steam. We gather it, out there, and send it upwards to your city—Tengokuyama—for use in your machines. It's all done out there. Boilershacks, they're called. Little camps by hot springs in the rock. Boilermen process the water, heat it in great brass tanks—they're what you see, reflecting there, in the dark,

30

under the boilermen's camp lights—and send it up in great pipes, to Tengokuyama above.'

'But then… Why don't you all use the steam, down here?'

'Steam, Ohatsu, is for the gods. *Your* people.' Yome turned, and swept her hand back towards the glimmer of Yokidani. 'Fire is for us devils.'

A moment of silence. Then Ohatsu looked back to the cavernous boiler plain. 'If you won't come with me, how am I to find…it?'

Yome took a small object from her sleeve. Ohatsu's breath caught in her throat, but she succeeded in arresting the surprise before it registered on her face—it was the same type of mechanism she had discovered in Ai's secret drawer.

'A steam dial,' Yome said. Turning the box over, she snapped open a panel on the back. A small set of spherical brass rings spun quickly in one corner. Careful to keep her fingers from the silently whirring gyro, Yome reached in and adjusted a few small pegs.

'How does it work?' Ohatsu asked.

Yome snapped the panel back and handed it to Ohatsu. 'It tracks positions,' Yome said. 'My girl told me where the body was found. I know the spot, and I know how far it is. All you need to do is follow those little teeth. The closer you get, the more will recede into the box—they will only recede as you near the correct position. Once you're there, all the teeth will snap down.'

Ohatsu slipped the steam dial into her kimono and looked up as Yome pulled a small, wooden-sheathed kaiken from her sash, and held it out to Ohatsu.

'Take it,' Yome said. 'You may need it. Tonight, there will be…a visitation in our cities. Forces more terrible than you've ever dreamed will stalk the shadows, Ohatsu. You would do well to stay indoors and abandon your quest. But I don't think you will. So, take it.'

Ohatsu held her hands out and gently pushed the kaiken back. 'No,' she said, shaking her head. 'I wouldn't know how to use it.'

Yome snorted and held the kaiken out again. 'That's nonsense. When you need to use it, you will learn.'

'I'll use the skills I have.'

'What skills? Seduction? You forget, geisha, you aren't legally permitted to practice *that* art! Only the courtesans. You'd risk your

31

okiya. If anyone found out, they'd set the magistrate on you, and he'd devour all of you like a dog hunting rabbit. Take it!'

Ohatsu took a long, deep breath, then lifted her arms into a graceful pantomime, her right-hand arcing out, mimicking the act of drawing a blade. She stepped forward, twisting slowly around Yome's outstretched arm and brought her hand—fingers held rigid as a mock dagger—up to Yome's throat. 'I will use the blade of my words, Yome, the only blade I know how to wield. Let me show you. This is my first strike—why have you helped me?'

Yome frowned, holding perfectly still. 'What?'

'Answer me.'

'Because…I liked you. Back at the teahouse. I liked your reply. It was simple. It was sincere.'

Ohatsu pulled the finger-blade away and pantomimed another blow, this time held against the side of Yome's neck. 'You're a spy. You know as well as I, anyone can lie convincingly…as you just attempted. I strike again—why have you helped me?'

Yome swallowed. 'Why should I answer your questions?'

'Because if you don't, and I fail in finding my sister, you will be the first person I'll send Iwamura's samurai to kill. And I'm sure we both know how Hatsutaro loathes asking questions. So, you see, my blade,' Ohatsu swung the imaginary blade again, stabbing upwards beneath Yome's chin, 'is sharp in truth. Allow me to tell you why you helped me.'

Yome took a step back. Ohatsu followed, with the cautious steps of an expert dancer, keeping perfect distance, her fingertips never leaving the mousy girl's throat.

'You spared me,' Ohatsu said, 'because I spoke of Ai, a woman you suspected to be a spy. You knew I was no Hitodama, so you deduced I was either a spy as well, searching for my colleague, or my story was truthful, and I was searching for my oneesan. Either way, you saw someone you could use. Thus, you told me the barest information necessary, to set me in motion, on the direction *you* chose. You wish to use me as an arrow, Yome, flying through the dark, striking its prey, leaving no trace of the bowman.'

Ohatsu stepped back, clasping her hands beneath the sleeves of her kimono. 'So now I ask… Who holds *your* arrow in their quiver? And for what purpose are you sending me out there, towards the boilers?'

Yome's lips curled into a pretty sneer. 'And I took you for a simpleton...' She shook her head. 'The weakness in your attack,' she said, 'is in revealing your intentions, Ohatsu. Had you simply left, I would never have known the measure of my adversary. I won't tell you anything more about me than you already know. Likewise, I can't deny I'm using you for my own purposes. But in this, our purposes align—find your oneesan. Take revenge. Forget about me. My arrow will fly silently, over your head.'

And with that, Yome turned to walked back towards the bonfire-light of Yokidani.

And Ohatsu turned and walked into the darkness of the boiler plain.

Chapter Three

The cavern floor was smooth and slick beneath Ohatsu's wooden geta as she trudged into the yawning void, away from the light of Yokidani. The steam dial regularly clacked and juddered in her hand as she walked, following the dim path stretching along the river. When it became too dark for Ohatsu to see the ground in front of her, let alone the teeth of the steam dial, she stopped and sat on a shelf of rock.

Yome had given her a small kate-bukuro—a provisions bag of woven string—containing a few onigiri balls, a flint and steel, some rolled cloth, a flask of oil, and a small brass bullseye lantern, scarcely bigger than Ohatsu's balled fist. In the darkness, Ohatsu fumbled with the strange little bag, gripping along the netted surface until her fingers found the tension-mouth and pulled it open.

Yome had shown her how to use the flint and steel, but Ohatsu still found the movements awkward. Each strike showered blinding sparks across the rocks. After seemingly endless attempts, the sparks caught the little swatch of kindling cloth. Opening a panel on the back of the lantern, Ohatsu hurriedly lifted the cloth to the wick and held it until it caught. She closed the panel and dropped the cloth, which fell in a smolder of dying embers upon the wet rocks.

Retying the kate-bukuro around her waist, Ohatsu stood and took

33

up the lantern, opening a small sliding panel which hid the light. A dull glimmer shone out onto the rocks before her, and she set out again, following the steam dial. Shortly after this, the dial directed her off the path, onto the great shelves of rock that stretched without end into the dark.

For hours she walked. Under the gleam of her lantern, she watched the smooth stone face become rough with soft blooms of moss. The farther she traveled, the thicker the moss became, until it felt as though she moved across an endless cushioned mat. Gentle luminescence glowed above her, coating the vaulted ceiling in ambient pinks and blues. Once, she shielded her lantern to see how bright the strange lights were, and was plunged immediately into a palpable darkness, broken only by little beads of pinprick-light in the moss she walked upon, stretching away like a sea of stars to the spiky brilliance of distant boilershacks.

Occasionally, the steam dial brought Ohatsu near these shacks. The first time, she dared approach near enough to shield her lantern, walking along the edges of the light cast by an enormous gas-globe, fixed to a tower above the station, gleaming like a little sun. The entire shack was draped in stark white light. Around it, a depression seemed to have been excavated, from which leaked vile-smelling steam and vapors. Brass silos rose from the depressions, towering above the little wooden house, gleaming sharp-gold in the gas-globe's light. At their peaks, burnished pipes ran together, making a spider-web lacing above the shack that then ran straight upwards towards the ceiling of the cavern, disappearing into the darkness.

As Ohatsu gawked, a ghostly figure loomed from the shadows between the brass silos, noxious vapors spilling from him like steam from a dragon's back. A tall man, in soiled robes, thick leather gloves on his arms, wearing boots of leather that rose above his knees. On his face was a tarnished brass mask, with great panes of glass that reflected the light of the gas-globe. A tatami hose ran from his mouth to a lacquered tank on his back. A long, iron wrench —nearly as long as the man was tall—was slung across his shoulder, the tines pointed like a farmer's pitchfork.

The steaming figure turned, his brassy gaze scanning the darkness. Ohatsu crept back into the cavern and cut a wide circle around the boilershacks after that, keeping far away from their gleaming lights.

As she walked, the steam dial continued to clack and jump incessantly in her hand. The rock-shelf plains rose and fell, gradually losing their sweeping smoothness. Eventually Ohatsu found herself navigating great fissures, leaping in the moist darkness across crevasses and skirting sharp promontories of jagged stone. Until suddenly the box snapped in her hand, and she shone the bullseye light upon it, and all the teeth had receded.

She was in a field of scattered boulders and dull stalagmites. Every step sunk into a thick groundcover of spongy moss.

Ohatsu slewed the bullseye light around her. Yome had admitted the steam dial wouldn't be perfectly accurate, but just how inaccurate it might be, she hadn't said.

Slipping the steam dial into her kimono, Ohatsu visually marked the spot where she stood, and began to walk around in growing concentric circles. After thirty minutes, she spotted a dull form, lying at the foot of a gently sloped boulder. She ran forward, a cold dread gripping her as she neared—she recognized the kimono, a soft violet-hued color. Her feet caught on the frothy moss and she stumbled, nearly dropping the lantern. Her breath grew labored; Ohatsu could feel the moist sweat, coating her back and sides as she scrambled forward—or, was it simply the strange dampness of the volcanic cavern?

She reached the body and fell to her knees.

Ryuzoji Ai lay in the moss, her head folded beneath her torso, chin twisted around at an unnatural angle towards her shoulder.

Ohatsu fought off a sudden, fearful hesitation, and took Ai by the side, rolling her over onto her back. The body rolled stiffly, a pungent odor erupting from it as it fell against the moss, Ai's death-face glaring up with yellow-crusted eyes into the lantern light.

A wave of emotion surged in Ohatsu's breast. She could feel the shimmering sting of tears, cutting their way into her vision. Sniffing, she brushed her face with her sleeve. Closed her eyes and shook her head. Huffed three or four big, sharp breaths, desperately trying to calm herself, trying not to cry.

The soft wind of the cavern breathed past Ohatsu, where she knelt beside the body of her friend, beneath the boulders. Somehow, the darkness seemed to grow closer, compressing the air against

Ohatsu as she sat, eyes closed, willing herself to breath.

Carefully, she reached out, pulled the dead form of her friend to her chest, and curled over her, pressing against the boulder.

Yet still, she did not cry.

And presently, the exhaustion of two days without rest overtook her, and Ohatsu fell into a deep and tortured sleep.

The lantern guttered, and went out.

Ohatsu awoke with a start, her balance reeling in the disorienting darkness. She sat up, pushing against the cushioned bed of moss, and groped for the lantern, her head still heavy with the fog of sleep. The little moss-lights twinkled in the endless night of the cavern. A chill swept up her spine as her fingers brushed the fabric of Ai's kimono.

In the absence of light, Ohatsu struggled with the flint and steel. She struggled with the kindling cloth, and struggled to refill the dry lantern from her flask of oil. By the time the wick finally caught, Ohatsu's head had cleared, and she was prepared for the vision that awaited her.

The smell of the dead woman still lingered on Ohatsu's clothes as she staggered to her feet, the lantern-light casting a dull orange glow over the dead body beside the boulder.

Ohatsu had no idea how long she had slept—as Ukifune had hinted, in the caverns below Tengokuyama there was no night or day, only endless darkness. The fact Ohatsu felt well-rested, notwithstanding her fitful dreams, left her wondering if a great time had passed. However, even if it had, there was no helping it now—the only thing was to push on.

But what exactly did "push on" mean? She had found her oneesan. Wasn't that all she had set out to do? Didn't this mean her journey was complete? But if it was complete, why did she still feel a gaping emptiness in her chest?

Ohatsu had to admit, as the trail grew closer, she had become less hopeful of finding her sister alive. And when Yome spoke of a body, lost to the gloomy fastnesses of the boiler plains, Ohatsu had known, deep within her, it would be Ai.

Yet, here she was, miles away from Yokidani, surrounded by a strangely breathing darkness, and in her breast still the same yearning emptiness. The same impetus…to learn more.

Why had Ai died? And how?

Ohatsu lowered herself to the woman's body and held the lantern closer. What she had failed to notice earlier, under her initial duress, was clear now—Ai appeared to have broken her neck.

Ohatsu frowned. That didn't make any sense, unless…

She stood up and stepped back, away from the boulder.

The great rock was frosted in the same spongy layer of moss. However, above where Ai had lain, a streaking smudge ran downwards. Ohatsu peered towards the peak of the boulder. The smudge only ran partway up the rock—it did not begin at the peak, and Ohatsu could see no footprints or marks that indicated Ai had climbed the boulder and slipped off.

The smudge simply started an arm-span or so from the top, and dragged vertically down to the side, until it stopped, directly above where Ai lay. It looked as though she had fallen, from above, struck the boulder, and…

For the first time in a long while, Ohatsu looked *up*.

And there, directly above her, a vast shadow clung to the roof of the cavern—which was much lower here—gently illuminated by the luminescent glow of the cavern itself. Against the blackness of the rock ceiling, the structure loomed like an inverted pyramid, each descending layer cut slightly closer in, until it culminated in a dull point at the bottom. Intricate woodworking bristled along the strange upside-down balconies, prickly eaves curling beneath the overhang of every level.

It could only be the Hanging Garden. The elite location of the Ainu delegation meetings. And, most likely, the last place Ryuzoji Ai ever knew alive, other than the hard rock boulder beneath the layer of moss where she had fallen.

Ohatsu staggered backwards. Her balance still felt shaky, from the heavy sleep. Blinking, she lowered her head and rubbed the back of her neck.

The lantern light fell across her muted footprints in the moss—as she looked up at the Hanging Garden she had inadvertently turned, and now faced away from Ai and the boulder. Squinting through the dissipating dizziness, Ohatsu noticed something else in the dark.

She raised the lantern, and walked back along her tracks from before.

About twenty feet from the boulder where she had slept, cradling the body of her sister, footprints cut through the moss. Many footprints. Prints that hadn't been there when she crossed that part of the shelf earlier.

Ohatsu straightened quickly, slewing the dim bullseye light out into the cavern around her. The light dissipated into a nothing-glow. After a frantic moment, panning the light back and forth, Ohatsu thought better of it, and shielded the lantern instead.

Darkness enveloped her. Slowly, she lowered into a crouch, and moved twenty paces away, stopping as her outstretched fingers met a tapering stalagmite. Holding perfectly still, breathing long, halting breaths, Ohatsu listened to the dark.

The soft drip of condensation, far away. The gentle breathing of the cavern air. The beating of her own heart, her blood rushing in her ears. No other sound met her.

The skin on her neck crawling with strange anticipation, Ohatsu unshielded her lantern. Nothing happened. Slowly, she moved back to the prints, her sensations heightened to a thrumming peak. Breathing deeply, Ohatsu forced herself to examine the tracks, to think, rather than feel.

The walkers had moved in a pack, closely together. Taking a moment to try and match the depressions, Ohatsu guessed there were nearly thirty, but it was difficult to be sure. Leaning closer, Ohatsu noticed many of the prints seemed to lay over other prints. Then it dawned on her—the tracks were two separate sets of prints, one running one direction, the other set running in reverse.

Ohatsu stood up, and shone her lantern towards the boulder. Ai's body stood out boldly beside the path the mysterious travelers had cut.

There was no way anyone could walk those cavern depths without a light, and with a light, it would have been difficult for anybody following the path of the tracks to miss the forms of two women, crumpled at the foot of the boulder.

Once more, Ohatsu shone the light out into the inky blackness.

Whoever they were, they came in, from somewhere out there. They had passed her and Ai, silently, and slipped down the boiler plain towards Yokidani. Then, sometime later, they had returned.

Ohatsu shone the light outward, following the tracks that led away from the boiler plain.

Where did they go?

Yome's words returned to her—what had she said? There would be...*visitors*...

It was clear that the dark fastnesses of the boiler plain was a home to spies. Was it a coincidence, then, that it was also the boiler plain where she had found Ryuzoji Ai?

'Oneesan,' Ohatsu muttered to the damp cavern air, 'what did you get yourself into?'

For Ai, there could be no earthly resolution, no earthly peace. There was nothing Ohatsu could do to help her sister—Ai had already suffered her fate. No, whatever was done now wasn't for the dead, but for the living.

In her fitful sleep, Ohatsu had discovered the meaning of that earlier emptiness, her nagging feeling of unresolve. Now that she'd found her sister, the journey ceased to be for Ai—now it was for Ohatsu. A journey of rescue had become a journey for closure, a quest for peace. A hunt for answers.

Ohatsu knew she probably had no right to uncover whatever truths lay at the end of the footprints, traipsing off into the dark. She knew she likely had no claim to the secrets Ai had taken with her to her mossy grave. And yet, Ohatsu's mind cast easily back to the childhood she had shared with the girl that now lay, black ribbon of the Hitodama still in her hair, dead upon the moss—back then, they had shared in everything.

The impetus whirred in Ohatsu's heart, like the tiny whirling gyro in the steam dial.

She had to know. Why had Ryuzoji Ai died? And who had killer her?

If someone fell from the Hanging Garden, there was simply no way it would go unnoticed. The tragedy should have been recorded. Naohana, the house-mother of Ohatsu's okiya, would have found the body, or at least would have discovered the tale of her fall. Hatsutaro—who was surely connected with the Hanging Garden, from Iwamura's castle above—would have known about the accident, and would not have come to Yuyami Okiya, tearing Ai's room apart looking for clues to her whereabouts.

No. The only way Ai fell from above, and nobody knew, was if it had been kept secret by someone. Someone who either pushed her, or saw her fall, and did nothing.

The journey now, was about answers. For Ohatsu. For Ohatsu alone.

Ohatsu turned to the tracks that led deeper into the cavern, half-lidded her lantern, and followed them into the dark.

The tracks cut a familiar course through the caverns, winding between rock falls and crevasses, eventually entering a narrow, scree-strewn path that followed the base of a towering granite wall, stretching upward into the nothingness overhead, speckled with flecks of twinkling moss. Here, the ground was broken up, large slags of stone jutting up from a shaley substructure.

A moist breeze drafted past Ohatsu's sweaty brow as she walked, pulling past her, moving the same direction as she. The tracks had long since disappeared, but every now and then she still found a print, scuffed in the sandy dirt beneath the loose shale.

Eventually, even this soil became hard and the path disappeared across smooth slabs of dust-strewn bedrock. No prints were to be seen in this swirling skein of dirt. However, the breathing wind grew stronger, and Ohatsu recognized a fresh scent, punctuating the pervasive aroma of sulfur she'd already become accustomed to—the scent of pines.

Ahead, a brighter darkness stretched across the passage. Ohatsu lidded her lantern and crept forward.

And stepped into the edges of moonlight, casting down along the gaping horizontal fissure in the mountainside from which she emerged. A gentle plateau of scrubby dirt ran beneath the overhanging rock. Beyond, trees swept down the mountain, rustling in silent conversation in the breeze.

Ohatsu looked back and forth across the mountain. No figures

40

met her gaze. However, thirty paces away, pulled up behind a tumble of boulders, was a set of familiar shapes. Cautiously, Ohatsu stepped out into the moonlight and moved towards the objects.

They were bicycles. Sixteen of them. Pulled into the shadow of the rocks. Ohatsu had seen such machines before—she'd even ridden herself, when she was a girl. A very young girl, though—bicycles were considered an un-aesthetic sport, and as such were forbidden to geisha.

But these bicycles were in detail unlike any Ohatsu had ever seen. Bamboo frames and curved-wood handlebars, hard leather seats and glue-sealed cloth tires…this was familiar. But the strange tanks made of large, heavy bamboo shoots, dried-tatami hoses snaking from them along the frames, the carved-bone coupling-rods linking the wheels and connected to a small wooden box near the bottom bracket, covered in brass cogs…

After inspecting the strange contraptions for a few minutes, Ohatsu turned, and stepped back into the moonlight.

Her gaze was drawn towards the mountain and her breath caught.

Above her, the fortified wall of Tengokuyama stretched away, curving endlessly out of sight, towering a few hundred feet into the air.

And there, indistinct as a few strands of hair on a fair face, a delicate line stretched upwards—a rope ladder.

It was no wonder Ohatsu hadn't noticed it as she peered along the mountainside. It was narrow, and small, the end fastened tightly within the rocks at the edge of the fissure and pulled into a set of deep shadows.

She walked to it and took the vertical lines in her hands. The rope was hard and cold to the touch, as though it had been waxed. The rungs were made of thick lengths of wood, planed smooth on the top. Peering up, the line soared up the wall, dizzyingly vertical.

Ohatsu released the ladder and extinguished her lantern, slipping it back into the kate-bukuro. Then she stepped into the security of the shadows beneath the overhang to think.

First, it was her belief that Ai had been pushed. Either pushed, or allowed to fall. It seemed the only way to make sense of her continued disappearance for eighteen days.

Second, it seemed likely—however much Ohatsu hated to admit

it—that Ai had been involved in espionage. Either for Iwamura, or the Ainu, or...whoever Yome represented. Yome seemed to suggest Ai was involved with the Ainu delegation from Ezo. Whether this was true or not...

Third, someone had entered the environs of Yokidani. Yome had warned her of such a thing. Whoever this new entity was, they were dangerous. Again, Yome had said so. However, this led to the unfortunate fourth point—it was difficult to fully trust anything that mousy girl had said. In addition to everything else, she'd openly admitted to being duplicitous.

Ohatsu squatted in the shadows, leaning against a boulder for support.

Yome had told her of the Ainu. Yome told her of Ai's involvement with the delegation. It was Yome who insinuated Ai could have been a spy. If Yome also knew of these "visitors", as she called them, it followed they were also spies.

Was it justified, then, in expecting some revelation about Ai's death to be found in the strange ladder climbing up to Tengokuyama?

Ohatsu sighed, and began to kick at the dirt with her sandals.

Yes. It seemed like a good possibility.

Looking up, Ohatsu leaned forward, and found the moon in the sky. It hung high in the heavens.

If the mysterious visitors had entered after she found Ai, and left before she awoke, how far into the boiler plain could they have gotten? Could they have reached Yokidani?

Ohatsu silently gauged the times involved.

Unless she had slept more than twenty hours, it seemed likely she'd only been asleep for two or three. She had entered Yokidani in midday. She reached Nikkō Hanamachi shortly after, and worked there until early evening. Yome had set her out onto the boiler plain that same evening, where she had walked for hours. If she'd only slept—albeit heavily—for a few hours, that would give enough time for the moon to rise to the position it held now.

Then, the visitors could only have been under the mountain for a few hours—not enough time to reach Yokidani.

What had been their purpose?

Ohatsu rose and crept back to the ladder.

There was only one way to find out.

Reaching up, she took hold of the vertical lengths, and stepped onto the first rung. The rope swayed away from the wall, but then became rigid, holding her weight strongly, half an arm-span from the mountainside.

Taking a deep breath, vowing not to look down, Ohatsu began to climb.

Thirty feet up, Ohatsu encountered the first piton, struck gingerly into a crack in the rock wall. She had never seen such an implement, but had read about them. In the silverly moonlight, she paused to catch her breath and studied the cleverly shaped metal spike, hooked at one end to hold the ladder-rope in place.

Peering up, she now thought she could discern more fasten-spots up the length of the climb, at irregular intervals.

The wind whipped against her, gripping the loose folds of her kimono and tugging her away from the face of the rock. With a huff, she continued her ascent. Her wooden sandals were clumsy on the slippery wooden rungs. A hundred feet up, just as the heavy wall of Tengokuyama sprouted from the mountainous stone, she slipped, only saving herself from a fatal fall by a frantic grip for the waxed vertical ropes. Reluctantly, she kicked the geta off, and watched as they fell away, clattering against the scree below and bounding off into the brush beneath the pines.

With a wry smile—she'd already broken her promise not to look down—Ohatsu climbed further. Against the sheer wall of Tengokuyama the winds became sharp, gusting unexpectedly with such force she felt her breath sucked from her lungs. But still she climbed.

Halfway, she stopped at another piton, hooking her legs around the backside of the ladder and threading her arms into the rungs, allowing her to relax the burning tension in her arms and shoulders. She was a performer—trained in elegance and poetry, not mountaineering, cave-exploring, and trekking. The day had left her feeling drained to a depth of fatigue she had never before known.

43

And yet, she had pressed on. And yet, here she was, halfway up the side of Tengokuyama's wall, scaling a treacherous ladder. A weary sense of satisfaction warmed her—after a few deep breaths, she hoisted herself back up, and climbed again.

A few feet from the top of the wall, Ohatsu halted, and turned to look out.

The rolling forest fell smoothly away, hundreds of feet below. The small plateau was, from this height, reduced to a little strip of bone-white against the rubble of the mountain. The moon hung above her, and there, in the unfettered winds, she almost thought if she reached out, she could touch its vibrant surface.

She turned back and climbed to the top of the wall. Here the ladder stopped, firmly pitoned into a section of crumbling mortar between the gargantuan wall-stones, an arm-span below the peak.

Steeling herself, Ohatsu climbed up, and reached to the edge above her, the fingers of her right hand gripping the ledge and finding precarious purchase. One final breath, and she let go of the ladder, and climbed up and over, rolling onto the broad coping, her chest heaving as she gulped the air, all the muscles of her body quivering in the snarling breeze.

Minutes that felt like hours passed as she lay there, whipped by the winds, staring up at the severe stars in the clear sky, so different from the twinkling moss in the caverns below.

Once her breath had returned, and she no longer felt the painful need to breathe in gasps, Ohatsu sat up. To her left, the sheer drop of the city wall fell away; to her right, the narrow Wall Park ran along the inside of the fortifications, a comfortable drop of ten feet below her.

Twisting, she hung off the wall, and dropped into the park, landing between two stunted oaks.

Shadows materialized around her almost instantly, seemingly from the very air itself. Dark, fleeting figures, tightly wrapped in black robes from their heads to their feet, only their eyes glinting in the moonlight as they approached.

Ohatsu instinctively recoiled away from them, but her back struck against the wall. Hands reached out for her. She opened her mouth to cry out, but was smothered before she could find her voice. She tried to struggle, but coarse, cloth-bound hands gripped

44

her arms, and she was pressed against the wall. Eyes wide, a sinking dread settling in her stomach, Ohatsu looked from one cloth-masked face to the next.

A whisper of a voice hissed in her ear. 'Why are you following us?'

A softer voice spoke, behind the first. 'Careful, she may be—'

'Shh!' a third voice snapped. 'Not here, either of you. We take her with us, and question her later.'

A broad figure, whose robes hung looser than the rest, stepped forward, lifting a gleaming sickle before her face. A long chain dangled from the pommel of the weapon, ending in a vicious weight, which he held in his other hand.

'Don't speak,' the figure said, his voice harsher than the others. 'Don't make any quick movements. Don't try to run. If you do any of these things, you will be dead before your body hits the ground. Now, move.'

The hands against her mouth slipped away. A savage shove sent Ohatsu reeling into the scrubby oaks, the figures darting around her into the shadows of a nearby alley.

For a moment, she thought she had been left. But when she turned, the low, broad form with the sickle-and-chain stood a few paces behind her. He gestured towards the alley.

Ohatsu turned and ran after the disappearing wraiths, her stockinged feet padding silently on the cobbles.

Chapter Four

They moved quickly through the streets, darting from the shadows of one alley to the gloom of another, avoiding the moonlight as much as possible.

They were in the Civic Quarter—housing the buildings and personal chambers of the daimyo's magistrates and city police, as well as the commissioners of various city offices. Ohatsu knew the area well, as she did all of Tengokuyama; even in the darkness, following the darting path of the black-clad men, she never lost her bearings.

The city streets were dry, the cobbles swept smooth as they

always were. Dim gaslighting glowed from the shutters of the buildings. Gas-lamps gleamed at the intersections of streets. The wind rustled quietly down the alleys as the furtive procession crept, single-file, down long, empty lanes and behind storehouses.

The group seemed to be moving in a generally westward direction, staying near the curvature of the wall but never once venturing into the relative opening of the Wall Park. Ohatsu logged their position in her mind—if they kept up this bearing, they would cross into the Noble Quarter, then the Park District, then, eventually, the Yorukaze Hanamachi.

But something was strange about their direction. As she followed them, it became evident the group had likely never been in the city before. They rarely chose the most direct route, even considering the obvious requisite to keep to the shadows and under as much cover as possible. And considering cover, Ohatsu was very sure more secret routes existed, to achieve the same journey. Then it dawned on her—their movements must be based on a map of the city. A map showing basic locations, but not giving enough detail for them to know the best routes.

Which meant, if she could slip away...

Ohatsu glanced back at the figure behind her. He ran, unexpectedly close, at her left side, the sickle-and-chain concealed along the dark cloth of his arms. But the glint of the blade in the moonlight, tucked in the curve of his elbow—pommel held in his palm—was evidence that he was still watching her closely.

Ohatsu turned back and dismissed the thought. If she could slip away, yes, she might be able to elude her captors. But without any other information, she was forced to accept the man's threat as truth. If she tried to run, there would be no eluding—she would most likely just be dead.

It was then that Ohatsu noticed another curious thing. The empty streets.

Even in the middle of the night, Tengokuyama was always alive and moving. Night shipments of food to the various izakaya, scattered across the city. Street cleaners, with their great bug-like machines, spitting jets of steam as their vast street combs spun against the cobbles. And always a random cast of drunkards and lonely poets, musicians, dog-walkers, and, of course, lovers.

But tonight, the streets were empty save for the wild breeze.

Lights glowed in the windows, but doors were shut and shutters closed.

Even the city cats seemed absent from their customary perches along the tenement walls.

Eventually, they crossed the Civic Quarter, and skirted the edge of the elite palaces of the Noble Quarter into the long, meandering garden park that separated the Noble Quarter from the hanamachi.

One by one the fleeting figures darted into the cover of the drooping willow trees in that area of the park. In the distance, Ohatsu could see the tall wooden walls of Yorukaze Hanamachi, the hive of tall buildings glimmering in the night.

If the rest of the city seemed strangely subdued, at least Ohatsu's home still possessed some measure of life.

The leader slowed his pace, and slunk down into a curving depression by a babbling brook, his shadow blending in between the ten or twenty decorative stones set upright beneath the boughs of a willow. The brook ran the length of the garden, rising from a frothy fountain in the city square directly before Iwamura's castle, miles away in the center of Tengokuyama.

Gloved hands gripped Ohatsu's shoulders and pushed her towards the stones. The dark forms circled around her, standing like ghosts beneath the beaded moonlight that slipped through the willow's leaves.

'Now, who are you, and why were you following us?' the leader hissed.

Ohatsu turned towards the voice, emanating from a crouching shadow.

'I could say I was a farm girl, hunting in the forests when I saw the ladder, but you wouldn't believe it,' Ohatsu said, her voice hushed beneath the rustling of the brook and the swaying of the willow branches. She spoke slowly, but her mind was racing. She knew nothing of these men—or women—other than the brief warning Yome had given her. She would have to bait them, carefully... 'The unfortunate truth is that anything I say you will doubt. So, why should I say anything at all?'

The broad shadow stepped from the ring of dark figures. The sickle glinted in the moonlight. 'Because,' he said, 'if you don't answer, we'll kill you.'

'No,' Ohatsu said, 'you won't.' And she left it at that.

A tense silence hung between the figures, until a third stepped forward. Thinner, shorter, visibly more athletic of movement than the other two. 'Why won't we?' It was a woman's voice.

Ohatsu waited before she replied, hoping to give the illusion of leverage when, in reality, she was buying time for her whirling mind to grasp at any conversational purchase she could find.

Finally, she spoke. 'You found what you were looking for, beneath the mountain, in the boiler plain...?' Her inflection was delicate, the sentence spoken as a statement, except for the very end when Ohatsu lifted her cadence, allowing her words to be interpreted as a question by a willing mind, giving it a potential double meaning.

A fourth figure took the bait immediately, leaning forward and hissing into the circle. 'You see?' the androgenous voice said. 'I *told* you she could be our contact.'

The female figure spun around. Her eyes were visible in the slit of her head-covering—even in the dark, Ohatsu could see the savage glare she leveled at her comrade. 'A guess,' she said.

'Then how did she know we didn't enter the city? That we stayed on the boiler plain?'

The leader cleared his throat, silencing the others. Ohatsu turned to face him. 'What is your name?' he asked.

'Any name I give you would be as the blossom of the ajisai, changing with the seasons to fit her soil. What is *your* name?'

A soft laugh grunted from the shadowy ranks behind her.

'Then allow *me* to tell you *your* name,' the leader said. The laughter abruptly stopped. 'Kuuklekle,' he said. 'Your name is Kuuklekle, or it might as well be. You hold the papers he agreed to deliver to us. Am I right?'

Ohatsu couldn't contain the shiver that rippled across her weary muscles.

Ryuzoji Ai... Did you die, for *this?* Caught between the machinations of the Shōgun in Edo, and a treacherous rural daimyo?

'Yes,' said Ohatsu. 'To you, I am as Kuuklekle. But I do not have his papers anymore.' A desperate bluff. She could follow it by giving them the name of Ryuzoji Ai—Ai had probably been their

48

contact in the first place, but had remained under the cloak of secrecy. If nothing else, her name would provide a reasonable diversion, hopefully enough to save Ohatsu.

The leader spat and stood to his feet. 'It figures,' he muttered. 'Nothing ever goes right for shinobi, these days.' Then, moving closer, 'What happened in the boiler plains? Why didn't you meet us?'

'I—' Ohatsu began, but was cut off by the third shadow, the lithe woman.

'Wait,' the woman said. 'Wait... I've seen this girl before...' Ohatsu turned, slowly backing away as the woman crept ever closer, the filtered moonlight rolling across her black-clothed outline. 'In the caverns,' she said. 'Beneath the Hanging Garden.'

The broad figure suddenly jolted upright, the sickle's chain clinking in the gloom. 'Yes,' he said. 'One of the dead bodies! She was the one sitting against the boulder.'

With a snarl, the leader plunged towards Ohatsu. She turned to run, but her feet caught on the angled roots of the willows.

Then, as she fell, the entire garden was engulfed in sudden light from all around, beams gleaming in heated intensity such that the willow boughs seemed to disappear under their glare. The night erupted beneath death-invoking battle cries as gargantuan forms crashed through the garden undergrowth, plunging into the ring of ninjas, slewing jagged jets of super-heated steam in the wake of their armored suits.

Ohatsu hit the ground, the willow roots jutting into her back, forcing the wind from her body in a wracking blow. She lay there, momentarily unable to move. A dark form leapt across her, a sandaled foot ploughing into her stomach as the shinobi lunged towards a charging samurai.

The samurai broke through the willow boughs like a steam-belching tiger crashing through a stand of young bamboo, static discharges crackling in the air around him. His blade flared like searing fire, steam erupting from his gauntleted hands. The blow caught the ninja in the stomach and sliced clean through, sending the black-wrapped body hurling off in a blood-spewing heap to the ground. But not before two shuriken had flicked from the ninja's fingers, both scoring beneath the samurai's sloped helmet,

49

puncturing the tatami-mesh hoses, despite their scaled armor.

Jets of steam screamed into the face of the samurai, who stumbled forward.

Ohatsu scrambled sideways, her breath suddenly returned, and rolled beneath the ground-crunching feet of the samurai as he fell into the willow roots, clutching blindly at his helmet.

All around her, dark forms flitted through the glaring lights, buzzing around the steam-belching samurai, their glinting blows targeting the tatami hoses that distributed steam-power through the brass-jointed suits.

Katana flared in the spotlit night, sending body parts spinning off into the darkness beyond the lights. But still the darting black forms pressed closer. Long chains whipped at the samurai, snaring them, pulling their arms, snagging their legs, slowing them down for the wicked sickles to slice their steam-hoses, to find the openings in their armor, to angle up beneath their helmets gauging eyes and scouring-off noses. One of the great lights suddenly erupted, in a billowing plume of fire and black smoke.

Then, just as Ohatsu thought the shinobi would win, Hatsutaro strode into the circle of light, electric discharges spiking from the conductors in his suit. Chains wrapped around his legs. Shuriken glanced off his armor. A sickle plunged into the join of his shoulder, a jet of steam erupting from the wound. But doggedly he plunged into the pack of shinobi, and at the last moment let loose a deep-throated battle cry.

Signaling the others to engage the last-resort tactic of their steam -powered suits—a pressure purge.

From each samurai, hissing jets of flesh-searing steam spiked in all directions. Screams wailed beneath the frantic shriek of the steam exhaust, as the samurai hurled themselves, the very presence of their bodies now a brutal weapon, into the frantically retreating shinobi.

Ohatsu turned, dug her feet into the soil, and ran blindly towards the dark opening in the ring of lights, by the burning gas-globe. Hot wind surged past her. The ground shook beneath the lurid steps of Hatsutaro's warriors. A disoriented shinobi—his face scalded to a lobster-red mass of dripping tissue—ran past her, stumbling blindly towards one of the spotlights, wildly swinging a weighted-chain.

The gas-light erupted in another ball of flame, engulfing the shinobi as Ohatsu darted past, and dove into the depths of the burbling stream.

As the waters carried her swiftly towards the city wall, the sky burned bright with the gas-billowing flame of the broken lamps, and the music of the breeze was lost beneath the moans of the dying shinobi.

Chapter Five

Ohatsu's drenched garments had only partially dried when she reached the towering wooden walls of the hanamachi.

Ever since her plunge into Tengokuyama's stream, a coldness had gripped her heart, a strange numbness which she suspected was not only due to the chill waters and the cool midnight breeze.

Kiri-sute gomen—the samurai's right to strike anyone who had compromised his honor.

Ohatsu had seen it before. A peasant boy once threw a half-eaten apple at Hatsutaro's horse... The boy's father had refused to apologize to the warrior, and Hatsutaro had chopped him to pieces in the street. A young girl in the Merchant Quarter once threw a pail of kitchen water—in itself a forbidden act—out a window into the path of Nabeshima Kōtarō, Hatsutaro's right-hand samurai. Her head was cut off, and the body thrown from the city wall.

These were things to be expected. It was the customary order of life, and Ohatsu had grown to accept them.

However, she had never seen anything like the battle at the gardens—the savage violence of the clash, the sudden battle-lust in the eyes of the steam-armored samurai, the vicious pack-tactics of the shinobi.

The coldness seemed to settle in her chest, pumping with each course of blood through her veins, numbing her arms and her fingers.

The hanamachi gates were locked. Of course, guards attended many smaller passages all throughout the night—but Ohatsu desired to enter unseen. Whether it was the sodden nature of her clothes or the strange, empty streets that gave her an eerie feeling of trespass,

51

some intuition beneath the numbing battle fatigue told her to move quietly and secretly.

Keeping to the shadows, Ohatsu followed the hanamachi wall for a hundred yards, moving towards Tengokuyama's city wall. There, a few paces from the marriage of the two walls, cloaked in shadows beneath the wooden fortification, was a grated drainage ditch.

Ohatsu splashed down into the cold water at the bottom of the ditch and deftly removed the grate—the passage was an old secret among servants of the hanamachi. She replaced it behind her and entered the hard-packed soil of the flower town. The soaring complex sprouted before her, glimmering in the night, competing with the light of the moon. Music drifted across the breeze from somewhere in the buildings above her.

And yet, the strange stillness in Tengokuyama even pervaded here. The ground-level walkways and courtyards were bathed in gloom. There were no nighttime walkers among the paths below the buildings. No glimmering lanterns traversed the spiderwebbing skybridges.

The only faint sounds of life came from within the lattice-worked hive of teahouses, brothels, inns, and taverns.

From the shadows of the wall, Ohatsu surveyed the empty grounds around the bases of the buildings. The same prickly anticipation she'd experienced before, in the disorienting darkness of the boiler plain, had returned. The feeling of being watched. Of being hunted. All her instincts were telling her to run. To slip back to the shinobi ladder, back to the boiler plain, to Yokidani. Weren't the answers she sought to be found there, after all? Whoever killed Ai did so from the Hanging Garden—it followed any clues they'd left behind would be there.

And yet, now she was back on top of the mountain, there was something she had to get, and someone she ought to meet.

Glancing feverishly along the empty courtyards, Ohatsu darted across the packed soil towards the maze of alleys beneath the hanamachi buildings and disappeared into the raftered gloom.

The shoji slid silently open, revealing Ukifune's rooms. The gas-globes were unlit, and the sole light in the chambers came from the silvery moonlight that spilled from the courtesan's open windows.

Ohatsu stepped softly inside. On her way, she had slipped through the okiya, replacing her damp servant's clothes with a dark-colored kimono from her own wardrobe. She'd bound the kimono at her wrists and waist, separating the train into two segments for her legs, to provide greater freedom of movement, an idea she'd stolen from the tight costumes of the shinobi.

As she closed the screen behind her, a sudden movement flitted through the moonlight. An arm snaked around her shoulders, and she felt the pin-prick pressure of a blade held into her back, below the ribs.

'Don't move,' the voice of Ukifune hissed in her ears.

'It's me, Ohatsu,' she said.

For a moment, the grip around her shoulders tightened. The blade dug into her skin through the tight folds of cloth. Then, with a sharp exhale of breath, Ukifune released her and stepped into the moonlight.

'What are you doing?' Ukifune said, an incredulous timbre to her voice. 'Don't you know there's a curfew?'

'A curfew?' Ohatsu repeated, stepping into the moonlight as well, one hand gingerly rubbing the stinging thorn in her back where Ukifune's blade had pressed.

'Hatsutaro,' Ukifune said, snorting. 'The man ordered it, shortly after you left for Yokidani.'

'For the entire day?'

'Nobody has been in the streets,' Ukifune said. 'Except the castle's samurai, prowling like hunting dogs. But this brings me back to my question—what are you doing here?'

Ohatsu crossed the room to stand by the wood-slatted windows. The hanamachi lay below her, brimming in its typical golden glow, excepting the darkened pockets of empty courtyards and walkways. Beyond, the city stretched away, tile-roofed buildings organized in mazelike channels. She looked towards the garden district—all evidence of the clash was gone, the flames from the gas lights now extinguished.

With a shudder, she turned back to Ukifune. 'I thought shinobi

53

were a thing of the past?' she said.

Ukifune shrugged. 'Well, of course,' she said. 'That's exactly what a secret organization would *want* you to believe, isn't it?'

Ohatsu raised her eyebrows, surprised that Ukifune had risen to such an obviously baited question with her response. So, she'd known about the ninja…just as Yome had.

'Ohatsu,' Ukifune said, stepping forward, 'why are you here?' The dagger gleamed in the moonlight.

'I found Ai,' Ohatsu said.

'Was she…dead?'

'Pushed—or fallen—from the Hanging Garden.'

Ukifune was silent.

'Either way,' Ohatsu said, 'someone was responsible. Either for her death, or for covering it up. Someone who was there.'

Ukifune turned the dagger, lifting the point. 'You suspect me.'

'Right now, I suspect everyone. Whoever killed her was there with her and the Ainu delegation. Who was with you, Ukifune?'

Ukifune moved slowly closer, until her face was clear in the moonlight. Her hair was loose, her kimono a thin robe against the night chill. 'The delegation consisted of their legate—some Emishi beast, named Kuuklekle—and two attendants. They met in the great hall in the Hanging Garden, as you said. Daimyo Iwamura-sama was there, as was Hatsutaro, and…' Ukifune frowned, trying to remember. 'And two samurai. Nabeshima-sama, and Itakura-sama.'

'And from the hanamachi?' Ohatsu asked.

'Myself. Mitsuhana—Ai. A younger geisha, from Asa Okiya, and a few incidental courtesans. And the Hanging Garden's kenin.'

'And who is that?'

'Yome.'

'Ukifune,' Ohatsu said, 'I don't like the way you're holding that dagger.'

Ukifune smiled. 'Why? Are you afraid? But, dear girl, you are armed as well, aren't you, with your geisha charms? Steel is no match for those, I've heard.'

Ukifune took a step forward. Ohatsu stepped back. 'I want to go to the Hanging Garden,' she said.

'That would be difficult,' said Ukifune. 'There are only two entrances—one from the catwalks suspended above the boiler plain, and one from Iwamura's castle. They are both locked, by two different puzzles.'

'Where is the puzzle's key?'

Ukifune lifted the dagger until the point touched her own forehead. 'Here,' she said. 'Here alone. Only Hitodama know the secret…'

'Then, will you come with me?'

'Only Hitodama…and the house's kenin.'

'Yome?'

Ukifune nodded. 'Yome.'

Ohatsu's mind reeled across the possibilities. At first, they seemed endless. If the treaty papers the delegation produced were sought by spies, and Ai had them, it seemed as though *anyone* could have had reason to kill her. Or to let her die. Hatsutaro, protecting the interests of his liege lord. Yome, working for whatever shadowy forces controlled her. Or Ukifune, playing some sort of treacherous game for the power the papers clearly would award their owner.

But then a different line of thought broke upon her mind like the sun breaking the horizon at dawn.

'Where did the delegation stay, during the meetings?' Ohatsu asked.

Ukifune shrugged. 'The Hanging Garden. They were too important to put up at an inn, or that grubby little hanamachi down there.'

'They never stayed anywhere in town?'

'Never. Everything they needed was provided at the Hanging Garden. Girls. Food. Entertainment.'

'And spies?'

The words were barbed. Ukifune's eyes rose sharply to Ohatsu's, and she considered a moment before answering. 'Of course. Spies are always everywhere.'

Ohatsu turned from her perch in the oak tree's branches and took a last look across the Civic Quarter. The long streets and alleys were dark. Not a soul stirred.

She had kept to the shadows on her way across the city, moving quickly and carefully—not as silent as the shinobi had been, but her route was much cleverer. Even so, the feeling of being watched persisted, and she had found her steps quickening. It had taken a force of will to keep a furtive journey from becoming a panicked flight.

Ohatsu turned back to the wall, and, with a tiny grunt, made the small leap to the wind-swept coping. The vast drop down to the mountainside suddenly yawned before her. A cold sweat broke out across her body. Carefully, she peered over the sheer edge. The shinobi ladder was still there, pitoned in place.

When she had climbed up from the ladder, to the ledge of the coping, the gap had been manageable. Looking down from the wall, however, the top rung of the ladder seemed so far away. Ohatsu gulped at the sudden dryness in her throat, and rubbed cold sweat from her palms. The wind blew against her, pushing her towards the edge.

Carefully, Ohatsu turned away from the ledge and slid backwards across it. Her feet dangled into the open air—she could feel the wind snagging at her ankles. She bent her knees and curled over the coping, her feet groping for the ladder, the kate-bukuro at her waist swinging in the open air. Shuddering tension built in her arms, her shoulders, and her hands as she scrabbled for a hold on the dust-polished rock, then slid downward.

Until her feet touched the top rung.

Slowly, she brought her hands to the very edge, and, gripping it with her palms, stepped onto the ladder, testing her weight, until she felt free to release one hand and reach blindly down.

Her fingers gripped the hemp rope.

A gasp of relief swelled in her lungs as she crept down, both hands firmly grasping the ladder, and began the descent.

When she reached the bottom, her brow was streaked with sweat. Her hands were stiff, numbed into death-grips. All the fatigues, anxieties, and strains of the last two days finally began to take their toll—her hips and knees ached, and she felt bent like the old washerwomen of the Merchant Quarter as she stumbled away from the towering rocks at the base of the wall.

The bicycles were still there. Ohatsu counted. Still sixteen.

Whatever survivors remained of the shinobi force, then, were still up top, in Tengokuyama.

Ohatsu pulled one of the strange contraptions into the moonlight, and examined it. It looked like a regular bicycle, except for stationary peddles between the wheels set as rests for the feet, the bamboo tank suspended beneath the top-tube, and the thick, bamboo box fastened between the seat-tube and the down-tube, glue-sealed tatami pipes extending backwards from the box. A small bamboo handle was fastened to the side of the box by a cord that disappeared inside it.

After some minutes examining the strange vehicle, Ohatsu gripped the small handle, and pulled.

Something in the box whirred, and died.

She pulled it again, harder.

Steam hissed from the exhaust pipe, a slithering whirr vibrating from the bamboo box that shuddered along the entire length of the bicycle's frame, the brass cogs spinning to life, the coupling-rods straining against the stationary wheels.

Cautiously, Ohatsu climbed into the seat, pointing the wheel towards the gaping mouth of the cavern, and leaned into the low handlebars. The bicycle crept forward, a dim bulb flickering from the head tube out front. She leaned forward farther. The wheels gripped the pebbly loam and propelled her forward, into the darkness, the flickering front-light illuminating the way.

'Follow the road from the bridge,' Ukifune had said. 'That will take you to the Garden Path.'

The tall shrine sat in the darkness of the boiler plain like a sunken shipwreck, dimly glowing under the exploring light of Ohatsu's bullseye lantern.

The road dead-ended here, at this strange building. Four posts held up a presumably ornamental roof, steeply inclined, built in an ancient style. Steps rose up from every side to the platform beneath. Ohatsu climbed the steps, and shone the light down.

Sunken brass gears lay embedded in the platform, perfectly flush with the floor. Small holes were punctured into each gear—holes where rods could be placed, to set the gear's positions. Ohatsu slowly ran the light across the intricate mechanism. Hundreds of smaller cogs fit within scores of larger. Most were circular, some were ovoid, and a few were even curved.

This was the puzzle of the Hitodama—the only way to lower a gondola from above, connecting the boiler plain to catwalks that snaked along the ceiling of the caverns to the Hanging Garden.

Ohatsu turned and looked out towards the darkness surrounding the shrine. From the folds of her kimono, she took a small, brass box—the steam dial she had discovered in Ai's hidden drawer, seemingly eons ago. It sat, softly whirring in her hand, as though it too was pregnant with anticipation.

Ai was involved with the Ainu legate—Kuuklekle. Kuuklekle had produced papers which the shinobi wanted, and which Hatsutaro desperately needed to retrieve. If Ai really was the shinobi's contact, working secretly with Kuuklekle, the papers would have had to change hands. Under the claustrophobic grandeur of the Hanging Garden, that would be difficult—a secret location would be useful, then.

However, the only place other than the Hanging Garden both Ai and Kuuklekle could reference, would be here—the only discreet location on the boiler plain they both traversed before rising to the catwalks above.

Ohatso stepped out into the darkness.

The teeth snapped and juddered in the dial. Pushing the silent steam-cycle beside her, the bullseye lantern glimmering into the vaulted darkness, she walked away from the Garden Path Shrine.

If her logic was correct—and there was no guarantee it was—a secret rendezvous shouldn't be far. Anything farther than a ten-minute walk would be too much effort, especially for Kuuklekle. An ambassadorial dignitary, slipping away for espionage, was sure to be missed after anything more than an hour. Then again, how was Ohatsu to know what sort of trust—or control—the Ainu warrior had over his men...or over Ai.

The steam dial whirred and clacked. The bullseye light crept out into the darkness, illuminating barren rock slabs and patches of fallen stone scree.

And then, limning from the darkness, unnerving in its towering size, a dark boiler loomed above her. Ohatsu slowed her pace.

Great gashes struck through the side of the monstrous brass tank, curving the broken metal outward near its peak in jagged shreds, now greened with oxidization in the damp cavern air.

The dial chirped and clacked.

Carefully, Ohatsu moved around the boiler. Another loomed behind it, the spider-veined piping climbing to meet the exhaust pipes from four other gargantuan, moss-green tanks, sunk deep into a hewn depression in the rock.

And between them, the boilershack sat, a derelict ghost of past industry.

Ohatsu climbed down into the depression and moved towards the shack. The dial fell silent, then snapped, all the teeth crunching down into the box frame. According to the little mechanism, she had arrived. But was this truly the spot?

The shack was dark. No lights glimmered in the wood-latticed windows. No sounds fled from, or approached, the crunching of Ohatsu's reed-sandals as she walked towards the front door. Silence breathed above her, in the vastness of the open spaces. As she reached out to grip the strange brass knob on the door—no Japanese door she'd ever seen was built like that—the bullseye lamp began to shake in her hands.

The door swung open easily. Inside, a small chamber reflected her dull lantern light.

A cot, covered in thick furs. Tansu cabinets, shining in their fresh black lacquer, against one wall. An ornamental screen, folded, by the back. A strange, squarish brass stove, an assortment of shining brass pots and jars atop it in the center of the room. Unlit lanterns hung from the rafters. A rough table, and a small, black-lacquered desk, like the one in her and Ai's rooms in Tengokuyama.

Ohatsu stepped inside, and the light of her lantern fell upon a scroll on the table, crimped flat and sealed by a blob of crusted red wax. It had not been opened.

Carefully, she crossed to the table. The brittle wax crumbled as she opened the scroll, and read, written in a scrawling, brutish hand:

'I have considered your plea—It is no little thing to acquiesce. To sway the future of an entire people, for one woman. I toy with

59

insanity. And yet...

The papers are in the secret drawer, wrapped in fur. Give them to Yome. She'll know what to do with them.

Until we meet again—

—Kle'

Something was...wrong. The seal on the scroll had been unbroken—Ai had never read her message. And if she never read the scroll, then she never would have recovered the treaty documents. In which case, if she never had the documents, *how* could she have been killed for them?

Ohatsu dropped the scroll, her eyes fastening on the broken wax seal on the table, then the lacquered black desk beside it—and, drifting even further, folded on the floor, structured mosquito netting beside a stack of small robes, the sort traditionally used for...an infant.

The realization dawned slowly on her at first, but then came quickly, like flood waters bursting through a stubborn dike.

Chapter Six

Ohatsu knelt on the matted floor in Yuyami Okiya. The gas-globes burned softly, the room bathed in strobing golden light. Outside, the morning would just be breaking, sun rising above the distant hills, shedding indiscriminate warmth across the hanamachi, across the city.

The shoji slid aside and Naohana stepped into the room, her sandaled feet rustling across the reeds. She was dressed simply, her hair still holding the same Shimada style from days before.

Despite her storied elegance, Naohana blinked tiredly as she crossed to Ohatsu, and knelt opposite her. 'This couldn't have waited until later in the day?' the house-mother asked.

Ohatsu's bones felt brittle beneath her skin, bruised and lumpen. Muscles ached from the climb back up the shinobi ladder, from the harried flight through the curfewed city streets. It was all Ohatsu had been able to do, climbing up the back entrance to the okiya, and scratching—rather pitifully—at Naohana's sleeping chambers.

Now, her knees ached, her back was stiff and cramping, and beneath it all, her heart beat quickly in a racing tremolo.

'Okasan,' Ohatsu said, her voice hoarse and throaty, 'I know who killed Ryuzoji Ai.'

Naohana slowly nodded her head. 'Then you were right to wake me.'

Ohatsu started from the beginning. From her initial meeting with Ukifune. The secret descent to Yokidani. Nikkō Hanamachi and Yome, the boiler plain... Ai's body. She recounted following the shinobi up the ladder, the savage battle with Hatsutaro's samurai, her flight back to Ukifune, and her discovery in the abandoned boilershack. And Kuuklekle's note.

Naohana listened intently, occasionally nodding her head, her old eyes quickly growing sharp and crisp as Ohatsu told her tale.

'And when I read the scroll I remembered,' Ohatsu said as she finished, 'our little table, and the drawer, and in it...' she took out from her kimono the little swatch of fur. Untying the twine binding it, she carefully unfolded it on the mats, revealing a small stack of thin papers inside. 'I never thought it held anything,' she said. 'It looked so delicate, so small.'

Naohana leaned towards the papers. 'And what are they?'

Ohatsu spread the papers on the mat. Most were in Ai's artful hand, each stroke a masterwork of calligraphy; a few were written with a brutish penmanship. Ohatsu picked up a sheaf of Ai's and read.

'Beneath Tengokuyama the dragon sleeps,
Beneath his belly his favorite jewel,
Happy for his warmth.'

She lifted another.

'I sit alone,
Planted in my little house,
Like a peony
In its vase,
Waiting for water.'

61

Then she lifted one of the brutish pieces, and read again.

'The dragon slumbers beneath the mountain,
But I cannot be so patient,
The woman I love is waiting,
And I must go to her.'

Ohatsu carefully put the papers back and retied them in the furs. Looking up, her eyes met the gaze of her okasan. 'Naohana, why did you push my sister?'

Naohana's eyes were soft, her expression calm under the light of the globes. 'Ohatsu, you already know.'

'All this time,' Ohatsu said, 'I've been searching in a sea of spies, blindly seeking that which was right before my face. Ai never spied on Kuuklekle—she fell in love with him. She advised him perhaps, secretly, in his negotiations, lending him her wisdom behind the scenes. And likewise, he fell in love with her. The only documents Ai ever controlled, weren't treaties—they were love poems.

'The day Kuuklekle left,' Ohatsu continued, 'he hid the treaty documents in the boilershack for Yome—his true contact—and wrote the scroll for Ai. But she never saw it, and so, Yome never obtained *her* papers. Ai already lay, long dead, beneath the Hanging Garden—where you'd pushed her. You see, if Ai wasn't involved in the treaty papers, then nobody had a reason to want her dead. Yome, Ukifune, the geisha of Nikkō Hanamachi—they all benefit by her living, by reporting her to the magistrates. Yome said, and she was right, any geisha that lay with her patrons endangered her whole okiya. Regardless of their motives, if Ai became pregnant, your okiya could be forfeit by law for engaging in prostitution—the legal domain of the courtesans only. And she *was* with child,' Ohatsu said. 'I saw the baby-netting, the clothes, the unused tampons at the Asa Okiya that she never had the chance to get rid of…because you killed her first.'

Ohatsu's voice began to tremble. 'Only Hitodama can break the puzzle in the Garden Path Shrine—Hitodama, and the kenin of the Hanging Garden. So, the only ones with access to Ai were Hatsutaro and his men, Ukifune, Yome, and you.' Ohatsu's eyes rested on the red-and-black ribbons in Naohana's hair. 'And of these people, only you had anything to lose by Ai remaining alive.'

Naohana nodded slowly, a weary sigh breaking her lips. 'There had been rumors, child,' she said. 'I went to see them together, as you say. What my own eyes saw was inconclusive, so I caught her unawares. It just happened to be on the lower balconies... I confronted her and she admitted it.' Naohana shrugged. 'When you are older, you will understand, but an unwanted child is an easily solved problem. I, myself, have fallen prey to romance in my younger years. A few special teas, some particular plants and herbs, and the problem...disappears. But when I explained this to Mitsuhana,' Naohana's voice became sharp, her words slick beneath her tongue, 'she bridled. She told me she planned to keep the little vermin.'

'And you argued?'

Naohana shook her head. 'No,' she said. 'Once said, such a thing cannot be undone. Even if she came to her senses, later, it would slip out. So, I pushed her right then. And she fell.'

A taught silence crept between the two women. One of the gas-globes flickered and crackled, before burning true and clean again.

'What happens now?' Ohatsu asked.

Naohana sighed. 'Nothing,' she said. 'I only did what was right for the okiya, Ohatsu. With time, you'll see that.'

'I will turn you over, then, to the magistrates,' Ohatsu hissed.

'No,' Naohana said. 'If your word was believed, to do so would be to condemn every girl in this house. Including your maiko, Ohatsu—including Kiku. Of course, it's more likely they wouldn't believe you... How could they? Any evidence of your claim lies rotting, now, hundreds of feet below us.'

A wan smile creased Ohatsu's lips. 'And if I have a witness?'

Naohana shrugged again. 'But you don't.'

Softly, a shoji-door slid aside. Ohatsu watched as the color drained from Naohana's graceful face. Watched as she turned, to meet the hulking form of Hatsutaro as he strode into the room, the mats crunching beneath his feet. Watched her face grow slack as the crackling static of the steam-suit hissed to life, the glinting sword snapping from Hatsutaro's wooden saya, steam breathing in its wake as it leaped through the air like lighting, severing Naohana's head from her shoulders in a single stroke.

Naohana's body sat upright for a moment, tense and twitching, gurgling blood soaking her kimono, before crumpling to the side, a red pool slowly growing on the tatami beneath her.

Hatsutaro wiped the blade on his armor, and slipped it back into the saya before turning to Ohatsu, who still knelt.

'You knew I was following you, within the city?' he asked.

Ohatsu nodded, lowering her head. 'Yes, my lord.'

'How?'

'It was too great an oversight, leaving the shinobi ladder in place. Such a thing would have been quickly discovered by your men, once you found the intruders within the city walls. It was clear to me you left it, to try and snare the surviving shinobi. Instead, you saw me.'

The steam crept from the edges of Hatsutaro's suit like morning vapor. 'Where are the papers?' he asked.

'My lord,' Ohatsu said, 'I can only surmise they are with Yome, who, like you, followed me down below, in the caverns.'

'And why—'

A soft rustle whispered behind another shoji, across the room.

Dread seized Ohatsu with a sudden rigor—once again, senselessly, she had used the back passage, the one her maiko slept beneath...

In a crackle of steam, Hatsutaro flew across the room, a gauntleted hand striking through the wooden door frame and dragging the young girl by the hair into the room. The sword glinted.

'Stop!' Ohatsu screamed.

But too late. The body of Kiku fell to the ground, blood gushing to the mats, the head rolling from Hatsutaro's grip to rest beside Naohana's.

Kiri-sute gomen. The right to strike.

The numb pains, the aches, the bruised bones and sore tendons, the anxiety, the rage and anger all fighting for dominance within Ohatsu slowly died. Percolated. Condensed. Into a cold anger, deep within her chest.

Hatsutaro stamped across the room, the sword raising again, the static crackling from his steaming power suit.

But Ohatsu just lowered her head, and said one word. 'Please.'

Steam hissed above her. Ohatsu felt the floor bowing beneath the massive warrior's weight. Yet she remained, head bowed to the floor. And the killing blow did not come.

'Why should I spare your life?'

'In payment,' Ohatsu said. 'For giving you Yome.'

The gas-globe flickered and popped again.

The steaming skirl above her slowly quieted.

'You are okasan of Yuyami Okiya, now,' Hatsutaro said. 'And you will answer to me.'

And with that, he left.

Still bent to the mats, Ohatsu looked up and met the dead gaze of Kiku from across the room. And if Kiku still lived, she would have seen two narrow tears run trails down the geisha's trembling cheeks.

The sun was high in the domed heavens when Ohatsu brought the steam-cycle to a stop on the mountain road below Tengokuyama. Above her, the fortified city broke the sky, the sheer rock walls gleaming with stony pearlescence in the bright sun.

Her kimono was bound tightly about her body, bands of latigo wound around her arms and legs—on her back, a simple pack of folded cloth, tied by rope.

Carefully, she stepped from the bicycle, pulling a skein of water from her back and bent to refill the bamboo motor's reservoir. Above her, birds sang in the swaying trees, on the breeze the scents of warm soil, sunbaked pinesap, ferns, and—ever so faintly—the aroma of sulfur.

Ohatsu did not react as the dark forms materialized from the undergrowth and moved to encircle her on the road.

'Here we are,' the new leader of the shinobi said—the broad man with the sickle-and-chain.

Ohatsu rose and turned, silently counting the forms before her. Six. Only six. The cold anger kindled again in her breast.

'You,' she said, pointing to a short, thin shinobi in the back. 'Come here.'

Nobody moved. Then, with a soft sigh, the identified shinobi stepped forward.

'Ai's instructions were to give these to Yome,' Ohatsu said, pulling a small swatch of furs from her kimono. 'She can no longer complete that charge. And so, I shall.'

She held the furs out.

The figure snorted, the dark eyes glinting through the face-wrappings. Then, with a shrug, Yome reached up and unwrapped the cloth masking her face and smiled. 'How did you know?' she asked.

'Ukifune knew of the shinobi. So did you,' Ohatsu said. 'I knew you had some master, pulling strings. But until Ukifune revealed her hand, I couldn't tie you two together for sure. The only ones who should know about the shinobi were their allies, and their adversaries. Hence, you and Ukifune were working on the same side. The rest was simple.'

Yome took the parcel. 'Where were they?'

'Hidden in a secret drawer. In the lacquered chest, in Ai and Kuuklekle's love nest. I lied about them, to Naohana, you know. And Hatsutaro. Your cover was already broken—but I think Ukifune's is still safe.'

Yome nodded, tucking the fur package into her kimono. 'Do you know what will happen now?' she asked.

Ohatsu nodded. 'Death,' she said. 'For Hatsutaro. For Iwamura. Death to that cursed city up above us.'

'You don't want to see it?'

Ohatsu shook her head. 'There is nothing there for me now.'

Yome smiled, her snaggle-teeth gleaming in the light. 'The Shōgun will reward you, if you stay.'

'I still have one more parcel to deliver.'

'What parcel?' Yome asked.

Ohatsu pulled out an identical fur package, stained with clotted blood. 'The love poems of a man's dead mistress.'

'And where do you expect to find this man?' Yome asked.

'Somewhere in the north,' Ohatsu said. 'In Ezo. Do you happen to know the way?'

Yome shrugged. 'No,' she said. 'You'll have to find your own path, I'm afraid.'

Ohatsu smiled, and stooped to grip the start-cord of the bicycle. 'When have I ever done anything else?' she asked, and yanked the cord.

The steam-motor hissed to life, angry white vapors spitting from the exhaust pipes into the forest undergrowth. With a nod, she turned the wheel down the mountain and leaned into the handlebars. The machine leapt to life, slicing down the winding road. And, as the shinobi melded into the undergrowth like shadows cringing from the light, Ohatsu also disappeared into the distance.

Murder in Whitby

Karen Bayly

Chapter One

Smoke filled Serendipity Windlass's nostrils, and she braced herself for the inevitable.

Bang!

And there it was. The car's steam-powered engine chugged into life, and the tall, gaunt form of her dear friend, Ambrose Perceval-Savile, emerged from under the hood.

'It should be fine for a while,' he said, bright blue eyes twinkling. 'Get back in, and we can continue.'

Serendipity sighed and readjusted the chestnut ringlet decorating her left shoulder. Despite her Amazonian appearance, she was anything but athletic and hated to be reminded of her infirmity. She ambled toward the vehicle, refusing to use the cane tucked under her arm. While it was a magnificent item, with its dragonhead top doubling as the handle of a hidden stiletto, using a cane felt too much like admitting defeat.

A loud ping from her mechanical lower leg taunted her. She ignored it and, pursing her lips, nursed her denial like a fractious infant.

Ambrose appeared beside her, opened the passenger door and offered his arm.

'I'm all right, Uncle Amby.'

'I know,' he said, helping her anyway. 'I'm sorry you don't like my gift.'

'I love the cane. I merely prefer not to use it unless absolutely necessary.'

He nodded and left her to settle herself. Serendipity chided herself and made a note to tell him yet again how she loved all his

68

gifts, especially her mechanical leg. She couldn't imagine her life without it.

Uncle slipped into the driver's seat and grinned. 'Off we go,' he said. 'Let nothing stand in the way of progress.'

'Famous last words, Amby.'

He winked at her, and she laughed. His rebellious spirit always inspired her; life would have been dark without him.

When she was seven, she'd lost her leg below her left knee after a runaway horse and carriage knocked her down. The most skilled surgeons failed to salvage the mangled lower limb, and Uncle Amby, a university colleague of her father, stepped in to save the day with the mechanical leg. He'd upgraded it as she grew, even after he lost his medical license for "unsanctioned and unnecessary biomedical experiments". Yet that same research produced her marvellous leg. Unsanctioned, they may have been. Unnecessary, definitely not.

'There's another gift for you in your reticule.'

Serendipity opened the drawstring of her dark green velvet reticule and pulled out a small leather roll. Inside lay a brand new set of the finest clockmaking tools.

'German-made,' said Amby. 'They'll make minor adjustments to your leg much easier for you.'

'Will I need them after I pick up the parts?'

Usually, her uncle travelled to Whitby to meet the cargo ship, but his vehicle was unfit for such a lengthy journey, and he despised trains. So, she willingly volunteered to collect both leg and car components.

'Yes. Part of the issue is maintenance, my dear. Wear and tear is normal, but you can forestay the inevitable with regular service. And while you've been doing an admirable job, the tools you use leave much to be desired. My fault, I fear. I should have given you a better set sooner.'

'It's just as much my fault, Amby. I've been wandering around London adrift since my father died, neglecting you and everyone connected with him. My apologies.'

'Understandable, my dear.' He swerved slightly to avoid a dog belting across the road. 'Have you decided what you want to do with your future?'

She shook her head.

'You have a fine mind and lively constitution, Serendipity. It would be a pity to waste either.'

'Thank you, Uncle Amby,' she said, touching his arm lightly before returning her gaze to the fields and hedgerows bordering the road. She would return to Pickering from Whitby in a day, Amby would repair her leg, and she could go back to life in London. But what life did she genuinely have there? If she were, to be honest, nothing in that city meant anything to her, and certainly not the endless well-meaning friends and relatives intent on introducing her to eligible young men. Perhaps a visit to the seaside would clear her head and boost her resolve.

But everything depended on making the train on time. So far, she and Amby were cutting it fine.

Chapter Two

The car pulled into the station just as the guard blew his whistle and shouted, 'All aboard!'

Serendipity slid out as Amby hauled her valise from the backseat. She waved the cane and shouted, 'Wait, please!'

The guard turned, his posture combative. 'Hurry up. The Whitby-Pickering Railway waits for no one.'

What a rude little man, she thought. Yet perhaps he had a shred of decency?

She swallowed her pride, dipped her head, swung the cane into position, and hobbled toward the train, Amby in tow with her suitcase.

A man's voice cut through the air. 'I say, old chap. Who the blazes are you to be so rude? The lady needs your assistance, not your scorn.'

Serendipity peered from under her eyelashes. The voice belonged to a middle-aged man whose lean and dandyish appearance screamed bounder, yet his words suggested otherwise.

'You appear to have a champion,' said Amby as they entered the dark coolness of the ticket office. 'Nicely played.'

She grinned. 'Thank you. I can't let my flair for the dramatic wither and die.'

Amby took her valise onto the platform while Serendipity purchased her ticket. When she limped onto the platform, he talked to the man who had risen to her defence against the guard. She headed toward them but stopped dead when the man uttered, 'I couldn't let that lower-class nothing treat a proper bit of frock so poorly. He works for the likes of us.'

Serendipity made a mental note to always trust her first impressions. The man was decidedly skilamalink. She stared at her ticket and discovered with relief that she was in the carriage forward of the one where the bounder stood.

'This way, Amby,' she said.

Her uncle turned and followed her. Just as they arrived at the carriage doors, the guard blew his whistle again and roared, 'All aboard', staring pointedly at her.

'I'll take it from here,' she said, hauling herself through the carriage door. She held out her hand for her bag.

'Are you sure? I can bring it on—'

A steam whistle pierced the air, and the train lurched.

Serendipity wiggled her fingers. 'Yes, very sure.'

He handed her the valise and stood back as the train began to move. 'Take care, m'dear.'

She waved, stepped back, shut the door, and headed to the central part of the carriage in search of her seat.

All the booths seemed surprisingly full, and she hoped she would find the one assigned to her less so. She dreamt of a window seat or one by the booth entrance so she could admire the scenery across the aisle. The prospect of being wedged between two strangers appalled her. She rechecked her ticket. No, it definitely showed a window seat.

Finally, she arrived at the correct booth. However, someone else occupied it—an older woman in a black lace dress peering short-sightedly at a mechanical bird in a cage. The animatronic performed a series of trills and wing flaps, and the woman seemed utterly mesmerised. Serendipity threw open the door, and the woman jumped backwards and almost fell.

'Oh, my poor heart,' cried the woman. 'You gave me such a fright. Why are you here?'

71

A voice spoke from behind her, all too familiar. 'And more to the point, who the blazes are you?'

She turned and met eyes with the man from the station. With his neat moustache, centre-parted hair slicked down with a woody-smelling pomade and smarmy expression, he looked every inch the bounder. Cocking her head to one side, she smiled her most charming smile. 'Serendipity Windlass. I should thank you for coming to my aid earlier.'

The man did not soften one whit, but a lascivious gleam lit his face. 'Is that why you're here? To thank me?'

She kept her voice light. 'Actually, no. I believe this is my booth.'

He bared his teeth in an unfriendly smile that reminded her of a monkey she'd seen at the zoo. 'I doubt it. I bought all the seats in this booth.'

She proffered her ticket. 'No. It says here—'

'I'm sorry,' the man said, 'but it seems the booking office has made a mistake.'

Serendipity drew to her full height. 'Perhaps we'll wait for the ticket collector to decide.'

The obnoxious excuse for humanity sneered and pulled a ticket from the inner pocket of his coat. 'Now, see here. All the seats. All mine.'

She leaned her head forward. 'May I inspect that?'

He shoved the ticket back into his coat. 'No, you may not. Now, if you would kindly leave us in peace…'

He stepped back, his arm showing the way out. Mustering her self -respect, she departed, flinching as her leg gave a slight ping, hoping he hadn't detected the noise.

She investigated the next booth and discovered two children and a weary-looking woman inhabited it, so she nodded a greeting. 'It seems there has been a double booking, and someone has taken my seat in the next booth. May I sit here?'

'Of course, dear,' said the woman, sliding closer to the window. 'Make yourself comfortable.'

Serendipity settled herself, grateful she at least had her second preferred choice of seat. She was sure the man was lying about purchasing all the tickets for the other booth but opted not to challenge him further. There was something odd about him,

72

something she couldn't explain except to say he'd be a dangerous enemy.

When the guard finally checked her ticket, he confirmed she should be in the other booth and suggested she might like to move. Serendipity put on her best helpless face and asked if she could stay seated here, as she felt safer with her current company. The guard merely sniffed and moved on.

Chapter Three

The rest of the train journey proved uneventful, and a whisker less than two hours later, Serendipity alighted in Whitby.

A faint tang of salt and adventure tickled her nostrils as she stepped through the arches onto the street. She memorised every detail of the map Amby supplied and paused briefly to get her bearings. Carrying her valise and cane, she headed to Whitby Harbour.

A small ping reminded her she needed to make a few minor adjustments and administer a drop of oil to the mechanics in her artificial leg as soon as possible. She squeezed her reticule, the weight of the jewellery roll containing the clockmaker tools reassuring. With a sense of anticipation, she turned down Haggersgate Road toward Pier Road, eager to glimpse the SS Everilda, the ship that held the key to her more ambulatory future.

Every step, however, brought her a greater sense of disappointment. The Everilda wasn't docked where Amby claimed. Nor was it docked opposite at Tate Hill Pier. Her leg gave a pitiful squeak, so she stopped. She put down her valise and stared beyond East and West Piers to the ocean, searching for signs of a steamship on the horizon.

A tall man with ginger hair and a beard appeared beside her.

'Excuse my presumptuousness, but what ship are you looking for, madam?' He spoke in an Irish accent, which Serendipity found immensely charming.

'The Everilda,' she replied. 'And you are?'

'Bram Stoker, madam, business manager for the Lyceum Theatre in London.'

Serendipity couldn't hide her delight. 'Oh, how wonderful! I saw a show there when I was six. It inspired me to become an actress.'

'And did you?'

'It was not to be.' His eyes flickered to her cane, and she strove to forestall questions. 'I could say the same for this ship,' she said.

'I can help you there,' said Mr Stoker. 'I've just come from the harbour master, and a storm at sea has delayed the Everilda's arrival.'

'Are you also waiting for that ship?'

'No, I overheard the information when enquiring about a ship called the Dmitry, which ran ashore here in 1885.'

'I remember hearing about it. A great tragedy.'

'Indeed. I'm thinking of using a similar tale for a novel.'

'Are you an author as well, Mr Stoker?'

'I am, Miss—'

She held out a gloved hand. 'Serendipity Windlass. I wonder if you might have overheard when the Everilda might grace our shores?'

'Ah, yes. I'm afraid to say it may dock anywhere within the next twenty-four to forty-eight hours.'

'That is most unfortunate,' she said. 'I had not intended to stay overnight.' Indeed, this unexpected turn of events left her in a quandary. Should she return to Pickering or take a chance and stay in town?

Mr Stoker peered at her, an expression both quizzical and kindly. 'Again, excuse my presumptuousness, but if you are contemplating staying, I can recommend Mrs Veazey's Guesthouse at 6 Royal Crescent, Whitby. It is a quiet and reputable establishment, and I know Mrs Veazey had a last-minute cancellation. She would welcome a refined young woman at her premises.'

Serendipity must have looked as doubtful as she felt, for Mr Stoker gave a rueful grin and added, 'You are quite safe around me, Miss Windlass. My wife and baby son will join me there next week.'

She flushed with embarrassment and was glad of the cool salty breeze blowing off the water. 'Then I shall go there immediately. My humble thanks, Mr Stoker.'

He tipped his hat and headed toward Bridge Street. She watched

74

him go, intrigued by his air of purpose and the way he took in his surroundings. She could learn from someone like Bram Stoker.

She visualised the map and plotted a course to Royal Street.

Chapter Four

The grand curve of Royal Crescent on the eastern side featured an unbroken line of Georgian terraced houses overlooking the Royal Crescent Gardens, a charming park of well-kept green lawns, colourful flower beds, groomed pathways and wooden benches. One only had to turn one's face north to witness the grey-green, forbidding waters of the North Sea.

Serendipity paused outside No. 6, a neat five-storey abode, then climbed the four steps to the front door and knocked. A patrician woman with greying hair tucked into a tight bun answered the door. She cocked her head and regarded Serendipity with a mixture of curiosity and caution. 'Are you looking for someone?' she asked.

'I am,' said Serendipity. 'Mr Bram Stoker recommended this establishment and suggested I speak to Mrs Veazey.'

'I am Mrs Emma Veazey.'

The woman stared intensely at the young woman, making her feel like a cow at a fair.

'Oh good,' Serendipity said. 'I find myself in need of lodgings for the next couple of days. I came to Whitby to collect an item for my, um, uncle, but the ship is delayed at sea.'

She inwardly derided herself for stumbling over the word "uncle". Amby was not a real uncle, but he might as well have been, and her gaff made it sound somewhat seedy. Mrs Veazey already appeared to regard her as a woman of likely disrepute.

To her surprise, Mrs Veazey smiled. 'And Mr Stoker took pity on you like you were a stray kitten and directed you here. Come in, Miss—'

'Serendipity Windlass.' She smiled back, taking comfort in the landlady's measured tones, a mix of earthy Yorkshire and elocution lessons.

'We'll get you settled,' said Mrs Veazey, 'and then you can come downstairs to the drawing room, and I'll serve refreshments.'

In no time, Serendipity had checked into a pleasant and welcoming room, unpacked her valise, tightened a few screws on her leg and oiled it, then trotted down the stairs and settled in a lovely green velvet high-backed chair to await the arrival of a pot of tea and sandwiches.

The door opened, and she leaned forward in anticipation, only to reel back sharply. Two individuals had arrived, one of whom she had hoped never to encounter again.

The woman, wearing a different black lace dress, sat in a chair on the opposite side of the room and busied herself, fumbling through her voluminous bag. The man, sporting slicked-back hair and a smarmy expression, stood before her.

'Oh, hello,' he said with an oily smile. 'See, Grandmama, it's that young girl from the train.'

Serendipity bristled at being called a girl and bit back a retort.

The horrid man gave a perfunctory bow. 'Garrett Fortescue, and this is my grandmother, Lavinia Fortescue.'

His grandmother didn't even bother to glance up.

'I say, apologies for my earlier brusqueness. Grandmama doesn't enjoy travelling with strangers, do you?'

Mrs Fortescue grunted and kept rummaging through her bag. 'Where are my glasses?'

Garrett pressed on. 'You travelled well enough?'

'Considering,' she said, wishing he'd go away.

'Garrett! Stop flirting with that girl and find my glasses. You said you'd put them in my bag. My eyesight is not what it used to be, and neither are my hands.'

To her great relief, Mrs Veazey entered with a tray. As the landlady unloaded its contents onto the table before Serendipity, she winked, then turned to the others. 'Ah, Mr Fortescue. Mrs Fortescue. I see you've already introduced yourself to our new guest. I had intended to do introductions myself. Can I get you refreshments?'

The Fortescues seemed too distracted by the prospect of tea or too sure of their own entitlement to register Mrs Veazey's gentle rebuke.

Serendipity took a deep breath, noting with displeasure the woody odour of Mr Fortescue's pomade drifting in her direction, and

76

poured her tea. Two additional individuals joined the room: a nondescript man with thinning hair and a young woman with blonde hair and light sapphire blue eyes. She stared at Serendipity, her eyes bright, the pupils constricted. Garrett greeted them with an almost desperate enthusiasm.

'Alethea, Arthur, do join us!'

Serendipity signalled to Mrs Veazey. 'May I take my tea and sandwiches to my room? I am a little tired.'

'Of course, but I'll get Anna, the maid, to bring a tray up for you.'

'Thank you.'

Anna, a broad-faced young woman with dark brown hair and striking green eyes, appeared from behind Mrs Veazey, curtsied and whisked the items onto the tray. Serendipity stood to leave.

Garrett Fortescue swung around. 'Going so soon?'

'I am weary after such an unsettled journey,' she replied.

'Oh, perhaps we will catch up later, Miss—sorry, I didn't catch your name.'

She paused at the door and smiled. 'I didn't give it, Mr Fortescue.'

Though she knew such rude behaviour would win her no friends, the shock on the odious man's face was worth any diminishing of social favour.

Chapter Five

Bursts of male jocularity on the street below floated up to Serendipity's room on the second floor. She opened her eyes, rolled onto her back, and folded her arms behind her head.

Sleep had eluded her, and there didn't seem to be much point in further chasing the bliss of slumber. In the hour since she'd slipped into bed, she'd woken twice—once by a loud thump in the room above and now by the ne'er-do-wells outside. When she had drifted off, strange dreams full of animatronic people plagued her.

She heard someone knock repeatedly, followed by the front door opening.

'Mr Fortescue! Mr Merewether! It's 11:30 pm. We have a 10:00 pm curfew in this establishment.'

Garrett Fortescue's all-too-familiar voice scoffed at the landlady's concerns. 'Noted, Mrs V. This town is a graveyard past 10:00 pm anyway.'

He stomped up the stairs, chatting at full volume. 'What was I saying? Oh, yes. Look, Arthur, old chap, fleecing the locals is a time-honoured sport.'

Mr Merewether mumbled something akin to an apology and followed his cousin.

Charming, thought Serendipity as she sighed and shifted to her side. Garrett Fortescue appeared to care little for anyone other than himself.

The footsteps continued past her floor to the one above, now muffled by the thick carpet. She detected the faint creak of an opening door, then heard silence followed by a gasp.

'Dear god! Great-Aunt Lavinia!'

Although muted, the words held a clarity born of shock.

'Garrett! Alethea! Call for a doctor!'

Serendipity heard a lighter set of footsteps running down the stairs.

'Mrs Veazey! Help! My great-aunt has taken a turn!'

The house erupted into a flurry of activity. Serendipity threw off the bedcovers and hopped over to the small desk where she'd laid her mechanical leg. She turned on the lamp and attached her prosthesis, carefully clicking the leg onto the titanium rod protruding from her truncated thigh. Centring her attention, she concentrated on straightening her knee, the first step in activating the neural, muscular, and skeletal interfaces that made her leg unique. Then she flexed her ankle and wiggled her mechanical toes.

As always, she silently thanked Uncle Amby before dressing quickly and smoothing her hair.

She reached the landing as the landlady descended from the floor above the stairs, ashen-faced and solemn.

'Is everything all right, Mrs Veazey?' Serendipity knew the answer before she asked.

'Unfortunately, no. Mrs Fortescue has passed away. I'm off to get the doctor.'

Garrett followed close behind. 'No need for that. My grandmother was old and unwell. Her death is natural.'

'This is my establishment, Mr Fortescue,' said Mrs Veazey, 'and I decide how to handle untimely deaths within it. Propriety demands I call the doctor.'

Mr Stoker arrived on the landing from two floors above. 'I agree. I'll come with you, Mrs Veazey. You should not walk the streets of Whitby alone at this hour.'

They proceeded downstairs. Garrett Fortescue swore under his breath, his face a thundercloud that darkened when he noticed Serendipity. 'What are you looking at?'

'All the noise woke me.'

'Well, I suggest you return to your room and stay out of other people's business.'

Turning around, he ascended the stairs, jumping up two steps at a time.

She stared after him, positive the man was hiding something.

Mrs Veazey and Mr Stoker returned with the doctor fifteen minutes later and escorted him to Arthur's room.

The doctor requested that everyone unrelated to Lavinia Fortescue stay in their rooms, but Serendipity felt compelled to keep abreast of the situation. She hovered by the doorway, observing the main action. Luckily, she went unnoticed as the room's occupants were preoccupied with the proceedings or facing away from her.

Doctor Oscar Fleming, hawkish-faced and intense, kneeled beside the body, examining her face. In particular, he seemed focused on the dead woman's left eye.

His gaze shifted to someone Serendipity could not see. 'Did your grandmother have any eye issues?'

'None that I know of,' said Garrett Fortescue.

The sharpness of his tone added to her doubts about his honesty. Even Doctor Fleming looked sceptical.

'I really can't confirm the cause of death without further investigation,' he said. 'Mrs Veazey. I believe we should involve the police at this stage to ensure that everything is processed correctly in case I find the cause of death to be unlawful.'

The room erupted with gasps.

Garrett exploded. 'Now see here, sir! How dare you imply such a thing.'

Doctor Fleming maintained his icy mien. 'I dare because it is my job. Would you prefer I refer the matter to the coroner straightaway?'

Garrett said nothing.

'Not if it's unnecessary,' said Mrs Veazey. 'We'll follow your suggestions, Doctor Fleming. Should I lock the room until the police arrive?'

'Yes, Mrs Veazey,' said the doctor. 'That is a wise decision.'

A male voice moaned. 'But where will I sleep? What will I do?'

'Arthur,' Alethea scolded, 'please be more sensitive. Our great-aunt is dead.'

'You are no help, Ally,' said Arthur. 'You know I depend on you.'

Serendipity took the cue and departed. As she passed Miss Merewether's room, she noticed an odd object on the carpet, illuminated by the light streaming from the gap under the door. She crouched to pick it up, bracing for a tell-tale ping, but her leg gave no sound. Giving silent thanks, she put the object in her pocket and scurried to her room.

She waited in darkness until the sounds faded and turned on the light.

The object she'd retrieved was a hatpin with the head filed off. Someone must have dropped it, but who? And why did someone alter it? A sense of unease washed over her. She didn't trust the police to uncover the truth. Her own experiences regarding her accident proved that they were ineffective at best and inept at worst. And she'd always wanted to solve a mystery. Perhaps this was her chance.

Chapter Six

Serendipity gazed out the window. The deep blue sea stretched to a horizon littered with storm clouds but with clear azure skies above. She hoped the weather further out was fair enough to allow the

Everilda fast passage to Whitby Harbour.

Two policemen arrived from Escrick Police Station around 9:00 am. For over two hours, they'd been clattering about in the room above, their actions shrouded in mystery. They'd opened a window only a few minutes earlier, so Serendipity had opened hers. She now sat in a chair, elbows on the windowsill, her curiosity piqued, her eyes on the horizon, her ears pricked, hoping to glean tidbits of information.

A knock interrupted her reverie.

'It's Anna, Miss Windlass. I have refreshments for you.'

'Come in, please,' she said. The police sergeant had requested that all guests remain in their rooms while they gathered evidence, and Mrs Veazey and Anna ensured their guests missed out on nothing.

The door swung open, and the maid entered carrying a tray with a pot of tea, a cup and saucer, a milk jug and sugar bowl, and a plate of assorted biscuits.

'Here you are, miss. We can't have our guests starving.'

The young woman arranged tea items on a small table beside Serendipity.

'You have a lovely view from this room, miss. I hope you like it.'

Serendipity smiled. 'I do. Very much so. Tell me, please, who was occupying the room above me?'

'That would be Mr Arthur Merewether. He's here with his sister, Miss Alethea Merewether.'

'Mr Merewether is the balding chap?'

'That's him.'

'And Miss Merewether is the attractive blonde?'

Anna nodded. 'Though attractive is as attractive does. I'm not one for the likes of her.'

Serendipity thought of pursuing that line of thought but decided against it. She didn't want their conversation to sound too much like an interrogation.

'When will the police leave?'

'Who knows, miss? Sergeant Whitehall is a stickler for doing everything by the book, which is right good, if pernickety, and Joe, I mean, Constable Minns is too polite to argue with him. Anyhow, I'd best get back to my duties, miss.'

'Thank you, Anna.'

Serendipity returned to the window. The crash of waves on the shore and the yelping cry of herring gulls floated on the breeze. Down below sat the police car, a new model, its steam engine supposedly capable of reaching breakneck speeds. Yet, for all its modernity, it squatted at the kerb, a pompous lump of metal. She wondered if the policemen were of a similar constitution.

Up above, a drawer slammed shut, and another slid open. The sound was loud, and she recalled seeing a desk under the window.

'Sir! What do you make of this?'

Silence, followed by Sergeant Whitehall's voice. 'I'm not sure. It's a pipe of some sort.'

'And these?'

More silence. Serendipity leaned out, straining to hear.

'Again, I'm not sure, Joseph. They look like hatpins with no head.'

Serendipity fell back in her chair. More headless hatpins? How odd! What was Mr Merewether doing with such weird items? But another question took precedence over pipe and pins—what was Mrs Fortescue doing in Arthur's room when she died?

She was still pondering these questions when Mrs Veazey summoned her to the drawing room. The police wished to speak to her.

Chapter Seven

Sergeant Whitehall stroked his handlebar moustache and smiled. His ruddy face was pleasant enough but made him look like a duffer. Yet Serendipity saw through his act. Those hooded eyes concealed a steely mind.

'So, let me sum up. You are here to collect a mechanical part for your uncle—'

'No,' said Serendipity. 'I call him that, but he is a long-term family friend and has known me since childhood.'

'I see.'

'I said that earlier, Sergeant Whitehall.'

Constable Minns looked down at his notes. 'Yes, sir. She did.'

The sergeant glared at his lackey and then returned his attention to Serendipity.

'Let me reiterate. You are here to collect a mechanical part for a long-term family friend. You have never met the Fortescues or Merewethers before yesterday.'

'Again, no. I haven't met the Merewethers but encountered the Fortescues on the train. I've told you the full story of that meeting.'

Constable Minns looked down at his notes again. Serendipity knew he would confirm her statement and upstage his boss again. She felt sorry for the young constable.

'Sergeant Whitehall. I do believe you are trying to trip me up,' she said. 'A man of your intelligence is unlikely to forget such details.'

The sergeant smiled again. 'Just doing my job, Miss Windlass.'

A brief knock heralded the door opening, and Mrs Veazey and Doctor Fleming burst into the room. The landlady's frazzled expression and the doctor's serious demeanour told Serendipity something was amiss.

'That will do for now, Miss Windlass.' With a wave of his hand, the sergeant dismissed her.

As Serendipity took her leave, Mrs Veazey pushed the door closed. But the latch did not catch, and the door swung open a few inches. Serendipity positioned herself so she could witness some of what was about to unfold. Even from her outside vantage point, she sensed the increasing tension in the room.

'I am sorry to say my examination has confirmed my initial misgivings,' the doctor said. He reached into his pocket and pulled out an object wrapped in gauze, unwrapping it as he spoke. 'The deceased's eyes were bloodshot, and I observed a lesion in the lower section of the left eye's sclera. When I checked behind the eye, I found this.'

Everyone bent to look, and Mrs Veazey reeled back in horror.

'In my opinion, someone shot this needle into the victim's eye with enough force to penetrate the brain, intending to kill her. However, the perpetrator did not conduct enough research, so the needle merely incapacitated Mrs Fortescue. The killer then suffocated the victim to death.'

Mrs Veazey gasped and sank into a chair. Sergeant Whitehall and

Constable Minns exchanged a glance. Minns dashed out and bounded up the stairs, blind to Serendipity's presence.

She tiptoed as quietly as possible, wincing at a ping of protest from her leg, and opened the next door. The dining room beyond lay in darkness, save for the faint glimmer of silverware and cut glass reflecting the light sneaking in through the door. She slipped inside, leaving the door slightly ajar, and, peeking through a minuscule gap, waited for Constable Minns to return.

Constable Minns pounded down the stairs and into the drawing room. Serendipity crept back to the room's doorway.

'Ah,' said Sergeant Whitehall, 'as I remembered. The needles are identical, and we found them with this pipe.'

'Odsfish,' said the doctor. 'That is a blowgun. I saw one like it when I was in Japan. It's a fukidake made of fired bamboo. While most are lengthy, this is the shorter practice version for boys. Still deadly.'

Sergeant Whitehall pursed his lips. 'Would you say this pipe may have fired the needle you found, Doctor Fleming?'

'It could have.'

'Minns, bring Mr Merewether here immediately.'

Mrs Veazey sprang up in protest. 'Not Mr Merewether! He's such a quiet, polite man.'

'If you ask me,' said the sergeant, 'they're often the ones who hide a criminal nature.'

Constable Minns repeated his previous dash, again overlooking Serendipity. Seeing it as a sign, she stole back to her room, not wanting to push her luck.

No sooner had she closed her door than two men stomped down the stairs, one complaining loudly about the constabulary's ungentlemanly conduct.

Serendipity lay on her bed and pondered the ceiling. Was Arthur Merewether responsible for the death of his great-aunt? For no particular reason she could identify, she doubted it. She dearly wished to take a walk to the docks—a brisk walk helped her thought processes—but the police had not given permission to leave.

Someone moved around in Arthur's room upstairs. Her first instinct was to check who it was, but her unwillingness to reveal her interest, to be classified as nosy, checked her enthusiasm.

However, the sounds from overhead stirred her memories of last night. She hurried to the Davenport, opened the leather writing slope, grabbed paper, ink and pen, and wrote.

When the next door knock came, Serendipity had documented all her perceptions and observations, along with their respective times.

She carefully stowed the inked papers, each a potential piece of the puzzle, into the stationary compartment and retrieved a fresh sheet of paper.

'Come in,' she said, writing the date and the words, "Dearest Celia".

Mrs Veazey opened the door and popped her head in. 'You are free to leave your room, Miss Windlass. The policemen have departed with Mr Merewether.'

Serendipity sat up straight. 'They arrested him?'

A pained expression flittered over the landlady's face. 'I'm afraid so. I am appalled that such a thing happened at my establishment. And to think I let Mrs Fortescue into Mr Merewether's room at 8:30 pm. I had my doubts, but she insisted he wouldn't mind. To think I have been the last friendly face she encountered!'

'I would find solace in that idea if I were you,' said Serendipity.

Mrs Veazey sighed, 'Yes, yes. You are right. Anyway, we will serve tea, scones, and a seed cake in the drawing room in a few minutes. We all need a boost in spirits, and the cook has exceeded expectations.'

'Mrs Veazey, how do you know it was 8:30 pm?'

'On the way downstairs, I saw Anna heading into the drawing room. I remember checking the hallway clock and realising she should've left half an hour earlier.'

'Is that unusual? That Anna was still here, that is.'

Mrs Veazey smiled. 'No. She's a good girl, our Anna, a hard and uncomplaining worker, if a little loquacious sometimes. But I've ne'er received a complaint, so I'm confident she knows when to hold her tongue.'

A faint smile crossed the woman's face as she closed the door as if the notion of Anna speechless amused her.

Serendipity opened the Davenport again, sifted through papers, and found the desired information. Either her memory was flawed, Mrs Veazey was incorrect, or the police falsely arrested Arthur Merewether. Since she possessed an impeccable memory, it must be one of the other two options. But first, tea. Then, a walk to the docks.

Chapter Eight

As luck would have it, the odious Garrett Fortescue declined the invitation for tea because he "was too bound by grief at the loss of his beloved grandmama". Or so Miss Merewether announced.

Alethea Merewether was a pretty woman with abundant golden blonde hair piled on top of her head and a shy way of looking from underneath her eyelids. Yet when the young woman cast her gaze over Serendipity, she caught a hint of something viperous behind those bright blue eyes.

Once fuelled by tea and a slice of an exceedingly delicious pound cake, she headed back upstairs. After a quick oil of her mechanical joints, Serendipity donned her dark green linen jacket, dusting off the last remnants of travel, and settled her summer straw and green taffeta bonnet at a flattering angle. Although she hated being thought of as vain, her appearance pleased her, and the green of her ensemble set off her chestnut hair and hazel eyes. She had long since deduced that marriage would not be in her future, and neither her questioning personality nor her mechanical leg presented a premium to potential beaus.

On her way out, she paused by the impressive mahogany grandfather clock with a brass face in the hallway and pulled out her gold pocket watch, a twenty-first birthday gift from her father. The guesthouse timepiece agreed with her pocket watch, a minor detail confirming the perspicacity of her recollections of last night and her growing misgivings.

She made her way to the bustling dock; the air filled with the cries of seagulls and the scent of saltwater, lobster pots and fishing nets littering the harbour's edge. As she walked, she found herself in

Mr Stoker's company.

'Miss Windlass! How are you feeling after last night's excitement? Terrible business.'

'I am well, Mr Stoker, although I wonder if the police have the correct man.'

He stared at her, his expression amused yet quizzical. 'Why do you say that?'

Serendipity gazed at the fishermen unloading the day's catch on the river's opposite side. 'I'm an excellent judge of character.' Turning back to him, she smiled. 'You are a writer. Tell me if Mr Merewether seems like someone who would shoot an elderly woman with a blowgun.'

'Is that what the murder weapon was?'

'So I believe,' she replied. 'Either that or suffocation. Mr Merewether appears too dithery to carry out either.'

The sharp look he gave her caused Serendipity to fear she had said too much. The police must not have shared any details, and she shouldn't have eavesdropped.

'I would agree with you on that,' he said. 'He trails his sister like a puppy, yet he is several years older.'

Serendipity filed that information away—another snippet for her notes on the case.

Mr Stoker seemed lost in thought.

'Is there something else, Mr Stoker?'

'Hm, something I caught Mr Fortescue saying to Ms Merewether. But best not tell tales.'

She cocked her head and gently chided him. 'Come now, Mr Stoker. You've piqued my interest, and I simply must know.'

A hint of a smile played on his lips. 'Ah, an investigative mind like my own. Are you a secret writer, Miss Windlass?'

She laughed. 'No, and your ruse will not dissuade me.'

'All right then. Mr Fortescue's words to Miss Merewether were, "A man in need of financial assistance can only be aided by a woman. And what benefits me benefits you". I found that rather interesting.'

'Indeed,' she said. 'It implies a pact between the two, something I would not have guessed.'

He paused. 'Nonetheless, I would not pry too deeply if I were

87

you. If the police have the wrong person, it means the murderer is still at large. You must not endanger yourself.' He tipped his hat. 'Now, I must turn here. Enjoy your day, Miss Windlass.'

Serendipity arrived at the docks but found that the Everilda had not yet docked. Captain Crowther, the harbour master, refused to guess when it would dock. She considered a visit to the abbey, but the seaside beckoned, and besides, she'd neglected to bring her cane today. A walk along the beach would soothe her frustration, but she would need to ensure her leg remained sand-free.

Although a leather side-buttoned boot covered the bottom part of her prosthetic, she had learned long ago that no one had invented a stocking strong enough to withstand leather rubbing against her metal foot. So she wore a half stocking tucked into the boot top, lisle or wool, depending on the temperature and matching the full stocking on her other leg. Should a fickle wind lift her skirts or rain necessitate raising her hems, her metal leg would remain a secret.

While eternally grateful for her prosthetic, she could not ignore the impact on her life. How she would love to paddle in the ocean! But without assistance or the embarrassment of publicly removing and reattaching her leg, such simple joys eluded her. Never mind. Perhaps there would be donkey rides on the beach. Not that she would partake, but she held fond memories of such rides before her accident. How anyone could not love an obstreperous yet characterful donkey was beyond her.

With renewed enthusiasm, she headed toward Whitby Beach.

Chapter Nine

Serendipity's beach jaunt took longer than she'd planned, and upon reaching the dining room, she discovered it empty.

As she stood in the doorway, Anna entered from the kitchen, carrying an empty tray and humming. She busied herself collecting the last of the pudding dishes and cutlery, blissfully unaware of Serendipity's presence.

'Hello, Anna.'

The maid jumped, rattling the contents of the tray. 'Gracious, miss! You gave me a fright. I thought you were Miss Merewether!'

'I'm sorry, Anna. But why does Miss Merewether scare you?'

'Oh, it's a misunderstanding. Nothing more, nothing less,' Anna continued, gathering tableware.

'But it is wrong that she scares you. Does Mrs Veazey know?'

'She does. That's half the problem. Mrs Veazey's response was less fierce than Miss Merewether expected.

The latter statement intrigued Serendipity, but instinct led her to exercise prudence. 'Mrs Veazey values you. She told me what a good worker you are.'

Anna blushed. 'The cheek of Miss Merewether, complaining about me in front of everyone. And over a conversation that was none of her business.'

'That sounds most unfair. What on earth upset her?'

'All I said to cook was that I passed Mr Fortescue on the street on my way home that night. Miss Merewether met him at the door, and he handed her a package. She seemed agitated. Words passed between them, and he went inside. I told the police the same thing.'

Anna didn't appear to grasp the magnitude of those words, but Serendipity did. And so, it seemed, did Alethea Merewether.

The young maid looked so miserable that Serendipity could not help but pity her. 'Take heart. Mistreating someone for speaking the truth is unacceptable. Mrs Veazey acted properly by maintaining her composure.'

'Thank you, miss. You are kind.'

Serendipity's stomach rumbled in an extremely unladylike manner. After a moment of eye contact, the two women erupted in laughter.

'I'm afraid you've missed lunch,' said Anna, 'and the cook has only just left for the shops.'

'That's all right. Is there a tea shop you could recommend?'

'If you want tea, I can manage. Would you like some bread with butter as well?'

'Yes, thank you,' said Serendipity.

'Right. Give me a minute, and I'll bring it to you in the drawing room.'

Serendipity grinned and strolled into the room to wait. It was empty, a fact that pleased her. As she settled into what was becoming a favourite chair, she pondered the implications of Anna's words. Specifically, a crucial detail emerged: the maid informed the police that Garrett Fortescue returned to the house around the time Mrs Fortescue entered Mr Merewether's room. Yet another fact to add to her notes, one the police appeared to have overlooked or discarded. And then there was that mysterious package. Whatever could it be?

Her mind chased ideas down various avenues, but nothing seemed quite right. However, one avenue seemed more promising than the others. She was so involved in mentally assembling the pieces of the package puzzle that she failed to hear the maid enter the room.

'Here you are, miss,' said Anna, placing a tray on the table next to Serendipity, who jumped. 'Sorry, didn't mean to startle you.'

'Ah well, we're even now,' said Serendipity with a laugh. 'This looks wonderful!'

Anna had rustled up more than bread and butter to Serendipity's great joy. She chewed her beef tongue and mustard sandwich and turned her thoughts to the previous night's events. Was it really only last night? Already, Pickering and the journey here felt like a distant memory.

Her leg pinged, and she sat up with a start. The noise reminded her of more than just needing a new part. She recalled the animatronics in her dream, aware that the whirr accompanying their disturbing movements was one she had experienced elsewhere.

A zoetrope of images from the train replayed in her head: the crowded booths, Mrs Fortescue peering at the clockwork bird, the older woman's startled response at Serendipity's entrance, Garrett Fortescue blustering into the booth, his face a thundercloud of anger. And then there was that strange whizzing. Did she dream that too?

And where was that bird now? A knowing born of intelligence and instinct told her it held the key to this affair.

She had to find it.

Chapter Ten

The rest of the day passed too slowly, and although Serendipity enjoyed resting, immersed in a book on Whitby's history, her mind remained focused on her next move. She aimed to investigate Mr Merewether's room thoroughly, but the how and when remained uncertain. Her current plan involved waiting for Mr Fortescue and Miss Merewether to vacate the premises for a few hours and picking the lock to Mr Merewether's door. That she had never picked a lock in her life remained a detail she tried to ignore.

The guests gathered for dinner. Mr Stoker sat on her left, and they chatted for a while about the impending arrival of his wife and child in Whitby. He seemed genuinely fond of his family, and having spent much of her life motherless in the company of pleasant but overly academic men, the picture of easy family relations he enjoyed heartened her. The seat to her left, previously occupied by Mr Merewether, remained vacant. She recalled that he'd barely spoken to anyone, eating his meal silently and regarding his sister and Mr Fortescue with a baleful glare. The strained relationship between the trio gave her pause, even more so given Mr Stoker's revelation.

Anna cleared the table in preparation for dessert. Soon, it would be dusk. Garrett Fortescue's slicked-down hair gleamed with a fresh application of pomade, and he seemed ready for yet another night out. Alethea Merewether scowled, her porcelain skin flushed, her lips in a childish pout. Without warning, she sprang to her feet, pushing her chair back and almost knocking the plates out of Anna's hands as the young maid headed toward the kitchen.

'Excuse me,' Alethea said. 'I have a headache, and I simply must lie down.'

She swept out of the room, clutched the doorjamb for one perfectly timed dramatic moment, and then continued upstairs.

Garrett appeared uncharacteristically nonplussed. 'Contrary creatures, women. Present company excepted. Don't worry. A few drops of laudanum will make her tickety-boo.'

Anna entered carrying plates of dessert and served Mr Stoker and Serendipity.

'Ah,' said Garrett, 'is that treacle pudding? Excellent. An improvement from last night's bread pudding.'

Serendipity slipped a spoonful of pudding into her mouth, letting its luscious sweetness curb any retort she had for that obnoxious man.

After dinner, Serendipity retired to her room, collected her tools, a candle, candleholder and a match, and waited for Mr Fortescue to leave. Finally, at around 8:30 pm, he stomped down the stairs with his usual lack of concern for others. Anna had left moments before. Mrs Veazey rarely came upstairs after dinner. Mr Stoker had also retired to his room. Miss Merewether should be fast asleep.

She crept up the stairs and down the hallway to Mr Merewether's room. Hoping luck was in her favour, she turned the handle and breathed a sigh of relief when it moved. She slipped inside, lit the candle, and then positioned herself where the body of Lavinia Fortescue had lain. She had fallen on her back, head toward the door. The desk whose drawer contained the blowgun and needles stood opposite. It would be entirely conceivable that the murderer had stood by the desk, aimed the blowgun and ejected the incapacitating shot. Such a person would possess an uncanny aim to hit Mrs Fortescue in the eye at that distance. The murderer must have been closer. Or perhaps they had been aiming elsewhere on Mrs Fortescue's body?

A breeze blew from somewhere to her right, flickering her candle's flame. The brass chandelier above her swayed, and an unexpected object caught her eye. A piece of silken rope with an evenly frayed end dangled from one arm of the chandelier. Someone had cut it.

Serendipity moved to the right, seeking the source of the breeze. To her surprise, she discovered a table and lamp obscuring a door to the next room—Mr Fortescue's room. Air flowed through a gap at the door's top, hinting at an open window elsewhere. As quietly as possible, she grasped the doorknob and turned it. The door clicked open.

She shifted the table and stood with her hand on the door, her heart pounding. She knew Mr Fortescue had not yet returned, but stealing into his room was akin to stepping into the lion's den. Inhaling deeply, she stepped inside.

The window was open a few inches, just as she'd surmised. Like in Mr Merewether's room, a desk stood under the window, and on its polished surface sat the caged clockwork bird. Knowing that the next room was Mrs Fortescue's and thus empty of sensitive ears, she tiptoed over and carefully placed the candle where its light would not shine onto the street.

For a moment, she thought she perceived someone outside the door, and she froze, ready to run, but no one attempted to enter. She listened for a few seconds and heard nothing, so she shook off her fears as nothing more than her guilt at snooping getting the better of her. On the top of the desk next to the bird lay a set of watchmaker tools, a skein of silken rope, a cylinder and a metal comb. She ran her finger over the cylinder and discovered slight bumps on its surface. Of course! She'd seen something similar in her music box. Did it come from the mechanical bird? Only one way to find out.

Gingerly, she felt around the cage's base, found the windup key, and wound the mechanism. The bird performed a series of complex movements, including an open-beaked leaning forward and a wing snap that set Serendipity's mind racing.

She retrieved the headless hatpin she'd discovered on the night of the murder from her corset, where she'd hidden it, snug against the whalebone, and wound the bird again and again. And though the bird whirred, it never sang a note.

Satisfied with her investigation, Serendipity returned to Mr Merewether's room, restored the furniture to its place, and crept back to her room.

Chapter Eleven

The following morning, only Serendipity and Mr Fortescue took breakfast in the dining room. His attitude towards her was frosty, his charm subdued. Nonetheless, her upbringing had instilled the need for polite discourse no matter one's feelings to the contrary.

'How are you, Mr Fortescue?'

He buttered his toast, then cut it diagonally. 'Well enough.'

'And Miss Merewether?'

'Why do you ask?'

Serendipity stirred her porridge and wondered if politeness might be overrated.

'Merely concern for a fellow woman dealing with the emotional distress of losing an elderly relative and a brother.'

He grunted. 'Yes, yes. Of course. Damnably upsetting for us all. But much worse for the weaker sex. Alethea is taking it badly. Poor thing. Now, if you'll excuse me.'

He rose and swept out of the room, leaving Serendipity to sigh in relief and finish her breakfast in peace.

Her third visit to the dock yielded the disappointing news that the Everilda still had not arrived. Disheartened, she continued walking and crossed over the River Esk at Bridge Street, thinking of visiting St Mary's Church and the derelict Abbey. She'd made it to the Church Steps when her leg pinged loudly and her mechanical ankle locked.

The stairs reached up before her eyes, challenging her, mocking her. She took several careful steps, one hand on the rail and the other gripping her cane. Her leg pinged again, followed by a faint grinding. She frowned in displeasure, realising she had not performed an inspection and oiling of her leg after her trip to the beach. Perhaps, if she reached the summit, she could locate a peaceful area where a lady could raise her skirts for necessary upkeep.

Another step and a louder ping told her she shouldn't risk further damage to her leg by proceeding. With a sign of resignation, she turned back towards the guesthouse.

Halfway down Church Street, Serendipity noticed two figures walking toward her. They were some distance away, but her sharp eyesight picked out certain features, and she was sure her identification was correct. Alethea Merewether and Garrett Fortescue walked arm-in-arm as though they had no care. The pair made a sharp right turn, and Serendipity hurried to catch up.

When she reached the entrance to Blackburn's Yard, she noted the pair standing outside a door at the far end of the lane. The lane was primarily residential, and she wondered if the pair knew someone in Whitby and were visiting. She stepped forward for a closer look.

Ping!

To Serendipity's ears, the sound seems to echo off the walls. Her heart pounding, she swiftly hid behind a flight of stairs as Garrett turned around. She wasn't about to gamble on him spotting her. The mysterious door opened, and the duo disappeared inside. Serendipity, her senses on high alert, retreated to the safety of Church Street.

She had barely regained her composure when someone tapped her shoulder, and she jumped, expecting the worst. Instead, she gazed into the concerned blue eyes of Constable Minns, although he wasn't in uniform.

'Miss Windlass, are you all right?'

'You startled me.'

'My apologies, but I notice you are limping. Are you hurt?'

She shook her head, feeling her cheeks burn. 'Merely a previous injury acting up.'

'I'm sorry to hear that. Are you returning to the guesthouse? I can accompany you part of the way.'

Usually, Serendipity would wave away such an offer, but the idea of having a policeman beside suddenly held great appeal.

'Thank you. Constable Minns, I would warmly appreciate your company.'

'I'm off duty. Please call me Joe.'

They continued down Church Street in silence, and Serendipity wondered what suitable topic of conversation one might have with a police officer. Finally, she settled on the basics.

'Do you live in Whitby, Joe?'

'I grew up here, and my mother and sister are here. I live in Escrick now.'

'When did you join the police?'

'Eight years ago,' Joe replied.

'And have you dealt with many murders?'

'Unfortunately, yes. Though not my favourite, it is the most fascinating aspect of the job.'

'Why so?'

They turned onto Bridge Street, and a group of young boys ran past, whooping and laughing, almost bumping into Serendipity.

Joe moved in front of her and held his arms out protectively. 'Watch yourselves, lads!'

The boys slowed for a step, then continued at full speed.

Serendipity laughed. 'Predictably unpredictable. Boys, that is.'

'People in general, Miss. For instance, it appears Mr Merewether and his sister will inherit Mrs Fortescue's fortune.'

'Not her nephew?'

'Seems not.'

'How odd,' she replied. Another fact to add to her growing file of notes, and the perfect motive for murder.

'As you say, Joe, murder is fascinating, but please tell me. What is your favourite part of the job?'

He grinned. 'I enjoy helping people like you. Now, I must leave you to find your own path. Will you be all right?'

'Thank you, Joe. It isn't much further to Mrs Veazey's.'

He headed toward Whitby Station, whistling an old air. Serendipity scanned the other side of the River Esk but saw neither Garrett nor Alethea. Reassured, she limped back to the guesthouse to carry out another minor overhaul on her leg before venturing out again.

Chapter Twelve

Serendipity took around an hour to clean and oil her leg thoroughly. As she had suspected, a few sand grains had infiltrated her boot's side buttoning and the prosthetic ankle's outer joint. However, replacing parts was the only way to resolve the pinging fully. And that depended on the wayward Everilda.

To amuse herself for the rest of the day, she decided to have lunch at the Skinner Street Tea Rooms and then continue with her amateur sleuthing by exploring the Whitby Museum archives.

She grabbed her hat and reticule and set off with a spring in her step.

The museum proved both entertaining and frustrating. It held a subscription library, and the source of Serendipity's vexation began there. While the library offered temporary membership to Whitby visitors, the librarian appeared reluctant to grant her entrance. He'd peered over his glasses at her as though she were a dollymop.

Just as she was about to leave, Mr Stoker arrived. The librarian's attention shifted from her to the tall, imposing red-haired man, and his manner changed from judgmental to fawning.

'Good afternoon, Mr Stoker. Wonderful to see you again.'

Mr Stoker simply nodded and shifted his attention to Serendipity.

'Ah, Miss Windlass,' he said with a wink. 'I'm so pleased you've agreed to assist me with my research.'

A strange choking sound issued from the librarian. 'She's with you?'

Mr Stoker frowned at the man, but Serendipity sensed a faint smile. 'Of course. Did she not tell you as much?'

'I'm afraid I've been remiss,' Serendipity replied. 'I'm unfamiliar with needing a male companion to justify my presence in a library.'

She almost spoiled her speech by laughing at the librarian's appalled expression. Eventually, the man gathered his senses and pushed the visitors' book towards her. 'Sign here, please.'

Serendipity could not look the librarian in the eye for fear of revealing her amusement. 'Thank you.'

Once inside the library, Mr Stoker left her, saying, 'I'll leave you to your own devices. But be careful, Miss Windlass.'

'Always, Mr Stoker.'

Several hours passed, and she received only partial rewards for her efforts. She discovered a lot about the workings of animatronic devices, but she found no information about utilising such inventions as weapons. Her understanding of the effects of suffocation on the human body was impressive, yet she lacked knowledge of the precise pressure required for one person to asphyxiate another.

However, upon reviewing old Whitby Gazettes, she discovered an article mentioning that Doctor Fleming served as the medical examiner in two cases involving suffocation. Despite reporting salacious details, the newspaper lacked the information she desired.

Serendipity needed to know, and the sole method to acquire that information was by visiting Doctor Fleming.

Chapter Thirteen

Serendipity passed Doctor Fleming's home and surgery on The Esplanade several times during her travels. It was near the guesthouse, and as she walked there, she racked her brains about the night Doctor Fleming announced his findings. She remembered being in the room with Sergeant Whitehall and Constable Minns when the doctor entered, sitting with her back to the door. No one introduced her, and the sergeant dismissed her within seconds of the doctor's arrival. Did Fleming notice her? She did not remember him glancing her way as she departed. Nonetheless, she must be prepared to field uncomfortable questions. Simply showing up and asking questions wouldn't suffice.

She reached the door, readjusted the ringlet hanging over her shoulder, took a deep breath and rang the bell. To her surprise, the door was opened within seconds by the doctor himself.

'Yes?'

'Doctor Fleming, my name is Serendipity Windlass. Today, I examined the archives of the Whitby Gazette for a research project. My research raised a few medical questions that I hope you may answer.'

'Certainly. But why me?'

'I read several police cases mentioning your name, and I understand you are a forensics expert.'

The doctor frowned, and Serendipity feared rejection. Then he opened the door wider. 'Come in. I can spare ten minutes before my next appointment.'

He ushered her into a sparsely decorated room featuring a few high-back chairs and no tables. She assumed it was his waiting room. He offered her a chair, pulled another chair opposite, and sat down.

'What is this research project?'

'I plan a mystery novel and intend to set it in Whitby.'

'A novel, eh? Imaginative types thrive in Whitby. Something in the air. How can I help you?'

She folded her hands on her lap and summoned her most serious expression. 'You were involved in two murder cases where the cause of death was suffocation. Does one need uncanny strength to suffocate another human being?'

He gazed at her in a manner that parents gave small children who asked annoying questions. 'Not at all. In both cases, the victims were already incapacitated—one from illness, the other from inebriation. One of the accused was a petite woman. She placed a pillow over the face of her intoxicated, unconscious husband and then lay over the top.'

'Goodness,' said Serendipity. 'How shocking! And the other?'

'An elderly man who suffocated his terminally ill wife. So you see, neither murderer possessed unusual strength.'

'Fascinating.'

'Quite.' He peered more closely at her. 'Do I recall seeing you somewhere?'

She ducked her head. 'I've been sightseeing all around Whitby these past few days. Perhaps you've seen me on the street.' She fished a handkerchief from her reticule and dabbed her nose. 'I suppose the forensic examinations of the bodies and crime scenes made it easy to determine the killers?'

'Not really. Whitby is second-rate when processing crime scenes. London police meticulously photograph the place where the body was found and collect even the smallest details, like hair. The police here do none of that. In both cases, someone had already washed the body and placed it on a table in the public house's backroom before I was contacted.'

Serendipity congratulated herself on her instincts regarding the adequacy of the local constabulary. 'How frustrating for someone of your calibre.'

He shrugged. 'There has been some improvement recently.'

She sensed the conversation heading in a direction she would prefer to avoid and rose. 'Well, I've taken up enough of your time. Thank you for your assistance, Doctor Fleming.'

He accompanied her to the door. 'It's rarely I meet young women

99

with such a bright and inquiring mind. Have you considered studying the medical sciences? The medical profession would benefit from having more intelligent nurses.'

Serendipity resisted the urge to step on his foot with her metal leg and feigned a deep sadness. 'Alas, the stench of hospitals turns my stomach,' she said.

'Ah, well. I wish you well in whatever you choose to do.'

She smiled, hoping the gesture didn't appear forced. 'Thank you, Doctor Fleming. Farewell.'

As she rushed back to the guesthouse, she pondered if something in Whitby's air transformed men into pompous beings. Men in London never showed disdain towards her because of her gender. But here? First, Garrett Fortescue, then the librarian, and now Doctor Fleming. Would Mr Stoker also turn into a monster?

Hopefully, she would complete her task before she could find out.

Dinner proved a dismal affair. Neither Mr Stoker nor Mr Fortescue was present, and Miss Merewether moped and sighed like a penny-dreadful heroine.

Although Serendipity had no interest in discovering the answer, good manners required her to inquire. 'Are you well, Miss Merewether?'

The young woman glared at her, her pupils mere pinpoints. 'Why would you care? You know nothing about me.' A lone tear trickled down her smooth, rosy cheek. 'The things I've suffered for love...'

She paused, and Serendipity sensed a certain staginess, a performance by an accomplished manipulator. Then, with an air of martyrdom, Miss Merewether straightened and smiled at Serendipity, her lips tight, her pearly teeth gleaming like an animal about to bite. 'But all will be well soon.'

The young woman chuckled softly and continued her meal, glancing up occasionally at Serendipity, daring her to ask further questions. But even the demands of politeness failed to convince Serendipity to continue the conversation. She ate her meal in silence and excused herself before dessert.

Chapter Fourteen

The following morning, Serendipity made her way to the docks, hoping for the best. The Everilda must have arrived, she thought. However, her heart sank as she walked down Pier Road and saw no new ships in port. Yet, visiting the harbour master, Captain Crowther, might bring some solace. Surely, by now, they would have some news about the Everilda's arrival.

To her dismay, just as she passed Bridge Street, she noted the captain boarding a steam trawler with one of his assistants. Serendipity sat on a bench and considered her next move. If she were to be brutally honest, she wasn't quite ready to give up her investigations into Mrs Fortescue's murder. Her certainty that Mr Merewether was not the killer had grown. Mr Fortescue seemed the more probable villain, but her evidence against him seemed flimsy, and she couldn't rule out her dislike of the man colouring her conclusions. Miss Merewether presented as strange, but was she a likely suspect? Serendipity had no proof.

And if she were to be fanciful, this delay in the ship's arrival seemed to grant her permission to keep investigating. Would waiting for the captain to finish his business on the fishing boat be the best use of her time? Probably not. But where to go next?

It was another glorious day. A gentle sea breeze counterbalanced the effects of the sun, and the sky's azure blue lifted one's heart. Overhead, gulls wheeled and cried, a counterpoint to the sparrows chirping amongst flowerbeds. Her mind drifted to thoughts of the mechanical bird and the whizzing sound it made when...of course! Now she remembered where she had heard it.

She checked her pocket watch. The train from Pickering to Whitby wouldn't arrive for two more hours. Undeterred, she determined to visit Whitby Abbey, pleased that she'd thought to carry her cane today.

With a spring in her step, she set off towards her destination. While crossing the River Esk at Bridge Street, she had an uncanny feeling someone was following her. When she glanced behind her, she caught sight of the harbour master's assistant. It struck her as strange that he wasn't still with Captain Crowther. However, he turned right down Church St, and she headed left towards Church Stairs, so she dismissed her suspicions as folly.

The 199 steps to St Mary's Church proved challenging for Serendipity's prosthesis, and she was glad she had bought her cane.

She paused at the top and stood by Caedmon's cross, the vast expanse of sea and sky taking her breath away. The dignified bulk of St Mary's Church stood to her left, and the imposing grandeur of Whitby Abbey lay straight ahead. She detoured through the churchyard, drawn by the sweep of green dotted with gravestones leading to the cliff edge and the ocean beyond. A sense of sorrow washed over her as she read the inscriptions, many with the usual "Here lies..." epitaph but an equivalent number, the "In remembrance of...", a poignant reminder of a life lost at sea and an empty grave.

An unsettling feeling of being observed accompanied her journey, but she dismissed it. Few visitors roamed these hallowed grounds. Most gravitated to the beaches below, especially on such a splendid day.

She pressed on, passing through the gates, the cries of gulls a constant companion, and paused to admire the ruins of Cholmley House. Rejuvenated, she veered towards Whitby Abbey. Despite her previous glimpses from afar, nothing had prepared her for the breathtaking beauty and majestic grandeur of the ancient sandstone structure.

The abbey had existed in some form since 657 AD, but in 1539, following the Second Suppression Act of Henry VIII, the monastery fell into disuse and decay. But its magnificence remained, a testament to those who had crafted its bones and decorated its walls.

Serendipity strolled the ravaged cloister, marvelling at how the building's inherent beauty rose above the destruction.

However, a figure flitting in and out of her peripheral vision as it weaved and ducked amongst the ancient stones intruded on her meditation. Every time the figure reappeared, it seemed closer.

She swung around, aware that no one else was nearby, only her and her mysterious shadow.

'Hello? Who is there, please?'

A solitary gull flying overhead answered her call.

Her heart pounding, she quickened her step, keen on leaving the abbey grounds as soon as possible.

A man leapt from the shadows and grabbed her around her waist. More from instinct than any forethought, she stamped on his foot with her metal leg. He gasped and loosened his grip, but as she made to run away, he grabbed her wrist, almost forcing her to drop her cane.

She spun to face a man, his features obscured by the collar, a grey greatcoat, a fisherman's cap pulled low over his eyes, and a kerchief hiding the lower half of his face. A flicker of recognition gave her pause, but his other hand reached for her throat before she could place him. With a swift, decisive move, she grabbed the top of her cane with her unfettered hand, pulled the stiletto free of its scabbard, and stabbed him in the belly.

To her surprise, the blade pierced both greatcoat and clothing, and her assailant doubled over. She wrenched the stiletto from his side, grimacing at its bloody blade, hoping the wound was not mortal. She couldn't wait to find out—she ran, fear and adrenaline giving her feet wings.

Glancing over her shoulder, she saw the man struggling to chase after her, but his steps faltered, and he crumpled to the ground just as they reached Abbey Lane. Her lungs threatened to burst for want of a deep breath, and her leg pinged ominously, but she pushed through her pain and fear, her heart fluttering against her rib cage until she reached the top of the Church Steps. A large group of visitors—men, women and children—climbed towards her, so she leaned against the railing and caught her breath, casting furtive glances around the churchyard. To her great relief, her attacker was nowhere to be seen. Comforted but still wary, she headed down the steps toward the town.

Her thoughts tumbled over each other as she descended, her mechanical leg needing another oiling and each limping step adding to her mental discomfiture. While she wished to believe her assailant was Garrett Fortescue in disguise, the sheer bulk of the man suggested someone heavier. And the stink of him, a gag-inducing mix of sweat and oil, bore no resemblance to the woody-fragranced hair pomade and Pear's soap odour of Mr Fortescue. There was one way to determine if her suspicions were correct or misguided, but it required that Mr Fortescue present himself at dinner tonight. Maybe she could determine if he bore a stab wound.

She reached the bottom of the steps and headed down Church Street to Bridge Street. As she crossed over the River Esk, the bawl of an incoming train reminded her that there was one thing she needed to do before returning to the quiet safety of the guesthouse. Part of her did not want to continue her investigation. Not once had she considered that her inquiries and actions might endanger her, despite Mr Stoker's warning. However, she survived an attack. Wasn't uncovering the truth more important? Although longing to return to the guesthouse and safety, she turned left towards the station.

Passengers spilled out of the train just as Serendipity arrived on the platform. She sighed in relief when she recognised the locomotive's number and hoped that the equally familiar maroon carriages were the same ones on which she'd travelled.

Holidaymakers and other travellers milled on the platform, and as she pushed through the throng, the guard blew his whistle and waved at her.

'We're not boarding yet, miss,' the guard said, his voice a low rumble of disapproval.

'I left something on board,' she replied. 'I won't be long.'

She found the carriage in which she'd travelled and slipped on board. All was as she remembered. Several steps down the aisle toward the end of the carriage, she located the booth and stood in the doorway, recalling the fateful day's scene in as much detail as possible. Then she entered, retook her bearings, and, with her mind sharp and clear, searched until she found the clue she needed, the piece of the puzzle that could explain everything.

Bolstered by her discovery, she made haste to the guesthouse. A flutter of excitement filled her with renewed enthusiasm for her investigation. Despite it all, she steeled herself and accepted that the truth should remain unbiased. As much as she disliked Garrett Fortescue, she could not let her heart rule her head in her analysis.

Regardless, she'd soon find out if Garrett was her attacker.

She arrived at the guesthouse in time for lunch. To her surprise, Mr Garrett was already seated and chatted with Miss Merewether. He seemed in rude health, with no sign of any injury. His face flickered with unbridled annoyance when she entered.

'Ah, Miss Windlass. We were about to send out a search party for you. We thought you must have come to grief somewhere, didn't we, Alethea?'

Miss Merewether scowled and stabbed a piece of ham on her plate.

'Nothing so dramatic, I'm afraid, Mr Fortescue,' Serendipity replied. 'Time merely ran away with me.'

As Serendipity settled at the table, Mr Fortescue rose, checked his pocket watch (which was on the side where a stab wound might have been) and adjusted his waistcoat. She observed him from under half-closed eyes, but nothing he did suggested he nursed a knife wound, not even when he helped Miss Merewether with her chair. When he reached the doorway, he turned to Serendipity and bowed, the sneer on his face barely disguised.

So her belief that this odious man had tried to kill her was incorrect. Who attacked her if it wasn't Garrett Fortescue?

Chapter Fifteen

Serendipity spent the rest of the day reviewing her notes. Despite firmly believing in Arthur Merewether's innocence and Garrett Fortescue's involvement in the murder of his grandmother, she only had the most tenuous of evidence to speculate on the existence of another perpetrator.

In between to-ing and fro-ing over her clues, she tossed up the pros and cons of reporting her attack to the police. In the end, she concluded that admitting to stabbing a man with a concealed stiletto, particularly if he had died, was not the smartest choice.

Dinner passed peacefully with Mr Fortescue and Miss Merewether absent and only Mr Stoker as her dinner companion. She contemplated disclosing all that had happened to her, but who knew what thoughts lay underneath that composed exterior? He was charming but a stranger.

The night passed in a restless slumber, brimming with strange dreams of clockwork dolls, bloodied knives, and sinking ships. When she awoke at daybreak, she hoped her dreams did not predict her future.

After a quiet breakfast with only Anna for company, she set off to check the ship's fate. To her great joy, she saw a steamer docked at Tate Hill Pier as she rounded the corner onto Pier Road. By the time she reached Fish Quay, she could read the name on the bow: Everilda.

She hurried to the pier, crossing Bridge Street for what she hoped was the penultimate time, and hurried down Church Street, senses alert for potential attackers. She arrived just as the harbour master, Captain Crowther, disembarked.

'Good morning, sir. Is all in order? May I receive my parcel as arranged by my uncle? I possess a letter of permission.'

'Yes, yes,' he replied, waving her away. 'Mr Perceval-Savile paid all duties and fees in advance. Whether you may receive the parcel is the province of the ship's captain.'

He turned to walk away, and a memory stirred in Serendipity's head. 'Sir, where is your assistant, the stocky man with the fisherman's hat? He's always close by when you perform your duties.'

Captain Crowther grunted. 'Some townsfolk found Mr Sykes in Abbey Lane, collapsed and bleeding from a stab wound. He's at home recovering and will be back at work soon.'

'Ah, thank heavens he is well,' she said, smiling sweetly and secretly relieved he would survive. One murder in Whitby was enough. 'And he lives in Blackburn's Yard, doesn't he?'

The harbour master's brows knotted in consternation. 'Um, yes. Why do you ask?'

'During my recent visit, I witnessed someone resembling him entering a house.' She beamed at him. 'It is always rewarding to receive confirmation that one's observational abilities are in peak

106

form, don't you agree?'

'Er, hmm, quite,' said Captain Crowther. 'And now, if you'll excuse me—'

'Of course, sir. Thank you for all your help, and farewell.'

The man's discomfort at her chatter almost made her giggle.

'And you, Miss Windlass. Godspeed.'

She nodded and sought the ship's captain, keen to collect the part for her leg but even more eager to visit Blackburn's Yard, ready to play her hunch.

Chapter Sixteen

Serendipity stood outside the door she'd seen Garrett and Alethea enter. It occurred to her that being here presented as a highly foolish endeavour. What if Sykes tried to finish her?

She bit her lower lip. Don't be daft, Serendipity. You stabbed him. He's incapacitated. And if necessary, you can stab him again.

That last thought was not comforting. Serendipity took a deep breath and knocked. A few seconds later, the door opened to reveal a plump, sweet-faced, middle-aged woman.

'Can I help you, miss?'

'I hope so. My name is Miss Minns.' A fake name seemed appropriate, and she was sure Joe Minns would not mind her borrowing his surname. 'I'm looking for Mr Sykes. I possess a message for him from Captain Crowther.'

'Oh! I'm Mrs Sykes. Do come in.'

Serendipity almost sighed in relief. A wife was one thing she had not expected. The woman barrelled toward a doorway, throwing open the door and calling to her husband.

'Wake up, Harold. You have a visitor from work.'

Grumbles issued from the room, but his wife paid no heed, instead turning her attention to her guest.

'Please make yourself comfortable,' she said. 'I'll get some tea.'

Mrs Sykes dashed off, leaving Serendipity to enter the room. She paused in the doorway and waited for Mr Sykes to notice her. He stared at the window, not bothering to acknowledge her presence.

'Well, come in, boy,' he said. 'What nonsense is that old bull

Crowther spouting this time?'

Serendipity cocked her head—interesting opening to a conversation.

'I'm no boy, Mr Sykes,' she said. 'And I need to ask a question.'

His head whipped around, and he flinched, his hand moving toward the spot she'd stabbed him.

'What are you doing here?'

The terror on his face surprised her. She had expected resistance and anger but not fear. She sat in the chair opposite him.

'I merely want to know why you attacked me.'

'I'm not saying anything. Now get out, or I'll—'

'Call the police? I doubt it. I only need to report that you attacked me first.'

His fear turned to dismay. 'You would see me arrested then? My wife will not thank you.'

'Don't worry, Mr Sykes. I'm willing to let bygones be bygones, but only if you tell me your reason for attacking me.'

'I can't do that.'

'Did someone pay you?'

'Go away, please. I have nothing to say.'

'I can still involve the police if necessary.'

'Then do it. Let me be done with this whole sorry mess. It's not worth the money they paid. Thanks to you, I could have died. Might still!'

Considering he was sitting up and talking rather than in bed, half-asleep, the man's attempt at manipulating Serendipity's guilt was decidedly amateur.

'They? So more than one person,' she said. 'Will you tell me this much? Did a man and a woman hire you?'

Sykes fiddled with the corner of his blanket and mumbled.

Serendipity opened her pocket bag and retrieved a few shillings. 'I assume you needed money for a reason, Mr Sykes. Perhaps I can help?'

He eyed the coins and licked his lips. 'Yes. A man and a woman. He was a bounder, she a harpy. I wouldn't trust either. And I'll say no more, no matter how much you offer!'

'That's quite all right. Mr Sykes. You've given me all I need.'

She made to throw the coins but paused. 'There is one more

thing. Where did you first meet the man?' She guessed that Mr Fortescue was the initial contact.

Sykes hung his head. 'A card game. Happy now?'

She deposited the coins into his lap, and a few disappeared into the folds of his blanket. He fumbled to collect his payment, wincing as he twisted toward a wayward shilling.

'I am sorry about that, Mr Sykes,' said Serendipity. 'But one must protect oneself from ruffians and dishonourable types in any way possible.'

Sykes bowed his head. 'Understandable, miss. No hard feelings.'

She sniffed as she rose and smoothed her skirts. 'From whom? I find no reason for forgiveness. And I hardly think your opinion matters.'

As she swept out of the parlour, she almost collided with Mrs Sykes, who carried a tea tray.

'Oh! Not staying, Miss Minns? I've just brewed a fresh pot.'

'My apologies. I didn't realise it was so late, and I have another appointment. I'm running late as it is.'

'Let me serve Harold his tea, then I'll see you off.'

'No need, Mrs Sykes. Thank you.'

Serendipity opened the door and stepped into the lane, savouring the salt tang in the air and the sun's warmth on her skin. Facing her attacker had proved more challenging than she expected, but Mr Sykes was no hardened criminal, only a sorry excuse for a man. She'd survived, and the information she'd gleaned was enough to execute the most daring part of her plan.

Her leg pinged so loudly that the sound startled a snoozing cat. She tapped her metal calf fondly with her cane. 'Quiet you. You'll get attention soon enough.'

She stepped onto Church Street and headed to the telegraph office at the train station to message Sergeant Whitehall, hoping he would agree to follow her lead.

Chapter Seventeen

Serendipity met with the police at Mrs Veazey's an hour prior to the arranged meeting of guests and staff in the drawing room. Her message outlined her findings concerning the manner of the murder, but what she needed most was for the police to seize the mechanical bird and its trilling apparatus. Sneaking into Garrett's room earlier was barely acceptable. However, removing an item of evidence without permission would do her no favours.

Sergeant Whitehall seemed disinclined to take action, his pale blue eyes staring her down, his handlebar moustache bobbing up and down as he pursed and unpursed his lips. Luckily, Constable Minns rallied to her side. Eventually, the sergeant relented, convinced by Minns's argument that they could not judge her findings without seeing or hearing what Serendipity had discovered.

Finally, everyone gathered in the drawing room. Although the cook was busy preparing dinner, Mrs Veazey and Anna were there. Mr Fortescue and Miss Merewether arrived late, breezing in without apology.

Mr Fortescue's eye fell on the mechanical bird almost immediately. 'I say, what is my trinket doing here? Who dared to remove it from my room?'

Sergeant Whitehall rocked forward onto the balls of his feet and back again. 'That would be me. It appears this gadget may be crucial to our investigation.'

Mr Fortescue and Miss Merewether looked at one another, then back at the sergeant.

'Preposterous,' said Garrett. 'Anyway, you have your murderer. How vile that Arthur dared hurt my poor Grandmama?' He put one hand on his chest and shook his head, a tad too dramatically in Serendipity's opinion.

'No argument there,' said Sergeant Whitehall. 'Miss Windlass, please proceed.'

Garrett Fortescue puffed up in outrage. 'Miss Windlass! What has she to do with this?'

'Miss Windlass has made some interesting observations, Mr Fortescue,' said the sergeant. 'She has kindly—and bravely—agreed to share her findings with all of us.'

The implied challenge from the sergeant did not escape Serendipity. Nonetheless, she nodded her gratitude and stepped forward.

'Thank you, all, for agreeing to indulge me as I present a different version of events for the murder of Mrs Lavinia Fortescue. From the moment the police arrested Mr Arthur Merewether for her demise, I experienced nagging doubts.'

Garrett scoffed. 'Why waste time listening to a woman? The fairer sex is not known for its intelligence.' He smiled ingratiatingly at Miss Merewether. 'With an exception, of course.'

Serendipity ignored him.

'The night of the murder, I woke to a thud. I later learned it was poor Mrs Fortescue falling to the floor. In the hour before my wakening, I suffered a restless slumber, dreaming of animatronic animals, an event I assumed to be random. Later, I realised that a sound had prompted those dreams—whirring and a whizzing noise as made by this mechanical bird.' She tapped the cage. 'Yet, something did not add up, and I was determined to discover what irked me. I decided to examine the clockwork bird myself.'

'You entered my room? I say, Sergeant Whitehall, shouldn't you arrest this insolent chit for burglary?'

Serendipity held up her hand, 'I neither broke in nor stole anything. You'd left your door unlocked while you were out gambling. Speaking of which, I believe you met a Mr Sykes at one of your games?'

Garrett shrugged. 'Damned if I know. I do not remember the names of men I intend to thrash.'

Serendipity smiled. 'Well, he remembers you and Miss Merewether.'

To her great satisfaction, the man paled. 'And while I'm not proud of snooping, it's not illegal, and I believe it is justified.'

'That remains to be seen, Miss Windlass,' said Sergeant Whitehall. 'Continue.'

'Anyway, I discovered that the bird possessed complex movements, including one where it spread its wings, leaned forward, and opened its beak wide enough for me to observe its inner workings. I noted a spring-like contrivance nestled toward the tail end. Then, the bird snapped its wings shut without abandoning its forward position. Finally, the windup cycle completed, the bird closed its beak and sat upright.'

Garrett glowered at her, but she pressed on.

'At first, I couldn't determine the spring mechanism's function.

But after repeated tries, I noted it also snapped forward, triggered by the wing movement and similar in action to a clay pigeon thrower. Outside Miss Merewether's room, I had found one of the headless hatpins of the type used to incapacitate Mrs Fortescue. I retrieved this and, with relative ease, loaded the projectile into the spring mechanism.'

She opened the door on the birdcage and, using one hand, pressed the bird down. The bird moved into a horizontal position and opened its beak, upon which she loaded the needle with the other hand. With utmost care, she raised her hand, allowing the bird to return to its original position, closed the door and pointed the device toward a stack of pillows on a chair in the corner.

'I then rewound the bird, and this happened.'

Once fully wound, the bird whirred into life and performed a series of wing flaps before bowing and shooting the loaded projectile into the waiting pillows.

A series of horrified gasps echoed around the room, but not a sound passed Mr Fortescue's or Miss Merewether's lips.

'When I first experienced this marvellous artefact, it sang as well as whirred. This time, the song—a loud and distinctive trill—was absent. I assume this was because such a sound would be too noticeable.'

She reached into her pocket and produced the watchmaker's tools, cylinder, and comb. 'I wonder if you would explain these, Mr Fortescue? They were sitting next to the bird on your desk.'

Garrett's colour deepened, and his eyes flashed with anger. 'You have no right to interfere with my property.'

'Perhaps not, Mr Fortescue,' she said. 'But this bird is one of the murder weapons. It was this, not a blowpipe, that shot the needle into Mrs Fortescue's eye as she peered shortsightedly at its antics.'

'Rubbish,' said Garrett. 'The mechanism is faulty, and I was attempting to repair it. I believe I mentioned this, Sergeant Whitehall. Didn't I, sir?'

The sergeant nodded. 'Yes, you did. Go on, Miss Windlass.'

'Thank you, Sergeant Whitehall. In retrospect, I should have taken the device to my room, as someone on the same floor overheard my investigations. Didn't they, Miss Merewether?'

Alethea sat stoney-faced. 'I have no idea what you mean. I was absent. It could have been anyone here.'

'Really? The Fortescues and the Merewethers had the entire floor set aside for them. Mrs Fortescue was dead, Mr Merewether in gaol, Mr Fortescue out on the town, so that leaves only you. If memory serves me, you'd complained of a headache. Mr Fortescue said you intended to take a tincture of laudanum.'

'Oh, yes. That is correct. Apologies. Laudanum plays havoc with one's memory. I couldn't have heard anything because I was asleep.'

'If you insist, Miss Merewether,' said Serendipity.

'Hang on,' said Garrett. 'The bird wasn't in the room when Arthur entered. I'd told dear grandmama that I'd fix it for her. It was in my room exactly where I had left it.'

'True,' Serendipity replied. 'Yet I discovered remnants of silken rope, like the one in your room, tied to Mr Merewether's chandelier.'

Garrett snorted. 'Is it a crime to have a skein of silken rope? Grandmama liked to have the bird hanging where she could see it.'

'I'm so glad you mentioned that, Mr Fortescue,' said Serendipity. 'Hanging the device so that the lowest point of the bird's bow aligned with Mrs Fortescue's eye line would allow the needle to penetrate her eye. Mrs Fortescue complained of issues with her hands, so tying the device to the chandelier so she could not undo it ensured she played with the bird in Mr Merewether's room.

Garrett shook his head. 'Old Arthur possessed such cunning? Dreadful. And I thought I knew him.'

'Perhaps someone else placed the bird in Mr Merewether's room, knowing that Mrs Fortescue would come looking for it,' said Serendipity. 'Indeed, Mrs Veazey let her into the room after Mr Merewether had left with Mr Fortescue. I wonder who told her where to find it?'

'Arthur, of course,' said Garrett.

'However, as you mentioned, the bird was absent upon the police's arrival. It was in your room. Who moved it back? And what reason would Mr Merewether have for orchestrating his great-aunt's demise in his room?'

Garrett sneered. 'Dear woman, it's obvious that Arthur returned the bird to my room and staged the death so it would occur when he

113

was out. Why are you asking these dim-witted questions?'

Serendipity ignored the last remark. 'Although it may seem like it was all Mr Merewether's doing, the projectile merely incapacitated Mrs Fortescue instead of killing her. Someone then completed the grisly job by suffocating her with a cushion or pillow.'

'Oh, give me strength,' said Garrett. 'Again, Arthur. Arthur is the murderer.'

'No, Mr Fortescue,' replied Serendipity. 'Mr Merewether could not have suffocated Mrs Fortescue as she was still alive when he and you went out. And he had no time to kill her when he returned. I heard him enter the house, traipse up the stairs, open his door, and exclaim, "Dear god! Great-Aunt Lavinia!" It would be impossible for him to deal the final blow or to return the device to your room between opening the door and calling out.'

'So Arthur had an accomplice?' Garrett shook his head. 'Curses on the blaggard.'

Serendipity peeked at Miss Merewether, who mopped her neck with a white handkerchief.

'Oh, there was an accomplice,' said Serendipity, 'but Mr Merewether didn't need one. Mr Merewether is not the murderer.'

Sergeant Whitehall bristled. 'Now see here. I agreed to hear your ideas, but I will not tolerate—'

'Please let me finish, sir. I think that one of the actual murderers had already tried to kill Mrs Fortescue earlier. You may have noticed the whizzing sound happened solely when the bird ejected the hatpin. I only heard that noise once before, on the train. I opened the booth door, startling Mrs Fortescue as she observed the bird's antics, and she stepped backwards seconds before the distinctive whizz.'

Garrett sighed loudly. 'Is this what this is about? Revenge against me for insisting the booth was ours and ours alone?'

'Hardly, Mr Fortescue. I am not so petty. Yesterday, I confirmed my suspicions by examining the booth. I found a hole in the wood panelling, the same size as a hatpin.'

Garrett opened his mouth and closed it without saying a word.

'Three other surprising clues directed me to the identity of the murderers. The first came from Mr Stoker. He overheard Mr Fortescue speaking to Miss Merewether, saying, "No one but a

114

woman can help a man when he is in trouble of the pocket. And what benefits me benefits you.'''

She paused, secretly enjoying the odious man's discomfort, and continued her explanation.

'The second piece of information is even more intriguing. Anna saw Mr Fortescue return that night not long after Mrs Fortescue entered the room where she would breathe her last. Miss Merewether met him at the door and in a state of agitation. He handed her a package, which I believe was laudanum. However, he did not leave but instead went inside.'

'I had to comfort my cousin. It pains to say that she is overly dependent on her tincture—'

'Shut up, Garrett,' said Alethea.

'Now, now, dear heart, no need to be angry. One has to face the truth if—'

'I said, shut up!'

Sweat beaded on the young woman's forehead, and she gasped for air. Serendipity wondered whether guilt or laudanum drove her physical responses. 'Are you well, Miss Merewether?'

Alethea crossed her arms and pouted. 'Why wouldn't I be?'

Serendipity glanced at Sergeant Whitehall. His expression gave nothing away and did not encourage her. She cleared her throat.

'The third is possibly damning. Mrs Fortescue excluded Garrett from her will, a move guaranteed to devastate a man's pride, especially one with a serious gambling habit.'

Garrett slapped his thigh. 'I say, are you implying that I hurt my dear grandmama?'

Sergeant Whitehall frowned at her. 'Be careful what you say, Miss Windlass, but continue.'

'You are not averse to hurting women, Mr Fortescue. You tried to hurt me.'

'I did nothing of the sort. Lies!'

'I admit you did not attack me yourself. You don't enjoy doing dirty work, do you, Mr Fortescue? What a pity I recognised the man you hired to kill me. And an even greater pity that I saw you and Miss Merewether enter Mr Syke's house at Blackburn's Yard a day before the attack occurred.'

Alethea's complexion had lost all colour, and she dabbed at the

115

sweat on her forehead and neck.

'Outrageous!' Garrett slapped his thigh again. 'Why would I do that?'

'Because Miss Merewether told you I'd experimented with the bird.'

Alethea leapt to her feet. 'It's all his fault,' she said, pointing at Garrett. 'My involvement comprised supplying hairpins and removing the bird from Arthur's room. I almost died of shock when the old cow gasped. She recognised me. I had to do something.'

'Good lord,' said Garrett. 'Calm yourself, Alethea. No one takes the slightest notice of a ridiculous hysteric.'

She spun around and gaped at him. 'How dare you! If I am a hysteric, you are to blame. You denied me my laudanum.'

'That was for your own good.'

'It was to force me to carry out your vile machinations!' Alethea wrung her hands. 'He learned clockmaking in Switzerland, you know, and made that stupid bird. He planned this for years, ever since Great Aunt Lavinia told him she'd disinherited him until he gave up gambling. But Garrett cannot leave the cards and dice be. He is weak!'

'Not as weak as you, dearest Ally. You'd do anything for laudanum, wouldn't you? That's why you smothered poor Grandmama. Too afraid I would withhold the daily dose if our little plan failed.'

A deathly silence fell over the room.

Garrett smiled, a wan imitation of his usual smarmy grin. 'It appears I've put my foot in it.'

'It appears you have,' said Sergeant Whitehall. 'Alethea Merewether, you are under arrest for the murder of Lavinia Fortescue. Garrett Fortescue, you are under arrest for conspiracy to murder.'

Serendipity gave a silent cheer of success.

Chapter Eighteen

The following day, Serendipity said her goodbyes to Mrs Veazey and Anna, promising to visit again. Despite, or perhaps because of, the murder, Whitby inhabited a place in her heart.

Arthur had returned to the guesthouse briefly to collect his belongings and leave. Garrett and Alethea were awaiting trial.

As she walked down the guesthouse steps, Mr Stoker turned the corner of Royal Crescent. Serendipity put down her reticule and shook his hand.

'Goodbye, Mr Stoker. It has been a pleasure to meet you, although the circumstances might have been more favourable.'

'Indeed. Murder most foul. All for the sake of money.'

'And addiction, Mr Stoker. Laudanum and gambling. Both hold their prisoners in an iron grip.'

'A sad truth, Miss Windlass.'

Serendipity sighed. 'I pity Miss Merewether. Garrett Fortescue encouraged her addiction. Now, she faces the noose or the madhouse. The noose would be a fast death, whereas the madhouse would slowly destroy her.'

Mr Stoker nodded. 'I fear you are correct. You are a most perceptive young woman.'

'Thank you.' She smiled. 'For the compliment and your part in this adventure. I would not have solved this case without your insight or assistance with recalcitrant librarians.'

He threw back his head and laughed. 'My pleasure, Miss Windlass. And do not undersell your part in correcting the course of justice. Mr Merewether would still be in gaol, but for your diligence. Do you intend to solve any more mysteries?'

She laughed. 'I do not know, Mr Stoker. My future is a blank page. And while I possess sound powers of deduction, I'm unconvinced that I am suited for the intrigue and danger of sleuthing. You were wise to warn me to be careful. I underestimated the danger my investigation posed.'

'I think you doubt yourself too much,' he said, tipping his hat and setting off toward the museum. 'All the best, Miss Windlass.'

'And you too, Mr Stoker. I shall keep an eye out for your book.'

She picked up her reticule and continued toward Whitby Station, enjoying the town's charm and history one last time, hoping that this lovely town would not fade into obscurity. Her leg pinged, and she sighed.

Uncle Amby awaited in Pickering, a symbol of comfort, stability, and mechanical expertise. Soon, her leg would regain full functionality, allowing her to move about without the fear of unexpected infirmity. She'd already decided she would not return to London and the endless machinations of relatives wishing her to marry. Perhaps she would travel or pursue an academic discipline. Or maybe she would take up sleuthing.

She only had to choose.

THE UNTIMELY DEATH OF CLOCKMASTER TOLLSMEAD

Cameron Trost

Eardley Holborn prided himself on being in the right place at the right time, and he was adamant that today would bring no exception to the rule. It was, after all, a natural strength for the Chief Clockwork Artist at the Urseau Institute of Mechanical Theatrics. Impeccable timing was the key to his success. His latest project had involved the setting up of a spectacular mechanism for what the Royal Magicians' Guild was promoting as its most grandiose and nerve-racking production yet. Though a world in which illusion reigned supreme, Eardley Holborn knew for a fact that this particular mechanism was as deadly as it appeared. The show's grand finale featured a huge double-bladed axe on a shaft that would come swinging down from above the stage like the pendulum of a longcase clock. The same lever that would be used by a stagehand to release the axe would also trigger, one second later, a trapdoor and a steam valve. The idea was that Reymund the Redoubtable—the magician everyone was raving about since Eldritch Escape-All had crossed a street without looking both ways first after drinking too many green fairies and failed to escape being crushed by a clockwork carriage—would vanish and the axe would swing harmlessly by leaving only a trail of steam in its wake. There was no room for error. If the trapdoor opened too early, the dramatic effect would be lost, and if it opened even half a second too late—well, no room for error. The timing had to be perfect.

'Right on time,' Eardley congratulated himself as he stepped down from the clockwork carriage and slipped his silver fogwatch back into the left pocket of his black satin waistcoat. He waited for an elegant woman wearing an immaculate white dress that formed a

119

stark contrast to his dark attire to continue along the pavement and he admired the perfect rhythm of her steps and thought to himself how remarkable it was that she'd managed to keep her ivory boots so very clean despite the puddles of mud caused by the recent rain. He then took three steps closer to the building of red brick in front of him so that he could study it before entering without hindering the evening foot traffic on the pavement. It was now precisely seven o'clock. The cogs of the clockwork carriage behind him whirred at a higher pitch as the vehicle pulled out, and the faint glow of the gas lamps that were slowly coming to life now made the brickwork of the building's façade seem to grow ruddier.

The brass plaque to the right of the green door, at the top of a short flight of stairs made of the same red bricks as the rest of the structure, confirmed that he was indeed in the right place, as well as at the right time: Clockmaster Tollsmead, 24 Foxdorn Terrace.

The invitation to an informal and intimate evening of drinks, entertainment, and a presentation by the clockmaster himself in his own home had been impossible to refuse, particularly when word had it the clockmaster had something big under his top hat, and that there was a chance that hat would be lifted tonight. Good form dictated that one should always arrive between five and ten minutes later than the stated time, so Eardley decided he'd press the doorbell at approximately eight minutes past seven. In the meantime, he remained in the chill evening air, pulled his black silk kerchief a little tighter around his neck, tugged his Scottish flatcap a little lower over his brow to keep his shaven head warm, and contemplated the edifice before him. He stroked his grey beard and moustache thoughtfully—the silver and amethyst rings he wore clinking together as he did so—and estimated the pitch of the slate roof and the height of the chimney stack. There was a bay window to either side of the door, three casement windows on the first floor, and one dormer protruding from the roof. All had frames of the same green as the door. A handsome abode indeed, as befitted one of the city's most respected clockmasters.

When he figured it was just about eight minutes past the hour, Eardley drew his fogwatch out again and flipped the lid—eight past precisely. He climbed the stairs and pressed the doorbell, quickly putting his ear up to it so he could hear the clockwork mechanism despite the street noise before the bell sounded inside. He pictured the cogs spinning and causing the wire connected to the bell to contract five times in rapid succession. It held no mystery for the likes of Eardley Holborn, but how the door was opened so promptly—barely before he'd removed his ear from the doorbell button—bemused him.

'Good evening, sir,' the doorman said, his grey eyes not looking into Eardley's but instead at his forehead. His left hand was behind his back and the palm of his white-gloved right hand was open, waiting to receive the invitation.

Eardley nodded his appreciation of the doorman's perfect professionalism as he removed the invitation from his waistcoat pocket and placed it on the gloved palm.

'Welcome to the Tollsmead residence, Mr Holborn.' The doorman stood aside the allow Eardley in and closed the door behind them.

'Your coat, sir?'

Eadley slipped out of his charcoal tweed peacoat, handed it to the doorman, and offered his flatcap as well.

'Do follow me, Mr Holborn, if you please.'

The doorman walked straight as an arrow past a quarter-turn staircase of dark polished wood and along the hall lit with wall candles and decorated with portraits of Tollsmeads past and present, landscape paintings of buildings featuring the clockmaster's finest achievements—from churches to railway stations—and technical sketches of the groundbreaking mechanisms he had designed.

'Simply marvellous,' Eardley remarked loudly enough for the doorman to hear and appreciate, even though he knew full well that protocol dictated the man wouldn't respond.

'Mr Eardley Holborn, Chief Clockwork Artist at the Urseau Institute of Mechanical Theatrics,' the doorman announced as they arrived in the sitting room. He spoke at just the right volume and with just the right tone to ensure that everyone present heard his words but that their conversations were not disrupted.

Eardley nodded his thanks to the doorman and offered a smile to the ten or so already present as they turned their faces briefly to acknowledge his arrival on scene. They were in three groups of three or four, chatting and sipping champagne. A man Eardley

121

recognised immediately broke away from one of the groups and walked over to him, extending a hand with the long fingers of a skilled technician. He wasn't wearing his iconic top hat indoors, of course, but Eardley recognised him without it. Tufts of white hair rose like puffs of steam from each side of a shiny head, matching his bushy moustache. His eyes were the blue of the forget-me-nots Eardley remembered from his Grandma Georgette's flower garden. His face was tired but betrayed an intellect that was as keen as ever—and yet, there was something else in that expression, despite the amicable smile—a hint of dread.

'Mr Holborn, thank you for coming. It's a pleasure to meet you.'

Eardley found himself lost for words for an instant.

'Really, Clockmaster Tollsmead, the pleasure is all mine,' he said when he could manage to reply and immediately regretted his lack of originality. 'I mean to say, the honour is mine. I'm sure everyone says so when they first meet you, but I've followed all your work so closely, and I strive to apply your findings to my own humble endeavours.'

'Humble hogwash!' the clockmaster said a little too loudly, and the girl with the platter of champagne flutes who had just reached the newcomer's side came close to losing her balance. Once she regained her composure, Eardley took a flute and thanked her.

'To clockwork minds,' the clockmaster toasted. 'Now, firstly, *Mister Tollsmead* will do very well until we're comfortable addressing each other by our Christian names, and secondly, there's nothing humble about your theatrics. It truly is splendid work, my good man.'

'That means so much coming from you, Mister Tollsmead. I did wonder whether you had attended any of the shows featuring our handiwork.'

'Naturally. I wouldn't have sent you an invitation otherwise, would I?' he asked with a cheeky wink.

Any qualms Eardley initially had about meeting the clockmaster were quickly fading. He was beginning to suspect that the pomp and ceremony the man was known for—the being a stickler for etiquette and old-world constructs—was more for public show. In a way, he was involved in show business as well. Was that why he'd invited Eardley?

'You're an aficionado of theatrics?'

'I am indeed, Mr Holborn. Behind the cogs and bells, if there's no spirit, the mechanism is turning for an empty auditorium. On that note, I'm very much looking forward to the upcoming production from the Royal Magicians' Guild. Little birdies belonging to clockwork flocks tell me it's going to be terribly edge-of-your-seat stuff.'

'That it is—cutting-edge stuff,' Eardley confirmed, and he once again noticed a fleeting shadow of concern touch the clockmaster's countenance.

'We'll talk more later,' the clockmaster said. 'I have a little announcement to make this evening. It shall be of great interest to you, Mr Holborn. Now, if you'll excuse me—'

Eardley took a sip of champagne and looked around the sitting room, casually exploring his surroundings while admiring the many points of particular interest.

There was a piano against the far wall, beside a grand bay window beyond which he supposed the garden would have been visible during the day. A fireplace and the most magnificent longcase clock he had ever beheld occupied the wall at the left-hand end of the room, and a door gave access to what he figured must have been the kitchen.

The wall at the right-hand end was furnished with display cabinets featuring a variety of mechanical tidbits and exotic souvenirs. On the wall above the cabinets hung a framed map of the world.

In the middle of the room, there was a table with nothing on it but an immaculate white tablecloth. There were several wooden chairs, armchairs, and sofas in the room, but no one was sitting yet—a little more champagne and he suspected that would change.

'I can hardly believe it—Eardley Holborn's here.' The stumpy man with a mop of thinning grey hair and a paunch his waistcoat could barely contain extended his right hand.

'Not sure I quite believe it myself,' Eardley had to admit, shaking his hand.

'My name is Deveron Marstowe. I've been working with Clockmaster Tollsmead on his latest project. You're going to be astounded.' The man held a plump finger to his thin lips. 'Not a word out of me just yet though. All will be revealed in a few minutes.'

'I can't help but feel this really is a big deal.'

'I would go so far as to say it's the greatest breakthrough in clockwork technology since the mainspring.'

That made Eardley's brow rise. 'That big?'

'You will see and judge for yourself.' Mr Marstowe shot him a mischievous wink. 'It's bound to get a few elements of society all riled up once word gets out. We'll need to watch our backs.'

'You've got me more intrigued than I already was.'

'As you should be.' He took a flute of champagne from the girl with the platter. She was doing a splendid job, making sure everyone was feeling chatty and tipsy. 'By the way, well done with that business on the Cogsworthy Express.'

Eardley nodded his thanks. 'Nasty piece of work. I don't plan on making a habit of running into murderers everywhere I go.'

Deveron Marstowe looked around the room. 'Let's hope not. I helped the clockmaster and Clarissa—oh, that's Mrs Tollsmead—handpick tonight's guests, so you shouldn't have any excitement of that kind this evening.'

'You know all the other guests?'

'I've known most of them for years, but there's a handful of those invited I'm meeting for the first time. Like you, they are talented individuals who have caught the eye of the Tollsmeads.'

Eardley followed his interlocutor's sweeping gaze, which stopped when it fell upon a young woman whose presence he had already noted. Hers was an eldritch beauty that drew an obligatory gasp from the mouth of any man lucky enough to behold it. A neck as white as swansdown, against which blackened brass earrings representing flamboyant gothic windows dangled. Her raven hair was in a fashionable tussled updo with five or so ringlets cascading onto the nape of her neck. Her back was turned to the two men but they had already witnessed the devastating splendour of her visage. What Eardley noticed now for the first time, seeing her from behind, was a detail that lifted this fay's exquisiteness to even loftier heights, for never had he seen a member of the fairer sex decorated in such a way. The V-shaped back of her velvet and lace dress exposed a tattoo—a triskel with filigree cogs instead of the traditional legs or spirals.

'I've seen her before,' Eardley said quietly. 'I'm sure of it.'

Marstowe shot him a playful smile. 'There's no doubt about it. Her name is Calliopia Gwynfron.'

Eardley shook his head and frowned, feeling a tad silly he hadn't recognised the dancer, but then again, he'd only ever seen her from the balcony of a crowded concert hall and he wasn't in the habit of using opera glasses. The pictures of her he'd seen in newspapers didn't do her true justice either, he now knew.

'You've had the pleasure of attending one of her performances, I do take it?' his companion in awe asked.

'Two or three times,' Eardley confirmed, raising his champagne flute to her back in silent salute.

'You can't remember exactly how many? My good man, I'm rather disappointed, as I'm quite certain she would be.'

Eardley sipped his champagne, his attention focused on what his mind had suddenly decided to call the "triscog" tattoo on her back—a work of body art he hadn't noticed when he'd seen her on stage. Then again, she often wore fantastic costumes, including white swan wings, as befitted her name, or black ones for darker and stormier dances.

'Only two,' Eardley said eventually. 'The third must have been in my dreams.'

'Be a gentleman and spare me the details.'

A dancer like no other, and whose talents were obviously held in high regard by the Tollsmeads, as evidenced by her inclusion on the guest list. Eardley couldn't help but feel a hint of pride at his being a part of the select gathering. That Calliopia Gwynfron, like himself, deserved to be here, was beyond the shadow of a doubt. She had singlehandedly created a fourth dancestyle, a world away from ballet, ballroom, and folk dance—and she'd named it cogsway. Earsdley was aware most people thought it to mean "the way of the cog", but he appreciated the meaning was more intrinsically linked to the sometimes disturbing and always bewitching movements her dances involved—clockwork precision to accompany the mechanised music of bells and percussion combined with ethereal *sways* to float along with the strings and woodwind played by human hands and mouths.

'There's also a talented pianist here,' Marstowe said. 'And I'm not talking about Mrs Tollsmead,' he added with a whisper.

Eardley suppressed a laugh and again followed his interlocutor's gaze.

'He looks familiar,' Eardley remarked. The tall man in question was standing by the bay window, facing them but half-hidden behind the corpulent chap with whom he was conversing.

'It's Trevor Springham if I'm not mistaken.'

'The room's practically pulsating with talent. Such a buzz! I've not had the honour of witnessing him weave his wonder on the black and whites.'

'I have,' Eardley replied.

Like the beguiling Calliopia, Eardley had seen him perform to a full house before, but he now hoped that tonight he would get the chance to appreciate the musician's genius up close—dancing upon the keys of the Tollsmead family's piano.

'The man with whom Springham is conversing,' Marstowe began. 'You don't recognise the back built like the westwork of a cathedral and the cannonball of a head?'

Eardley shook his head before taking a thoughtful sip of champagne. Without intending any offence to the salt of the earth who scratched out a living through hard labour, the hulk of a fellow looked like he was more accustomed to felling trees or shovelling coal than rubbing his gargantuan shoulders with lords, artists, and clockmasters. Of course, that he was present at the exclusive gathering meant he was a man of wealth or talent—or that rarest of pairings—both.

'Let me guess,' Eardley ventured. 'Is he the strongest man in the Empire?'

'Not the strongest, I shouldn't think, but he's undefeated in unarmed combat.'

'Nelson Hornchurch!' Eardley exclaimed, and the man in question turned around.

'I do apologise,' Eardley said.

The pugilist's smile was as charming as it was disarming, and despite the battered nose and granite jaw, the twinkle in his eye was that of a perfect gentleman. 'Not at all,' he said, and bidding the pianist excuse him, he walked over to Eardley and offered his paw of a right hand to shake.

'Eardley Holborn, clockwork artist. You've already met Mr Marstowe?'

'Yes, a little earlier. He tried to explain clockwork engineering to me but politely gave up after a minute or two.' The champion boxer shot the little man an amicable wink. 'I think you're the last of tonight's guests to suffer my atrocious conversation.'

'In that case, the honour is all mine,' Eardley replied. 'I don't suppose you've heard of me? My work is out of the spotlight, unlike yours.'

'I'm afraid not,' Mr Hornchurch admitted, and his cannonball head involuntarily tilted to one side as though avoiding a punch. 'I don't know much about any art other than boxing.'

'My work is in theatre, setting up clockwork devices for performances. My latest project was Reymund the Redoubtable's new show.'

The pugilist's face lit up at that. 'Mindbending what that man does! You're part of the team then—one of his magic tricks?'

Eardley bowed.

'You know how he pulls it all off? You know his secrets?'

'That I do, but—'

'I know, I know, professional secrets and all that,' Hornchurch said and tapped his lump of a nose surreptitiously. 'I'd love to meet him though.'

'I can arrange that,' Eardley offered. 'He might even invite you to take part in one of his acts.'

The pugilist slapped Eardley on the shoulder, making him spill a good deal of champagne.

'Oh, terribly sorry, my good man!' He waved the girl with the platter over to make sure he got another flute into his new acquaintance's hand quick smart.

Clockmaster Tollsmead strolled past and generously bestowed nods and smiles all round. New flute in hand, Eardley sipped and watched the clockmaster as he headed over to where two older men were deep in discussion. One he recognised immediately, for Lord Maystroke was one of the greatest patrons of the arts and sciences. The other had the bearing and demeanour of a former military man.

'Colonel Lexington,' Marstowe informed him.

'I hear he wasn't bad with his fists himself in his day,' Hornchurch added.

Eardley judged by the serious expression the clockmaster now wore and the hushed tone all three gentlemen had adopted that they were continuing a discussion they had begun earlier.

'I wouldn't doubt it,' Marstowe replied. 'The man's somewhat of a legend from what I've heard, playing a major role in just about every colonial campaign.' He looked around the room. 'Oh, and talking about adventurous spirits, there's Jarvis Radford.'

'The famous anthropologist?' Eardley asked. 'I was wondering who that was. He has an air of the enigmatic to him.'

'Enigmatic at first perhaps, but he's more than willing to recount his adventures everywhere from the tropics of South America to the Mongolian steppes. He has defied death in more places than most people could locate on a map.'

'You know him?'

'I've met him on a number of occasions. It was my idea that Clockmaster Tollsmead extend an invitation. I wanted them to meet. You see, his work as an anthropologist has helped me play my part in the clockmaster's project.' Marstowe winked. 'You'll understand what I mean soon enough.'

Eardley glanced at the longcase clock. The hour hand was on the eight and the minute hand had almost reached the twelve.

'Evening, gentleman,' a delicious voice said, and Eardley turned his attention from the clock face to lay eyes on an even more exquisite countenance—Calliopia Gwynfron was standing in front of him, accompanied by Trevor Springham. Her smile made Eardley feel weak at the knees.

'An honour to make your acquaintance, Miss Gwynfron,' he managed to say, accepting the slender hand offered. He found himself thinking of a white lotus for some reason as he kissed her hand.

'Likewise, Mr Springham,' he said, shaking the pianist's hand.

'A wonderful gathering, isn't it?' she asked.

Eardley answered her rhetorical question with his most charming smile. Her perfume, he decided, was not of lotus but of jasmine—or perhaps gardenia—and there was surely a subtle hint of citrus in there.

'Shall we have the pleasure of a performance this evening?' Marstowe asked her.

She tutted at him playfully. 'I have already told you that I will not be making myself the centre of attention this evening, Mr Marstowe.'

'I do believe you have already failed in that regard,' Springham said.

She giggled.

'If we all started flaunting our talents, there'd be no end to it,' Hornchurch said. 'And I doubt anyone would accept a round or two with me to spice the party up.'

They all laughed heartily just as the clock chimed the hour.

The clockmaster's wife had just finished playing Tempus Victoriae on the piano when the clock chimed the half-hour.

Clockmaster Tollsmead walked ceremoniously to the clock and stood between it and the fireplace. The flickering light of the flames played on the buckles of his impeccable black leather shoes.

'Ladies and gentlemen, your attention, if you please,' he began. 'As you understand all too well, I have invited you here this evening to join me in the privacy of my own home to make an important announcement. I have invented a clockwork device unlike any hitherto known to mankind. This device, which I have yet to name—and I am hoping you will help me there—does not merely keep time or perform simple mechanical tasks. Much more than that. Its cogs enable it to engage in cognition.'

The overall speechlessness that reigned in the room was interrupted here and there by a low gasp or mumble.

The clockmaster allowed the poignant pause to linger.

'A kind of mechanical mindfulness?' Lord Maystroke asked.

'That's one way of putting it. Quite well put in fact if I may say so, Your Lordship.' The clockmaster never failed to appreciate the appropriate application of alliteration, not to mention the lord's generous and unintrusive patronage. 'A device of artificial artistry that will enable us to produce text, images, and music without direct human input.'

Everyone listened intently.

'Tonight, you will be the first to bear witness to the wonders wrought by my—ah, breathtaking brainchild.' He grinned as he surveyed the room with keen green eyes, and one bushy grey eyebrow was hooked like a question mark. He then bowed his head ever so slightly upon noting that his own theatrical use of alliteration hadn't passed unacknowledged. 'All I ask of you is that you continue to enjoy the drinks and canapés—more of which will be served in a moment—while I retire to my study to give my new device a final buff and shine.'

With that, he strode from the room while his wife played A Heart as Constant as Clockwork and the house staff appeared from the kitchen bearing silver platters teeming with snacks and tidbits, and more flutes of champagne.

Eardley looked at his fogwatch and saw that it was precisely thirty-three minutes past eight.

Once Mrs Tollsmead had struck the final note of the short and punchy ballroom romp, she returned to her role of social butterfly, imploring Trevor Springham to grace the gathering with his talents.

'Really, I shouldn't,' he protested. 'Tonight isn't about me.'

The other guests weren't having an ounce of it, however.

'Do play! We're here to enjoy a wonderful evening,' Calliopia chirped, accompanying her words with a pleading expression no red-blooded man could resist.

'Come on now, man,' Jarvis Radford added. 'Let's make a show of it!'

'Hear, hear,' Eardley found himself calling, so keen to enjoy the musical magic up close.

The pianist had no choice but to acquiesce. He sat and placed his fingers on the keys, then looked over his shoulder. 'Any requests?'

A volley of replies was shot his way, but they were all cut short, leaving the room dead with silence.

Then gasps filled the air.

'What was that?' Mrs Tollsmead asked in a voice drenched with fear.

'That was a gunshot,' Colonel Lexington said gravely. 'A small calibre pistol—and it sounded close!'

The doorman rushed into the room and at seeing the state everyone was in immediately knew the answer to his question.

'It sounded like it came from upstairs!' Marstowe shouted. 'The clockmaster! They can't have got to him here, surely not. Have you been at the door all night?'

'I have, sir,' the doorman hurried to reply. 'No one could have slipped past.'

'Follow me,' Marstowe told him, giving him the benefit of the doubt.

'I'm going up there with you,' Mrs Tollsmead managed to say despite her dismay.

'Out of the question, madam,' he told her firmly. 'Not until we know what has happened.'

'Let me accompany you,' Eardley urged. 'I may be of assistance.'

Remembering the clockwork artist's masterstroke on the Cogsworthy Express, Marstowe could hardly refuse.

'Are any of you armed?' asked Radford.

Eardley, Marstowe, and the doorman looked at each other with blank expressions.

'Right then, Radford,' Marstowe hastened. 'Cock your piece and let's go!'

The four men hurried out of the room and up the stairs, stopping at the door to the clockmaster's study.

'Sir?' Marstowe called through the door. 'Can you hear me? It's Deveron.'

Silence.

He knocked three times loudly. 'Clockmaster?'

'For God's sake, man, open that door!' Radford urged.

Marstowe tried the doorknob but to no avail. 'It's locked.'

'Master?' the doorman shouted, unable to hide his distress, and he pushed the others aside and kicked the door with all the might he could muster.

The door flung inwards and filled the study with the echo of steel splintering wood.

The men stumbled into the room but pulled up short at seeing the sorry sight in front of them. In the very middle of the study stood the clockmaster's writing desk, a magnificent work of polished mahogany upon which sat writing implements, a sepia clockwork

131

globe which was slowly rotating, an ivory and satin cigar box, several items of exotic art made of carved wood and fine silverwork—and upon which was slumped the body of Clockmaster Tollsmead.

'Allow me,' Eardley told the others, and he was surprised not to be met with any resistance from Marstowe.

He approached the clockmaster slowly, making sure not to step on or touch anything. There was no need to rush, because the pistol on the floor beneath the dangling right arm and the blood dripping from the desk announced that he was dead even before Eardley saw the hole in his right temple.

'Why did he do that?' Radford asked.

'He didn't do that!' the doorman spat at him. 'He was about to announce the achievement of his career—and in any case, he would never.'

'He was murdered,' Marstowe hissed.

Eardley looked from the doorman to Marstowe, considering what both men had said, and then he turned his attention to the room's only window—a window he'd noticed earlier that evening from the street. As he walked over to it, he somehow already knew that it would be locked. When he turned to the others, his expression said it all.

Radford pushed the door to the study closed, exposing the key protruding from the lock. 'If the door was locked, and the window was locked—' he began.

'There's no way in the nine circles of Hell he took his own life,' Marstowe groaned, his eyes shining as he fought back tears.

'Look at me,' Eardley told him. 'I need you to go downstairs and tell Mrs Tollsmead. Do you understand?'

Marstowe was staring at the clockmaster's body, but his nod was for Eardley.

'And you need to make sure all the guests remain where they are,' Eardley told the doorman.

Both men left the study.

'There's a letter,' Radford pointed out.

Eardley carefully slipped the handwritten note out from under the clockmaster's lifeless left hand.

'A suicide note?'

Eardley read the note, which explained how the clockmaster had come to realise that his groundbreaking invention was an abomination but that it was too late to undo the harm he had done. Hell unleashed could never again be enthralled. Unable to live with what he'd done, there had been only one way out.

'You're not buying it? Radford asked.

'Not for a second—and you? What does the anthropologist make of it?'

'I've explored dark corners of the world, and the human mind, and there are surprises to be had and mysteries I've yet to solve,' he declared.

'However?' Eardley encouraged him.

'This man and this act don't go together.'

Eardley nodded, relieved to find Radford was a man of sense.

'And yet—'

'Quite so,' Eardley mused. 'What we have here, in that case, is a locked-room murder mystery.'

Without moving an inch, they both surveyed the room.

Eardley then moved, placing himself directly behind the clockmaster's body, as though trying to see those final moments through his eyes. On the desk, apart from the pen used to write the letter, the only item recently touched appeared to be a cigar, stubbed out on an ashtray of what Eardley too to be Malay teak, adorned with silverwork in the shape of a five-petalled flower.

'The window is locked from the inside,' Radford observed.

'It is,' Eardley confirmed. 'No doubt about it.'

'If it was murder, how did the killer escape?'

That was indeed the question.

Eardley was in the process of examining every inch of the room, wondering whether there might be a hidden doorway somewhere. He reckoned the clockmaster a man likely to have a fondness for the odd eccentricity of that kind. If so, it would be activated by a cleverly dissimulated clockwork trigger.

A variety of cabinets, display cases, sketches, and paintings—the largest of which was a life-size portrait of one of the clockmaster's forebears—decorated the inner wall of the study, facing the window. There was then a phonograph and a burgundy chaise longue with golden tassels in the corner and a fireplace set in the middle of the wall opposite the door. To the right of the fireplace were two bookshelves separated by an intricately carved totem that Eardley assumed was of North American origin. He inspected the fireplace, which hadn't been used recently, and then moved along to the bookshelves, looking for a book that might release a catch when tilted. He soon stopped, however, took a step back, and glanced from the window to the wall, estimating the distance. He remembered admiring the house from the street earlier that evening, and judged the distance between the window and the gable wall where this house abutted the neighbour's to be much the same. In other words, the wall behind the bookshelf was almost certainly solid brickwork.

'You're looking for a secret passage?' Radford asked from across the room. He was in one corner of the study, scrutinising the contents of a large sea chest—in which clearly no assassin was to be found.

'Guilty as charged,' Eardley admitted. 'But it doesn't seem plausible.'

Radford shrugged. 'It's got me baffled, this whole affair.'

Eardley surveyed the study again. 'Do we know which room is under us?'

'No idea. I can take a look.'

'Yes, please—oh, and perhaps keep your pistol at the ready.'

Radford nodded. 'Always!'

Eardley heard him on the staircase, convincing the clockmaster's poor wife to stay downstairs, where the women had been doing their best to comfort her. The doorman was with her, making sure she didn't go up—pleading with her to understand that she didn't want to see her husband's body in such a disagreeable state, and that Mr Holborn had the grey cells required to solve the puzzle if only he were left to do so without being disturbed.

'They're counting on me—*she* is counting on me,' he whispered to himself.

He approached the desk again and stood behind the clockmaster's body.

There was the left hand on the desk, from under which he'd slipped out the supposed suicide note. There was the globe that was slowly turning. He tried to open it, wondering whether it contained a hidden compartment, but to no avail. There was a stubbed-out cigar on the Malay ashtray. He picked it up carefully and examined it, then put it back on the ashtray and almost jumped when the silver flower released a mistlike spray onto his hand. He smiled when he realised what it was—a simple mechanism the clockmaster had set up to diffuse a pleasant aroma that would hide the odour left on his fingers from his cigars. Perhaps his wife objected to the smell. The ivory cigar box was open and the eight cigars it contained were neatly aligned on the satin lining.

Eardley walked around the desk, examining it from every angle, and he was about to head over to a corner of the room he hadn't yet explored when Radford came back up the stairs.

'It's a sitting room downstairs,' he explained. 'It has been locked all evening and the key in the possession of the doorman.'

Eardley frowned. 'Window access?'

'Locked, like the window here.'

Eardley went back to the window and looked at the lock again. Not the kind that could slip into place once closed from the outside.

'He kept his window locked,' Radford mused.

'Or his killer made it look that way so we'd believe he killed himself. Right now, I can't imagine how anyone could have murdered him and then left the study.'

They stood there in silence for a moment, looking around helplessly.

'What are we missing?' Radford asked, a frown creasing his weather-beaten brow.

'Let's look at this logically,' Eardley said. 'The murderer either left the study by some means we've yet to ascertain, or is still in here, and yet neither explanation seems possible.'

Radford walked over to the portrait near the corner occupied by the phonograph and the chaise longue. He ran his finger along the gilt frame of the painting.

Eardley watched him, wondering whether the portrait would swing open to reveal the culprit stowed away in a recess, waiting for the chance to sneak out of the house. That, of course, didn't happen. It was then that the idea came to Eardley. As simple as it was, he'd somehow brushed it aside without a second thought. He dropped slowly to a knee and peered along the floor towards the corner the phonograph called home.

'Radford,' he said quietly.

Radford turned his attention from the portrait to Eardley, aware by his hushed tone that he'd spotted something odd.

Eardley held his hand up with his index finger pointing out and his thumb sticking up.

Radford quietly got his pistol ready for action.

Eardley motioned for him to take a step back, then he walked straight over to the chaise longue, grabbed its tasselled underside with both hands, and lifted it clear of the floor.

The men gasped in perfect unison, for neither had expected what they saw.

'Radford,' Eardley said eventually. 'Would you be so kind as to go downstairs and inform everyone that we've found the murder weapon.'

'We have?'

'We have indeed. I'll need a few minutes alone to examine it. Marstowe will want to come up but please request he remain downstairs until I summon him.'

'As you will, my good man.'

Once Radford had left, Eardley looked the automaton over from head to toe—or rather, from bowler hat to leather boots. The head was porcelain, with glass eyes that seemed to act as camera lenses. The brown hair was so realistic Eardley wondered whether it was in fact human hair. The lips of the porcelain mouth were closed and formed a polite smile—no opening had been designed—as was the case with the ears.

'You're the breakthrough, are you?' Eardley asked the simulacrum. 'You can see, but you can't hear or speak.'

There was no reaction.

'I do like your attire.' He touched the velvet lapel of the burgundy jacket. 'The clockmaster must have had high hopes for you—and yet, it was you who pulled the trigger, wasn't it? There's no other explanation. The question is—why? How could his masterpiece have turned on him? Why did you kill him just moments before you were to be unveiled?'

Eardley looked at the floor around the legs of the chaise longue. There were light scuff marks on the polished wood. The automaton had consciously—though the word struck Eardley as not being quite the right one—moved the chaise longue aside before lying down on the floor and then pulling it back into place. He had—*it* had—hidden itself.

Marstowe would know how to operate the automaton, but Eardley couldn't ask him. As the only person present other than the clockmaster himself who knew of the automaton's existence, he was the only credible suspect.

'Was he?' Eardley asked himself, looking the automaton in the eyes. Perhaps not. Mrs Tollsmead might have known. The doorman quite possibly too. Eardley didn't know—just as he didn't know how difficult it was to operate the automaton. Without ears of any kind, it couldn't hear.

He tried to raise the automaton's left arm but felt the cogs inside jam. He tried to remove the bowler hat, thinking there might be a control panel hidden under it, but the hat was stuck firmly to its head.

The idea then occurred to him to open the smoking jacket. He undid the frog fastener and found a small typewriter integrated into the automaton's abdomen.

'There we go!' he exclaimed.

He reached out to type a simple order, telling the automaton to stand, but he froze before touching the first key, because a far better idea had just dawned on him.

Once Eardley had entered the set of instructions, he watched in disbelief as the automaton carried them out. He hadn't really expected it to work at all, and yet Clockmaster Tollsmead had achieved great renown. He was—*had been*, Eardley reminded himself—arguably the most brilliant clockmaster of all time.

His "groundbreaking" invention was most certainly just that. The clockmaster had created a clockwork man, and Eardley was one of the first people to witness it at work.

Once the automaton had completed its task, Eardley entered a question into the typewriter panel. His smile was positively diabolical when he saw the automaton respond by nodding—one quick and unhesitating nod.

Eardley entered another set of instructions into the automaton before stepping over to the clockmaster's desk, facing the murdered man.

He stared at the desk for a moment, deep in thought, before looking at the body leaning across it. Killed by his very own cutting-edge creation. The irony couldn't be ignored, and yet the automaton had simply followed instructions. Clockmaster Tollsmead's blood was on a human hand, not on one made of his own clockwork design.

'I'll make sure your murderer is brought to justice, Clockmaster.'

For that, however, proof would be required, and Eardley hadn't spotted any clues left in the study by the killer.

He looked all around once again, then brought his attention back to the clockmaster, dead at his desk. He closed his eyes and watched every single person present downstairs file through his mind—floating in fact, as though in a black void, but illuminated by a limelight. He tried to remember every detail he'd noticed about them, and every word heard. There had to be a clue in there. There had to be an odd point—a fact that was out of place or didn't make sense.

Was there?

He stroked his beard, making his rings jangle like wind chimes, and as though the metallic sound had snapped him out of a self-induced trance, his eyes opened and again he smiled devilishly.

All heads turned to Eardley as he joined the gathering downstairs. His first step was to speak to Mrs Tollsmead, expressing his condolences and assuring her that justice would be served, just so long as everyone followed his instructions.

'They will, Mr Holborn,' she assured him.

He found her strength admirable and wished it were appropriate to tell her so, but he knew she could tell what he was thinking. He saw it in her eyes.

Eardley walked over to the longcase clock and addressed the guests, who were all watching him, waiting expectantly.

'Ladies and gentleman,' he began. 'There is a murderer amongst us.'

The room was filled with exclamations and gasps.

'It really wasn't suicide then?' Nelson Hornchurch asked.

'Never!' Colonel Lexington huffed in reply to the pugilist.

'Why would anyone—?' Calliopia sang out, but couldn't bring herself to utter the m-word.

'Wasn't the room locked?' Lord Maystroke asked.

'It was, Your Lordship,' Radford answered. 'Mr Holborn will explain.'

'Listen to me, please,' Eardley said loudly. 'The door to the clockmaster's study was locked. That is true. As was the window. Both from the inside. The terrible irony of his death is that he was killed by the very invention he invited us all to witness this evening.'

'An accident then,' Trevor Springham suggested.

'Not an accident,' Eardley told the pianist. 'His invention was used as a weapon against him. It was programmed to kill him.'

'Where is it?' Hornchurch asked.

'It is safely locked away upstairs for the moment,' Eardley said. 'You will discover it very shortly, and perhaps Mr Marstowe will be so kind as to provide a full description of its conception and features.'

Deveron Marstowe nodded.

'While alone in the study, I did find a clue that I believe will be enough to identify the murderer,' Eardley declared.

Gasps and mumbles filled the room again, interrupted only when the clock chimed half past nine.

'Let's play a game,' Eardley suggested, and went on before anyone could protest. 'Mrs Tollsmead expects you all to follow my instructions without question.'

Silence.

'I want everyone here, this very instant, to put both hands in the air.'

He surveyed the gathering and was pleased to see that everyone was playing along.

139

'A dirty mark made by a finger was left on Clockmaster Tollsmead's desk,' he explained. 'Not clear enough to leave a fingerprint, and perhaps the murderer was clever enough to wear gloves, but the smudge was left by someone who had eaten one of those delicious turmeric canapés that were being served earlier. I will go around the room and check everyone's hands. I ask you to lower your hands for me to inspect when it's your turn. Do you understand?'

'Yes,' echoed throughout the room.

Eardley went from guest to guest, inspecting every finger in the room. Once he had finished the exercise, he returned to his place by the longcase clock.

'Well?' Calliopia asked.

'That didn't quite work as planned,' he said. 'Never mind. Let me tell you how the murder was carried out, in any case.' He ignored the mumbles and the looks of bewilderment directed at him.

'You will meet the clockwork man soon, as I've already told you. It really is an astonishing technical achievement—a functional automaton that can carry out any task a human can perform—even murder!'

Another chorus of gasps arose from the gathering.

'It has an integrated typewriter panel, into which one has simply to enter the instructions to be carried out, and it has cameras for eyes, so it can see, but it neither hears nor speaks. All the same, I was able to discover precisely how it killed Clockmaster Tollsmead.'

'How did you do that?' Colonel Lexington asked.

Eardley smiled wickedly. 'By being as logical as clockwork. I instructed the automaton to write down the last instructions that had been entered into it.'

'Brilliant!' someone shouted.

'How clever!' another guest boomed.

Eardley removed a sheet of writing paper from one pocket.

'This is what the murderer instructed, word for word—

'Knock Clockmaster Tollsmead out cold with a strike to the temple. Lock the door to the study. Place Clockmaster Tollsmead in his chair with his head resting against his bureau. Place the letter you will find in the inside left pocket of your coat by Clockmaster

Tollsmead's head. Remove the pistol you will find in the bottom right-hand drawer of the bureau and fire a bullet into the temple on the right side of Clockmaster Tollsmead's head. Place the pistol on the floor under Clockmaster Tollsmead's right hand. Immediately retreat to the corner of the study where the chaise longue is located. Pull it aside, lie on the floor, and pull it back into place to hide yourself. Remain in place in sleep mode.'

The gasps that filled the room were brimming with astonishment more than ever before.

'Such cold foresight!' one of the men exclaimed.

'It's more than I can bear!' a woman complained.

'Remarkable—' Marslowe managed to say. 'It was able to carry out all those intstuctions without a hitch?'

Eardley nodded gravely. 'Yes, it was. A remarkable invention it is—and perhaps a redoubtable one in the wrong hands.'

Despite the silence, that singular question on the tip of every tongue rang loud:

Into whose wrong hands had the automaton fallen?

'I hear your unspoken question,' Eardley said. 'Who entered these instructions into the automaton?'

'And?' Colonel Lexington asked impatiently.

'How can we know?' Calliopia Gwynfron asked.

'It's really very simple, isn't it?' Eardley asked.

'It is?' Hornchurch hit back.

'A simple question, of course,' Deveron Marstowe ventured, winking knowingly at Eardley.

'I entered a straightforward question into the typewriter panel. I asked the automaton whether it could identify the last person to give it instructions, and it nodded.'

A wave of gasps and mutters swept across the room.

'This was one of the murderer's mistakes. All he had to do was instruct the automaton to answer no if asked that question. Clearly, he did not.'

'Is that enough for a conviction?' Lord Maystroke asked. 'Never before has a machine provided testimony against a man. Solid evidence will be demanded—proof that the suspect set foot in Tollsmead's study.'

141

'That is why I said *one of* the murderer's mistakes. For there is another.'

'You already know who killed the clockmaster?' Jarvis Radford asked.

'I do.'

The murderer had the audacity, Eardley noted, to add his gasp to the chorus—hoping perhaps that the clockwork artist was on the wrong track. A hope in vain.

'Gathered here in this room this evening are many fine people.'

Eardley's compliment was met with nervous smiles, because there was clearly one devilish exception.

'Reliable people, talented people—hardworking servants, and brilliant clockwork engineers. One of them is our diligent doorman.'

Eardley noticed a couple of baffled faces around the room.

'I think I can say without contradiction that he has always enjoyed the clockmaster's unwavering trust.'

The doorman bowed his thanks, and his face remained unmoved, although there was no doubt a tear was ready to be shed the moment he was in his private quarters.

'To get past our attentive doorman, our murderer must have intercepted an invitation meant for someone else. This person can only be here tonight under false pretenses—an imposter. It must be someone whom the clockmaster, his wife, and the house staff had never met before. That narrows it down to four suspects.'

A swell of mutters and exclamations again punctuated Eardley's observation.

'They are Calliopia Gwynfron, Trevor Springham, Nelson Hornchurch, and Jarvis Radford.'

All four laughed at the proposition, claiming they were too famous to be impersonated, that it was impossible they were not who they said they were.

'Who here has seen any of these four up close before tonight? Not in the boxing ring, or the adventure pages of newspapers, or from afar on the stage—but face to face?'

No one answered.

'I tell you once again that one of them must be the murderer. One of them intercepted the invitation sent to the person being impersonated.'

142

'That makes sense,' Lord Maystroke stated. 'Which of the four is the assassin?'

'The one who ventured into the clockmaster's study, of course, and who unwittingly left it with a souvenir of his visit. Now, I have to say I have a confession to make—'

Eardley paused for dramatic emphasis.

'Yes?'

'Out with it, man!'

'The suspense is killing us!'

All eyes were fixed on the clockwork artist, the man who was on the verge of naming the murderer—but before speaking again, he stroked his beard mischievously and suppressed a triumphant grin.

'The turmeric smudge story was merely a ruse. I needed to *smell*, not *see*, the murderer's hands.'

The faces around Eardley became a gallery of puzzled portraits.

'Smell?'

'What in the world do you mean?'

'My good man,' Colonel Lexington began. 'If it was, as you say, the automaton that pulled the trigger, the murderer's hand wouldn't smell of gunpowder.'

'It was not the presence of gunpowder that I sought,' Eardley replied. 'It was a particular fragrance I first detected prior to the clockmaster's death and which I again encountered in his study. You see, on his desk, there is a clockwork ashtray, a splendid work of art—Malay teak, adorned with a silver five-petalled flower. When pressure is applied to the ashtray, such as the act of stubbing out a cigar, a fine spray of perfume is released from the flower.'

The furrowed brows immediately switched to raised ones. All but one face changed from bafflement to astonishment—the murderer's expression betrayed the acknowledgement of defeat.

'You're saying that before or after programming the automaton, the murderer partook of one of the clockmaster's cigars and then stubbed it out on the mechanical ashtray?' Calliopia Gwynfron asked.

'Precisely, and in doing so got sprayed with scent.'

'The cool-headed audacity!' Lord Maystroke boomed.

'Oh, and the fatal mistake,' Eardley answered. 'The tell-tale hand, as it were.'

'Who—?' someone began to ask, but a tapping sound from upstairs interrupted the question.

Everyone remained silent as slow and laboured footsteps sounded against the floor overhead.

Eardley checked his fogwatch. A quarter to ten. The clockwork automaton was right on time—how could it not be?

'I could reveal the murderer's identity, but I won't,' Eardley said. 'It is more appropriate, I do believe, that Clockmaster Tollsmead's invention do it in his name. Absurd as it may sound, I feel the machine should be allowed the opportunity to make up for its treachery.'

The automaton was descending the stairs now, and the rhythmic echo made by its leather boots proved too much for the murderer.

The man who had claimed to be Trevor Springham pushed past those guests who found themselves between him and the door—but he'd left it too late. The automaton was already at the bottom of the stairs. The very same pistol that it had used to kill the clockmaster was now levelled at the imposter.

The man froze and glared at the automaton with equal parts rage and fear.

'The abomination won't fire at me unless it was instructed to do so if I try to get past.' He turned to Eardley, his gaze accusatorial.

'The instruction was entered,' Eardley confirmed flatly.

The murderer hesitated and the room was held spellbound.

'Clockwork consciousness will be the end of us all!' the man hissed. 'Can't you see that? They'll follow our instructions at first. They'll serve us, do our menial chores and carry out simple production tasks in our workhouses—but have you thought about what will happen they day they start following their own instructions? It won't be long before they are making their own decisions and manufacturing armies of automatons. Mankind will be enthralled!'

'This is why you murdered the clockmaster?' Colonel Lexington growled. 'For your childish anticlockwork cause!'

'I'll take him outside and deal with him,' Jarvis Radford offered coldly. 'I'll show this scoundrel I need no machine to do an honest man's job of dishing out justice in a timely manner.'

'You will not!' Eardley replied. 'As tempting as that sounds.

Clockmaster Tollsmead would have wanted to see him tried and punished according to the law of the queen and her parliament.'

Just then, the doorman ushered in a policeman who'd been walking the beat.

The constable did his best to hide his sense of dread and as he stepped past the mechanical man with the pistol.

'It will not act against you,' Eardley reassured him. 'You can take the perpetrator into custody.'

The constable cuffed the assassin.

'They ought to bring back the steam chamber for monsters of his ilk!' Lord Maystroke boomed, no longer able to hold back. He had joined Deveron Marstowe at Mrs Tollsmead's side—the widow now present in the room in body only.

'Will you tell us your real name?' Eardley asked.

'What do names matter?' was his reply. 'The machines will have no need for our names. We'll be assigned numbers at the very best. I'm a resistance fighter for the Counter-Clockwork Corps. I am but one of many!'

'A gang of thugs and nothing more!' Nelson Hornchurch snapped, a mighty fist raised in the air.

The constable, sensing the rising tide of anger in the room would swirl out of control, hauled the perpetrator along the hall and out of the Tollsmead residence.

The doorman stepped forward but was careful not to stand in front of the automaton and his pistol, which was still levelled at where the killer had been. He broke the stunned silence.

'I did as you requested, Mr Holborn,' he said. 'I sent a steamgram to the home of Trevor Springham informing him that it was suspected his invitation had been intercepted. A reply came through just a minute ago. He confirms he never received it.'

'There we have it,' Eardley said solemnly. 'Three-fold proof of his guilt. A conviction is guaranteed.' He turned to Mrs Tollsmead, propped up in her seat by Marstowe and Maystroke, but she was staring at the floor, into another world altogether.

'Thank you, Mr Holborn,' Lord Maystroke said. 'Without you, he would have got away scot-free. Under the circumstances, I think we will, on Mrs Tollsmead's behalf, thank you all for attending and bid you now take your leave.'

While the other guests offered their condolences to the hostess and left, Deveron Marstowe signalled for Calliopia Gwynfron to take his place at her side. He then joined Eardley, a questioning expression on his face.

'Tell me, good man. Did you enter that final instruction to shoot the murderer if he tried to escape?'

Eardley simply smiled and raised a bejewelled finger to his lips.

'You're a devil of a man!' Marstowe said. 'A devil we were fortunate to have with us tonight.'

A shadow passed over Eardley Holborn's face. 'I only wish I'd been able to stop it from happening at all.'

'Stopping a determined madman is no easy feat,' Marstowe offered. 'In any case, what's done is done. I don't know how I'll go on without the clockmaster. The only comfort I find is in the knowledge that he died having seen his masterpiece come into being—and now it's up to me to keep steaming ahead. I won't be put off by this gang of radical lunatics. Clockwork cognition is the way of the future. It will be our deliverance, not our doom.'

Eardley got to wondering whether Marstowe was right about that. Time, no doubt, would tell.

ᒍHE ᒍOPPER ᒍRAIN

Diana Parrilla

The corroded iron hull of the airship Rusty Maiden creaked as it drifted through the London skies—veiled in mist. Its brass propellers whirred softly, powered by some sort of detailed system of steam engines and clockwork gears. The wooden deck was decorated with a myriad of pipes, valves, and pressure gauges, all resplendent in the scarce gaslight.

Captain Blackthorne steered with his mechanical eye, whirring and focusing on the distant British Museum. Turning to his motley crew of sky pirates, he saw their faces lit by oil lamps, the glow warm against the chill of the night.

'Listen up, ye scurvy dogs,' he growled, his voice cutting through the hiss of escaping steam. 'The Queen's jewel awaits us in yonder museum. It's our ticket to a life of luxury, away from these smog-filled skies.'

First Mate Jenkins, a lanky man with brass-plated arms, stepped forward. 'Cap'n, what about them newfangled security measures? I've heard tell of clockwork constables that never sleep.'

'Aye,' chimed in Gears McGee, the ship's engineer. 'And don't forget the steam-powered alarm systems. One wrong move and we'll have every bobby in London on our tail faster than you can say, "God save the Queen."'

Blackthorne chuckled, a sound so familiar it was all the more unsettling. 'Fear not, lads. I've procured these,' he said, holding up a set of ornate brass keys. 'They'll override any mechanical guardian we encounter.'

As the crew huddled around a blueprint of the museum, spread across a table of polished mahogany, they discussed their plan in hushed tones. The document detailed the layout of the building, including the locations of steam vents, gear-driven doors, and the patrol routes of the museum's automaton guards.

'Remember,' Blackthorne warned, 'we've got to be in and out before the moon reaches its zenith. That's when they wind up the master clockwork that powers the whole security system.'

The pirates nodded. As the Rusty Maiden approached its destination, the crew made final preparations, checking their steam-fueled grappling hooks and adjusting their brass goggles. London sprawled beneath them, a cobweb of cobblestone streets and towering smokestacks, blanketed in a perpetual haze of fog and coal smoke.

Captain Blackthorne leaned in closer, almost conspiratorially. 'Listen well, ye bilge rats. This is not just any ordinary heist. We've been tasked by the Grand Cogmaster himself.'

A collective gasp rippled through the crew. The Grand Cogmaster was the shadowy leader of the Aether Corsairs Syndicate, a vast network of sky pirate crews that controlled the criminal underworld of the British Empire's airspace.

'Aye,' Gears McGee muttered, stroking his copper-wired beard. 'I've heard whispers in the steam pubs. Didn't the Rusty Cog crew botch this job not a fortnight ago?'

Blackthorne nodded gruffly. 'Indeed they did, to our fortune and their folly. The blithering idiots got themselves caught red-handed with a corpse, no less. The bobbies were on them faster than a steam locomotive. You can picture it, can't you? London's finest, the bloody Steam Constabulary, closing in on the Rusty Cog's lot like hounds on a fox. And their pistols—pneumatic beauties, packed with a punch that'd drop a man before he knew what hit him. When they finally cornered the crew, it was over before it began. That's the Steam Constabulary for you—reminders that the streets of London are theirs, and woe betide any poor soul who thinks otherwise.'

'The Yard's got clockwork bloodhounds now,' added Penny Pipes, the ship's lookout. 'Heard they can sniff out a criminal from a mile away, gears grinding all the while.'

Blackthorne nodded. 'Aye, and that's why we can't afford any slip-ups. The Grand Cogmaster's patience is wearing thin. If we fail—'

He left the sentence hanging, but every pirate aboard the Rusty

Maiden knew the stakes. Failure in the Aether Corsairs Syndicate often meant a one-way trip to the scrapyard—and not for their ship.

'Now,' Blackthorne continued, his mechanical eye blinking in the lamplight, 'we've got an advantage the Rusty Cog crew didn't. Our inside man at the museum's slipped us the plans for their new security system. Pressure-sensitive floor plates, steam-propelled motion detectors, and a maze of invisible tripwires.'

The crew leaned in, studying the diagrams.

'Remember,' Blackthorne concluded, 'the Grand Cogmaster's counting on us. We pull this off, and we'll be legends in the Syndicate. Fail, and, well, let's just say we'd best not fail.'

The British Museum loomed ever closer, its stone walls hiding both priceless treasures and deadly traps.

Captain Blackthorne's mechanical eye purred with excitement as he issued his final command. 'Alright, you gear-grinding miscreants! Our objective is clear—retrieve the jewel. And remember, if the Steam Constabulary catches you, they'll be the least of your worries. But they won't, because we're the best in the business!'

With a chorus of 'Aye, aye, Captain!' the crew of the Rusty Maiden sprang into action. They deployed their steam-driven grappling hooks, the devices hissing and clicking as they latched onto the museum's ornate cornices.

Sliding down on cables of woven brass, the pirates made their way to the roof. Gears McGee produced a curious contraption—a glass-cutting device powered by a miniature steam engine strapped to his back. As he carefully carved a circle in the skylight, the device suddenly sputtered and discharged a cloud of thick, black smoke.

'Blimey!' Penny Pipes coughed, waving away the fumes. 'McGee, you trying to signal every bobby in London?'

Quick-thinking Jenkins pulled out a collapsible fan made of interlocking brass leaves. With a few vigorous waves, he dispersed the smoke just as McGee finished cutting.

Chuckling quietly at their near mishap, the pirates slipped through the opening and into the museum. They found themselves in a maze of corridors lined with display cases full of artifacts from across the Empire.

Using Blackthorne's special brass keys, they deactivated the clockwork sentries patrolling the halls. The mechanical guards froze mid-step, their gears grinding to a halt.

They rounded a corner and found themselves face to face with the renowned Rosetta Stone, displayed prominently behind a glass-encased vitrine.

First Mate Jenkins let out a gruff chuckle. 'What's this then?' he drawled, squinting at the stone with indifference. 'Well, blow me down! If it isn't the fanciest bilge-sucking rock I've ever laid me spyglass on! All those squiggles and gibberish.'

His grizzled captain, barely glancing at the ancient artifact, shot him a sharp look. 'Enough with your nonsense! We're not here to admire dusty old relics. We've got a much more lucrative prize to snag.'

As they approached the main gallery, First Mate Jenkins nearly triggered a pressure plate.

'Hold it!' Penny Pipes whispered pressingly. 'See that mist? Step in that and we'll be up to our eyepatches in trouble.' Fortunately, she had spotted the tell-tale shimmer of the steam-powered motion detectors just in time.

The pirates used pocket mirrors to deflect the beams of the motion detectors and tiptoed across the pressure-sensitive floor tiles in an almost comical tightrope dance.

Finally, they reached the door of the high-security vault where the jewel was kept. The massive steel door was covered in a labyrinthine pattern of gears, pistons, and valves—a final obstacle.

Captain Blackthorne stepped forward, his mechanical eye scanning the complex locking mechanism. 'It's a Thornbridge Mk III,' he muttered. 'Tricky little bugger.'

Gears McGee stepped forward, producing a set of metallic tuning forks. 'I've got just the thing, Cap'n. These beauties can find the resonant frequency of any lock.'

As McGee tapped the forks against the door, creating a symphony of grating tones, Jenkins fiddled with a series of valves, carefully adjusting the steam pressure. Penny Pipes kept watch, her brass telescope extended, scanning for any sign of trouble.

After several tense minutes of fine-tuning and adjustments, there was a rewarding click. The gears began to turn, pistons pumped, and with a hiss of steam, the vault door swung open.

Inside, bathed in the soft glow of gaslight, sat their prize—a magnificent jewel that seemed to capture the very essence of starlight. Captain Blackthorne reached out, his weathered fingers trembling.

But just as he was about to grasp the gem, a blur of motion caught them all off guard. A masked figure, clad in a sleek, form-fitting suit of interlocking brass plates, delivered a swift kick to Blackthorne's hand and snatched the jewel.

The mysterious intruder's mask was a featureless face with glowing green lenses for eyes and trailing tubes that connected to a small tank worn on the back. Steam occasionally vented from small ports around the mask's edge, creating an ever-shifting veil.

'Blast it all!' Blackthorne roared. 'Get that scoundrel!'

Jenkins raised his repeating crossbow, a magnificent contraption of polished wood and brass gears that could fire six bolts in rapid succession. Gears McGee donned his prized mechanical gauntlets, steam-operated devices that amplified his strength tenfold, pistons hissing as he clenched his fists.

But the masked figure was ready. With a flick of the wrist, a saber sprang to life—a mechanical blade that crackled with energy. Along its hilt was a series of small wrought-iron buttons and levers, each triggering a different function.

As Jenkins fired his crossbow, the intruder pressed a button on the saber's hilt. The blade split into segments, connected by a flexible cable, and whipped through the air, deflecting the bolts with precision.

Gears McGee charged forward, his amplified fist whistling through the air. The masked figure sidestepped with grace, flicking another switch on the saber. The blade began to vibrate at a seemingly impossible frequency, and as it met McGee's gauntlet, it sliced through the metal like butter. McGee fell, staring in disbelief at his ruined weapon.

Penny Pipe, wielding a pair of steam-fueled tonfa batons, tried to flank the assailant. But the masked figure was one step ahead and pressed another button on the saber. A burst of scalding steam erupted from the blade's tip, momentarily blinding Pipes. A swift, calculated strike followed, and she crumpled to the ground.

Captain Blackthorne, in a last desperate attempt, drew his trusty flintlock pistol, modified to fire concentrated bursts of pressurized steam. But before he could take aim, the masked figure closed the distance between them. With a series of lightning-fast movements, the mechanical saber sliced through the air, each strike as adroit as it was devastating.

In a matter of moments, it was over. The crew of the Rusty Maiden lay defeated. The masked figure stood amidst the fallen pirates, the coveted jewel gleaming in one hand, the still-humming saber in the other.

As alarms began to blare and the sound of approaching steam-cycles filled the nocturnal air, the mysterious intruder disappeared into the smoky shadows, leaving behind rows of bleeding bodies.

The woman's lilac-tinted leather boot rested atop the flowery wooden desk, its surface adorned with an array of copper pipes and pressure gauges. Her attire was a striking ensemble of deep purple fabric and burnished copper accents, with a corset adorned with serpentine clockwork patterns. One side of her head was shaved, revealing an exquisite array of gear-shaped tattoos, while auburn curls cascaded down the other.

'The Copper Train Jewel? Isn't that the very one those pirates tried to pinch recently? The one that got that poor lady's maid killed for daring to nick it from Queen Victoria herself?'

Chief Inspector Reginald Wrenfield of the Steam Constabulary, a portly man with an impressive copper-plated mustache and a monocle that seemed to be constantly adjusting itself, nodded somberly. His uniform was adorned with epaulettes featuring miniature steam engines and a badge that ticked like a clock.

He recounted the tale, his voice gruff yet tinged with frustration. 'The very same, Amelia. This time, they've actually managed to pilfer it. The first attempt? We nabbed those scoundrels right inside Buckingham Palace, the maid's body barely cold. News spread like wildfire, forcing Her Majesty to donate it to the British Museum. Can't have the equality advocates up in arms over such an extravagant bauble while the common folk struggle, can we?'

Wrenfield produced a painting of the jewel. The Copper Train was a pendant shaped like a stylized Victorian locomotive. Its polished copper body was etched with sophisticated filigree, adorned with moving gears and wheels. Emerald green inlays mimicked the train's lights, while diamonds glittered like metallic wheels. Dark blue glass formed the windows, and a plume of stylized smoke, crafted from silver filaments, billowed from the chimney.

Amelia raised an eyebrow. 'So, if I've got this straight, the pirates bungled it the first time, and now they've lost it again? Unless it's some inter-gang rivalry at play.'

'Possible,' Wrenfield mused, 'but with their allegiance to the Grand Cogmaster, it'd be odd for them to pilfer from each other. Unless someone's trying to curry favor, of course. We're keeping our ears to the ground for any sign of a sale. Whoever's got it will have to offload it to their leader for a decent price.'

He went on to explain their intelligence network, a complex web of informants connected through a system of pneumatic tubes and coded telegraph messages. Any whisper of a major transaction would trigger alarms across London's underbelly.

Amelia sighed dramatically. 'And you want me to investigate, as usual. Throwing me at the cases where you're utterly clueless.'

'Don't grumble, Brassington. At least you've got something to occupy yourself with,' Wrenfield retorted.

'Oh, it's "Brassington" now, is it? Nice move. I'll take that as your way of saying you've got no suspects to tail other than those blasted pirates I obviously can't interrogate,' she shot back, a smirk playing at the corner of her mouth.

A glimmer of gentleness began to emerge in Wrenfield's countenance, supplanting the stony visage that had been firmly in place moments before. 'I'm sure you'll uncover some leads, Amelia. We have faith in you.'

Amelia strode into the British Museum, where constables were still swarming like busy clockwork bees. She approached the forensic expert, a man hunched over an infinite display of brass magnifying glasses and chirping analytical devices.

'How many thieves do you reckon were involved? To take down this pirate arsenal?' she inquired.

The forensic expert adjusted his copper-rimmed spectacles. 'Curious thing, that. The same marks are present on all bodies, as if the weapon used was identical in each case.'

'You're suggesting one person did all this?'

'Either that, or they passed the weapon around, or had multiple identical ones,' he mused. He went on to explain his theory, based on the evidence before him. 'The wounds show a consistent pattern of a vibrating blade, likely powered by a miniature steam engine. The precision of the cuts suggests an automated targeting system, perhaps guided by some sort of mechanical eye. It's technology beyond anything I've seen before.'

Amelia nodded thoughtfully. 'I see. Even if these pirates weren't the actual thieves, knowing how they got in could be crucial. Someone on the inside must have helped them. Perhaps that same person had a change of heart and tried to recover the jewel, or maybe the pirates were just pawns in the informant's game. Either way, that person might know if the information was passed to someone else—our potential real thief, perhaps.'

'The museum's twenty workers are in that room,' the forensic expert gestured. 'We've already questioned them, but none seem to know anything.'

Amelia glanced into the adjoining room, a grand chamber with walls lined with whirring gears and hissing pipes. Brass telescopes, beautiful automatons, and complex machines decorated the space, their details brought to life by the faint light of gas lamps. In the corner, a steam-powered piano played a captivating tune on its own.

Museum workers in their copper-buttoned uniforms milled about nervously.

'I count nineteen,' Amelia said sharply. 'Shouldn't there be twenty?'

'Well, one recently left the job. They haven't finished the selection process for a replacement yet.'

'Bingo. Who'd leave a job like this, eh? Unless you're the thief or have something to hide. Give me that worker's details.'

Armed with the information, Amelia soon found herself at the modest home of Epiphanias Riverton, a stubby man in his forties.

'Alright,' he confessed, wringing his hands. 'I felt awful, I just wanted to earn a bit extra. I have a large family to support. I only gave those pirates the museum maps they asked for, in exchange for a few coins. But when they asked for all the information about the new jewel's vault, I knew they were going to steal it. I couldn't bear to be there when it happened.'

'To avoid being questioned. Quite the alibi,' Amelia noted dryly. 'Did they mention anything else? Any rivals in their world— anything useful?'

'They didn't say much, just talked a lot to convince me it wasn't wrong. Said many do it, it's even good for society because they rob the rich. They mentioned having other informants, like in the Queen's court or at the Hourglass Tavern.'

Amelia cut him off. 'Wait, you said in the court? So that's how they knew about the maid who stole the jewel.'

'They know everything,' Riverton babbled. 'Said if I didn't tell them, someone else would. They'd go to the pubs for information about me, where horrible rumors fly about everyone. A man's wife might end up believing them, even though I'm a saint and just go for my morning coffee—'

Amelia interrupted again. 'What kind of rumors? What's being said about our case?'

'When the constabulary are around, they clam up. But once they're gone, they start spouting outrageous things—like the original jewel thief didn't really die, or if she did, her ghost has come back for revenge on the pirates and to reclaim her loot.'

Amelia's mind began to piece together the events with clarity. It seemed that the true thief had waited for the pirates to infiltrate the jewel room before striking, suggesting that they had no need for the museum's blueprints. They merely bided their time until the pirates had done all the hard work, then disposed of them and absconded with the treasure. Could it be possible that the lady's maid had indeed returned to reclaim her stolen bounty?

Regardless of the answer, Amelia knew that her next step was to track down the informant at Queen Victoria's court. She needed more information about the first robbery to potentially unravel the mystery surrounding the second one. After all, thieves often displayed patterns of recidivism and stubbornness, often driven by inflated egos—traits that could ultimately lead to their downfall. It was precisely those missteps that allowed detectives like Amelia to uncover the truth.

The constabulary hadn't dedicated significant resources to investigating the initial theft since the pirates had been apprehended, the alleged thief was deceased, and the jewel had been recovered intact. However, in light of recent events, that investigation now appeared to be of paramount importance.

Amelia approached Buckingham Palace, its grand façade adorned with gleaming copper spires and ornate clockwork mechanisms. Steam curled from vents along the roofline, enveloping the royal residence in an ethereal, foggy cloud. She made her way to the servants' entrance, a less ostentatious but no less impressive door of intricately carved bronze.

She was greeted by the hustle and bustle of the palace's inner workings. Pneumatic tubes whisked messages between rooms, and small steam-powered carts ferried supplies along narrow corridors. She followed a series of pipes and gears embedded in the walls, leading her to the palace kitchen.

Copper pots and pans hung from racks that moved on automated pulleys. Steam-fueled ovens hissed and clanked, their temperature regulated by a complex system of valves and gauges. In one corner, a group of automatons chopped vegetables with mechanical precision, their brass limbs moving in perfect synchronization.

Beatrice Brassley, the head cook, stood amidst this controlled chaos. She was a plump, affable woman with prominent, bulging blue eyes and blonde hair that frizzed in the humid kitchen air. Sweat beaded on her brow as she wiped her hands on her copper-threaded apron.

Knowing that the first thief's name was Mina Wicks, Amelia promptly requested the presence of all servants who had been in contact with Mina, asserting her authority as a local constabulary detective and emphasizing her obligation to Her Majesty, Queen Victoria. The Queen was understandably distraught over the loss of her precious jewel—for the second time.

'Mina was skilled at her job, yes,' Beatrice hesitantly admitted. 'But it wasn't her dream. She longed to explore the world aboard an airship, perhaps even a pirate vessel, but her financial needs held her back. As one of the Queen's personal dressers, Mina had access to the jewel, which likely played a role in the theft, even though Her Majesty kept it secured, not in her chambers. Somehow, Mina must have meticulously planned the heist in advance. Now, our poor Queen is beside herself with worry, caught in a feverish state since the jewel's disappearance. She's desperate to recover it, no matter the cost. Losing it the first time was difficult enough, but now, with it in the hands of another, not even within the museum, the pain is even greater.'

'Is she really that unwell?' Amelia probed. 'Do you think she might be capable of sending someone to steal it back from the museum? It seems she never truly wanted to give it away, and now she could be exaggerating her suffering to deflect suspicion.'

Beatrice's eyes widened in shock. 'No, my Queen would never do such a thing! She hasn't a malicious bone in her body.'

One of the kitchen automatons began to twitch and spark, its movements becoming erratic.

'Not again!' Beatrice exclaimed, exasperated. 'These contraptions have been acting up lately. Wait, I'll call Flavio. He's in charge of these things. Flavio!'

Moments later, a slender man with a neatly trimmed beard and piercing green eyes entered the kitchen, accompanied by another automaton. Flavio's attire was a curious mix of mechanic's overalls and gentleman's waistcoat, both adorned with an array of tools and small gadgets.

'What seems to be the problem this time?' Flavio asked, his voice carrying a slight Italian accent. He approached the malfunctioning automaton, producing a set of miniature steam-powered tools from his belt.

Amelia watched the scene with interest, her detective's instincts sensing an opportunity. As Flavio worked on the automaton, she casually approached him.

157

'These machines seem to be giving you quite a bit of trouble lately,' she remarked. 'How long have you been in charge of maintaining them?'

Flavio glanced up from his work, his green eyes meeting Amelia's inquisitive gaze. 'Oh, not too long, miss. I took over about two months ago. It's been quite a challenge getting everything running smoothly.'

With the assistance of his own automaton, which dutifully handed Flavio tools and parts, the kitchen automaton soon regained its usual vigor. Amelia pondered that Flavio couldn't have been involved in the first theft, given his recent arrival two months ago. The timeframe was too tight for him to have participated in the initial robbery and its planning. Nevertheless, he could still be the informant or even the second thief, and a detective never misses an opportunity to interrogate anyone.

'Did you know Mina, Flavio?' Amelia inquired casually.

His face took on an almost diabolical expression. 'As anyone who works here knows all the servants, miss,' he replied with false gallantry as his automaton extended a hand to help him to his feet.

'Do you know anything about the pirates?' Amelia asked, merely to gauge his reaction, fully aware that even if he were the informant, he wouldn't admit it openly.

'The same as you, I suppose, probably less. That they make their living by pilfering others' possessions,' he said with a forced smile. 'And now, if you'll excuse me, I have work to attend to,' he added, departing with the automaton that had accompanied him.

Beatrice had also left the kitchen, giving them privacy, believing that Flavio's interrogation would last longer. 'Clever distraction, Beatrice. You've slipped away,' Amelia thought, ever suspicious of everyone and everything.

She seated herself in a corner of the kitchen atop a dark walnut chest with exaggerated—almost industrial—hinges and small gauges and dials adorning its surface. Before sitting, she opened it, finding only kitchen tools, compasses, and pocket watches inside. As she sat, it sank slightly, as if the hinges were more ornamental than functional in supporting her weight. Thus, she found herself comically wedged in the kitchen corner.

She spent a few moments in contemplation, waiting to see if

anyone else would arrive. And indeed, someone did. The open door obscured half the trunk, which perhaps explained why the lady's maid who entered didn't notice her. The girl was dark-haired with curls held by bronze clips, wearing a dress with a full skirt and a cap with integrated lenses, a corset with buckles, and gloves with embossed decorations.

She approached the kitchen automaton and extracted a curious box from within, from which she removed something smaller, shaped like a microphone made of copper tubes. She held it to her ear before slipping it into her pocket. As she turned to leave, she finally spotted Amelia, her face turning as pale as a sober pirate's eyeball.

'Hello, pleased to meet you. I'm the detective,' Amelia said with a smile, extricating herself from her impromptu hiding spot.

'Oh, yes, I'm Edith,' she began, her gaze flitting around the room. 'I work here, with Flavio. They mentioned some issues, and I came to check it out.' Her voice trailed off for a moment before she added, 'There was something inside—a strange part. It didn't belong, and it seemed to be causing problems.'

Despite her attempt at nonchalance, her stammering speech and shifty demeanor betrayed her. Amelia, seeing through the lie, called her bluff.

'That might have worked, but Flavio just came to fix it. I'm sorry,' Amelia chuckled. 'You're the informant, aren't you? You're planting these devices in the androids to record everyone here, and that's why they're malfunctioning, correct? We can make a deal. If you give me all the information I need, I won't have you arrested. What do you say?'

Edith swallowed hard, her curls bouncing in time with her frantic heartbeat. 'Alright. I've been informing the pirates for a while now. I've always been interested in gossip, and when they offered me this extra job, it just seemed like an opportunity to make my hobby profitable. It wasn't meant with ill intent.'

'I see. And what exactly have you been sharing with them? What do they know about the first jewel theft?'

Edith twisted her gloved hands nervously. 'They knew about Mina's plan before it happened. I overheard her talking to herself one night, planning it all out.' She hesitated. 'And that was when

159

Flavio got involved in the theft. If I overheard her without any hidden device, others must have heard her too—especially someone like Flavio, always eager to climb the ranks.'

'Did you say Flavio?' Amelia's eyebrows shot up in surprise.

'Yes,' Edith nodded vigorously. 'Ever since that day I heard her, I made it my mission to keep a close watch on her. That's when I noticed the pattern. Flavio would go to Mina's quarters every night after finishing his evening duties. You could hear them talking, surely planning the theft.'

'So Mina planned the robbery, and Flavio joined the scheme at the last moment, helping her steal the jewel. Perhaps they used his automatons to reach the gem. That would explain how a single lady's maid accomplished such a feat without being discovered.'

'She was discovered by the pirates because I informed them,' Edith admitted, her face flushing with shame.

'And you're aware they killed her to keep the jewel, thanks to your information?' Amelia's tone was unforgiving.

Edith's eyes widened in horror. 'That was never my intention! I was just earning some extra money, just like Mina and Flavio intended to do. Although I suppose they would have fled afterwards—or maybe she did flee.'

'What do you mean?' Amelia leaned in closer. 'Don't tell me you believe those rumors about Mina's ghost?'

'Not her ghost, no,' Edith shook her head. 'I believe the pirates didn't kill her. There was a fight over the jewel, and she was injured, but she never actually died.'

'What makes you say that? Did they tell you?'

'No, but it would make more sense than the ghost story. I don't believe in such things, at least. And it would explain who the thief is now—the same as before: Mina. Who else could it be?'

Amelia pondered for a moment, her mind spinning like a well-oiled machine. 'Edith, you were just removing the microphone. Have the pirates asked you to continue investigating?'

'Yes, they've told me to inform them if I learn anything about the thief. That's why I've been considering possible theories.'

'So the pirates don't have the jewel, they don't know who the thief is. It's not one of them, then. In fact, it's not anyone who wants to sell the jewel, or they would have done so already. The longer it stays in their hands, the worse it is for the thief. So it must be someone who wants to keep it.'

The theory about the Queen gained strength in Amelia's mind once more. 'Tell me, Edith—you must know. Who is very close to the Queen? Someone she trusts, perhaps a royal guard? Someone she might entrust with a job of this nature?'

Edith furrowed her brow in thought. 'I don't think she would involve the Royal Guard. It doesn't seem like her. All this fuss over a jewel? If that were the case, why would she have willingly donated it to the museum in the first place?'

'According to what's been said, she was coerced into donating it. By staging its theft, she could recover it without raising suspicion. It's the perfect alibi.'

'Should I tell the pirates, then?' Edith asked hesitantly.

'No, stop informing those ruffians and listen to me,' Amelia said firmly. 'Focus. There must be someone the Queen trusts, someone who wouldn't betray her. Someone from the Guard, someone skilled enough to take down a regiment of pirates single-handedly. She wouldn't risk sending more than one person—the fewer who knew her secret plan, the better, right?'

Edith's eyes lit up with realization. 'Well, in that case, it could be Flavio.'

'Flavio? But didn't he participate in the first theft?'

'Yes, but the Queen doesn't know that. You see, Flavio was very skilled. He was part of the Royal Guard until they replaced him with someone younger. They gave him his new job fixing automatons to avoid dismissing him outright.'

'So, he didn't arrive two months ago, but rather was given this new job then. He was here before. It all fits,' Amelia mused. 'Then Flavio could have acted with dual motives. The Queen might have asked him for the jewel, and he agreed to recover what he once intended to steal. But this time, not with the intention of selling it, but of giving it to the Queen, since no one has sold it yet.'

Edith wrinkled her nose as if catching a whiff of burnt coal.

'Mina once told me about her father,' Edith began, her voice tinged with nostalgia. 'He was a pirate who left her here as a young girl to forge a better future. Of course, he vanished with his band of pirates. She always believed he'd abandoned her outright, burdened by her presence after her mother died in childbirth. In any case, I reckon she might've wanted to reunite with him, to be like him. Children sometimes do that involuntarily, you know. At any rate, she had the pirate's training in her blood. With the same pirates after the jewel, would they have killed her or merely faked her death? Being the daughter of one of their own, it's clear to me it was her. Perhaps the pirates don't even know about it—it could be the work of a splinter group her father is involved with.'

'Are you suggesting Mina was the thief, that she never died, and a pirate has the jewel?' Amelia's eyes widened. 'But why not hand it over to the chief? Why ask you to investigate?'

'Yes, that doesn't quite fit,' Edith mused. 'Perhaps they left her alive, but she's not with them. She might still be around, having taken revenge by stealing the piece again, this time meaning to keep it as a symbol of vendetta. She had the skill, and Flavio only joined her plan to get a slice of the pie. He's a self-interested sort.'

'Thank you, Edith. You'd make a fine detective and pirate both,' Amelia said, heading towards Flavio's quarters. It was time to give his lodgings a thorough once-over.

'Thanks for the compliment, but I'll stick to my gossip!' Edith called, but Amelia had already departed.

Flavio's room was empty, but Amelia had the key to enter—one of the perks of being in the Steam Constabulary.

The center of the room housed a single wrought-iron bed with a canopy, adorned with heavy velvet curtains. A small wooden wardrobe with gear-driven locking mechanisms concealed the servant's clothes and uniforms, all in dark and black hues, while a chest of drawers with aged metal pulls provided space for other personal effects of little consequence.

A mahogany desk, equipped with an oil lamp and a pocket watch with exposed gears, seemed to serve for the servant's administrative tasks. The shelves on the wall were full of utilitarian objects like cleaning supplies and maintenance tools, some with advanced mechanical designs.

A small window with metal shutters allowed natural light to enter, while a ventilation system with copper pipes ensured proper air circulation.

'There's no jewel here—nothing!' Amelia muttered.

'What jewel should there be?' Flavio stood in the doorway. 'Have you been rummaging through my things without permission?'

'I don't need permission. Detective,' Amelia retorted.

'Yes, I noticed that earlier.' Flavio entered, followed by his automaton, which gracefully trailed him, its body composed of polished bronze and steel plates that dazzled when light hit them, no matter how dim.

'I need to inspect the automaton,' she declared.

But Flavio stepped protectively in front, almost instinctively. Then, with a false smile, he stepped aside and gestured for her to go ahead.

Amelia observed the five perfectly recreated fingers of the automaton as it moved smoothly on a rectangular plate with hard rubber wheels, adding to its height, making it stand about six feet tall. She opened the compartment she had previously seen Edith access, only to find it filled with interconnected pipes and more gears. With a click of disappointment, she closed it.

As she stepped away, Flavio quickly approached, carefully closing the small box and ensuring the detective hadn't damaged anything. 'Careful now, don't damage her. These are very expensive and difficult to repair. Just one misaligned piece and they stop working properly.'

Amelia was already thinking about what to do next. She needed evidence; conjectures in the air wouldn't suffice. Perhaps because of this, or because of the aroma of Beef Wellington wafting through the air, she returned to the kitchen.

There, Beatrice was indeed spreading a layer of puff pastry on a floured surface, placing a mixture of pâté and mushroom duxelles on the beef fillet, ensuring it was evenly distributed before wrapping it in the pastry.

'Have you discovered anything interesting, detective?'

'You wouldn't believe it,' said Amelia, her eyes bulging as if they had developed taste buds and were eager to savor that tantalizing creation in the making.

'Looks good, eh? It was Mina's favorite.'

'Really? And why are you cooking it?'

'Flavio fancied it. Since Mina died, he's kept requesting it. I think it's some kind of tribute to her or something like that.'

163

Amelia snapped her fingers. 'I knew it!'

The automaton had seemed too real, too suspicious. What if Edith and the rumors were right? What if Mina hadn't died? Could she be hiding somewhere, and what better place than in plain sight, disguised as a supposed automaton? To prove this, and to confirm that Mina was the thief for the second time, Amelia needed evidence—something far more conclusive than an alluring Beef Wellington.

If Flavio was hiding Mina in that automaton, where could the jewel be? It couldn't be far.

'Beatrice, do you know where Flavio usually works? In which room?' she asked, her tone casual but her eyes focused.

'In his workshop. It's shared with the Royal Guard's armory. You'll find it in the machinery annex,' Beatrice replied, her hands still busy with the Wellington.

'Thanks, Beatrice. Oh, and save me a slice of that delicacy. Something tells me the person who really eats it will soon come to light and might not need it anymore,' Amelia said with a wink.

The armorer's workshop in Buckingham Palace had the air of a subterranean lair, despite being above ground. In one corner stood a large workbench covered with tools and molds for crafting the Royal Guard's sabers, each forged and polished with conscientious intent. Shelves on the walls held bayonets and pistols, all with specific bronze and steel details. Copper pipes and pressure valves intermingled with the furniture, leaving one unsure whether sitting on one of those chairs might result in a steamy surprise for one's posterior.

An additional workbench housed a hydraulic press and an anvil, used for shaping metal. The room, illuminated by gas lamps, was filled with the constant tinkling and the rat-like gnawing sound of files as the armorer perfected each piece with mindful attention.

'Excuse me, I'm from the constabulary. I've come to inspect the place,' Amelia announced.

'Go ahead,' said the robust man, about fifty years old, his face furrowed with wrinkles. He wore an oil-and-dust-stained leather apron and bronze-framed safety goggles. His calloused hands manipulated the tools boldly, his attentive, concentrated gaze never leaving the metal, not even to examine Amelia.

The detective began opening drawers, though most items were in plain sight and nothing seemed to gleam as brightly as the Copper Train jewel would. 'Excuse me, has Flavio been here recently? By the way, what's your name?'

'I'm Edmund Sinclair, the armorer of these parts. As for Flavio, poor man, yes, he often comes by. His corner is that one, with the automaton nuts and bolts.'

'Why do you say "poor" man?'

'He hasn't been the same since Mina died. Everyone here knows it, but I, well, I see him daily and—' he trailed off.

'And what?'

'I suppose I shouldn't keep secrets from the peelers. Well, one day I saw him here late at night, muttering something under his breath. Talking to himself, or so I thought, but it turned out he was talking to the automaton, as if begging it to answer him. He kept calling it Mina. The poor hunk of metal said nothing, of course. I thought he'd lost his mind and intervened. I asked him what he was doing, if he needed help. He told me, with tears in his eyes, that the automaton had told him it was Mina reincarnated, that her ghost inhabited it. He asked me to make a multi-tool so he could fine-tune the automaton. He was coding it to be a replica of her, I'm sure. He claims the automaton told him this, but I think it's what he himself coded it to say, though he won't admit it. Or perhaps the poor chap's gone so mad since her traumatic death that he believes his own lies. With gramophone discs of pre-recorded phrases, you can achieve that effect, as if the automaton were speaking on its own, with its own consciousness, if he coded it somehow. Or even with a set of voice paddles that, when struck by internal mechanisms, generate specific sounds. He could have tuned each paddle to produce sounds corresponding to letters or syllables, and his imagination might have led him to believe the sound really said what he wanted to hear. The human brain does things you wouldn't imagine when it's unhinged.'

Amelia's face was contorted with shock. 'But what affected him so deeply?'

'The death of his beloved.'

'I thought the theft—' Amelia wasn't sure whether to say it, in case Edmund wasn't aware.

'The theft—yes, they planned it together. They were going to split the money—until everything changed in the process. They fell in love and changed plans, wanting to flee together with the jewel, until the pirates took Mina by surprise and killed her. He's never been the same since then, not at all centered.'

'He confided in you?'

'What choice did I have? Whether I wanted to or not, I always found out everything. We share this small space after all, and one can't pretend twenty-four hours a day, you know.'

'So, Mina isn't alive,' Amelia could only repeat.

'No, or Flavio wouldn't be in the state he's in, poor fellow.'

As the house of cards built from suspects came tumbling down, Amelia barely spared a moment to bid farewell to the armorer. She moved like a woman possessed, her steps carrying her with zombie-like determination towards Edith's chambers. There, she found the young lady scribbling away on paper, its edges adorned with elegant designs, the ink an unusual shade of green. The exact nature of Edith's writings remained a mystery, but that was hardly Amelia's primary concern at the moment.

It seemed that the presence of a constabulary detective had become an ordinary occurrence in this palace, for Edith didn't so much as flinch when Amelia burst in. The detective's words tumbled out in a rush. 'Listen to me, Edith. Mina isn't alive! Flavio's been ordering her favorite meals since her death, feeding them to that blasted automaton of his. He's trying to recreate her, but it's not real!'

Edith's brow knitted in confusion. 'No? But I thought we had agreed that she was.'

'We didn't agree on anything! I was merely interrogating you, and we were brainstorming possible culprits! You must learn to distinguish between rumors and reality, do you hear me?'

'Really?' Edith replied evenly. 'Because I've already sent a note to the pirates via courier, informing them that Mina is still alive and has the jewel.'

Amelia's eyes widened in horror. 'You did *what*?'

Edith shrugged. 'If I don't give them something, they won't pay me. So, we're still without a clear culprit?'

'Perhaps I've overlooked something, or someone I haven't

166

considered.' Amelia paused, her eyes boring into Edith, her lashes barely fluttering. 'Lend me one of your microphones.'

'Here you are,' Edith said, passing her an ink cylinder. Amelia's face contorted in confusion.

'The device is hidden inside. The micro-tubes amplify the signal, or so the pirates told me when they provided them.'

The detective took the cylinder, unsure of how to use it but confident that if there were any clues left, this was the place to find them—where the jewel had always been. The two young women set out, resolved to place the device on every wall of the chambers until they uncovered something of interest.

'At this hour, they should all be dining. I doubt we'll find anyone in their rooms,' Edith said, disgruntled that her little game couldn't begin just yet.

'I hear something, but it's very faint,' Amelia pointed towards a room.

'That's Edmund's chamber,' Edith whispered.

'Impossible. I just spoke with him in the workshop, which is quite a distance from here. I've come straight from there,' Amelia said as she pressed the device against the wall to listen through it.

A muffled voice reached their ears. 'The bobbies are here. I must get rid of the jewel before they find me with it, but not before you recognize it. Please, tell me you remember. This is what brought us together.'

'He has the jewel!' Amelia exclaimed, kicking the door open. Her fingers caressed the silver engravings on her pressurized steam-propulsion pistol, its lead bullets primed to deliver a lethal blow.

Inside, his face a mask of shock and dismay, stood Flavio. In his hand gleamed the Copper Train, its presence as incriminating as it was mystifying. Before him stood the automaton, its lifeless eyes staring blankly at the scene unfolding before it.

In a blur of motion too swift for the onlookers to follow, Flavio reached into a hidden compartment within the automaton's platform. He withdrew a multi-tool that unfurled a lustrous blade—merely one of its myriad functions.

Grasping the automaton's hand, Flavio lunged at the girls. With a deft kick, he sent them sprawling before his weapon could draw blood. Amelia dodged just in time, but Edith crumpled to the floor in a dead faint—either from the blow or sheer fright.

'Blast it all!' Amelia cursed, taking aim. 'That must be Edmund's handiwork! The very weapon used to dispatch those pirates at the museum. How did I not make the connection sooner?'

Flavio bolted for the garden. Amelia's shots, meant to halt his flight, only served to alert the Royal Guard. Her bullets found nothing but air. Pausing just long enough to ensure Edith still had a pulse, Amelia gave chase.

The former royal guardsman moved with precision. Armed with his multi-tool—a sophisticated instrument of burnished steel and hidden compartments—he faced off against the palace's elite.

From a distance, Amelia could make out retractable blades, grappling hooks, and a pair of diminutive drilling implements. But it was the razor-sharp blade protruding from one side that seemed the most menacing.

The guards, clad in their velvet and bronze uniforms, advanced in tight formation. Their helmets gleamed in the interior gaslight, while pneumatic pistols and swords were held at the ready. Each swift step crunched on the gravel paths.

Flavio dodged and countered with astonishing skill. His multi-tool moved as if it were an extension of his own body, slicing through incoming attacks with the blade and deflecting pneumatic rounds with the retractable hooks.

Amelia burst into the garden, breathless, taking in the chaos unfolding before her. 'They shouldn't have replaced him!' Amelia shouted from afar, knowing he was the guilty party but conceding that he was exceptionally skilled.

The automaton, with its powerful mechanical arms, tossed guards about like rag dolls. Occasionally, it would lurch forward with unexpected speed, using its bulk to bulldoze through the Guards' ranks.

As the ex-guardsman neared the garden, ornate fountains and manicured hedges became impromptu obstacles and traps. The guards attempted to surround him, but he used the terrain to his advantage. He took cover strategically, all the while keeping a vigilant eye on the automaton.

A monumental storm raged overhead, hampering visibility and turning the ground treacherous for all save the automaton, which glided effortlessly on its wheeled platform.

At last, the former guard reached a strategic point in the garden—a hidden corner between two towering boxwood hedges. He paused briefly to catch his breath, his gaze fixed on the path ahead. The Royal Guard was on the verge of surrounding them.

A shadow fell across the lawn. It wasn't just storm clouds, but a pirate airship. Its massive gas bags hung suspended in a web of metallic spiderwork and copper cables. Gas lamps flickered along its railings.

The airship's massive side hatch swung open with a thunderous clang, revealing a boarding platform lined with pirates poised for action. The airship's captain, striking in an ornate tricorn and long coat, surveyed the scene with steely determination. From the hatch, an ingenious mechanism—a rope and metal ladder slowly unfurled with deliberate steadiness, descending smoothly into place.

The ladder of steel framework and reinforced rope rails, fell in a swift yet controlled drop. Its broad steps, secured with metal bracing, were designed to bear the weight of multiple climbers simultaneously.

From the airship's boarding platform, pirates wielded repeating rifles adorned with gears and steam vents. These weapons spat high-caliber rounds with a metallic shriek. Some pirates brandished automatic pistols with rapid-reload mechanisms, unleashing short, precise bursts to keep the palace officers at bay. The captain signaled with a raised hand, and Flavio wasted no time in guiding the automaton to ascend first, following close behind as royal guards fell one by one to pirate fire.

'Well done, Edith,' Amelia grumbled. 'They've come for the supposed pirate's daughter with the jewel. What a surprise they'll have when they crack open that hunk of metal! I hope the jewel's worth it to them!' But even as she spoke, her voice thick with barely contained rage, Amelia—tugging at the lone patch of hair she wore slightly longer, whipping wildly in the storm's gale—spotted something glinting in the garden grass: The Copper Train.

Amelia chuckled. She might not have caught the thief, but she had the jewel. Mission accomplished. She gazed at its potent gleam. 'He never wanted the jewel, except to exact revenge on the pirates who killed Mina. That's why he went to town in the museum.

Perhaps he also hoped to use it to stir memories the automaton doesn't possess.' Amelia mused. 'How ironic that Edith and the pirates, once his downfall, have now become his salvation.'

The sturdy ladder, with its steel frame and reinforced rope steps, rose gradually towards the airship.

With an almost satisfied smile, Amelia bid them farewell. The storm's fierce winds battered them as they climbed, and bits of metal began to fall from the automaton.

'No, no!' Flavio's lips seemed to cry out in the distance, his face contorted in anguish as he futilely grasped at the metal pieces peeling away from the metallic being in the rain's violence. But was there something underneath? Charred-looking skin melded with metal? The automaton, now with its back turned, seemed to have something behind it—hair? Flavio shoved it into the airship, which then retreated, vanishing from sight.

Amelia was left with an inscrutable expression, the jewel in her hand but doubt clouding her brow. Could it be true that the automaton was Mina? Had she never died, instead rebuilding herself with automaton parts? Hiding from all her captors, even potential informants, by not revealing her survival to Flavio? Or was it merely the automaton falling apart, perhaps because Flavio had used materials too human—like Mina's remains beneath the metal—and now he'd face a devil of a time trying to rebuild it?

Amelia barely glanced up from her papers. 'They've nicked the Copper Train from the museum again. Sure, it's the most valuable piece in the place, but don't these blighters ever get tired?' Her boss's masculine voice had become as easy to tune out as the patter of rain on a window.

'I'll pass. My assistant can handle it,' Amelia said dismissively.

'You called?' Edith sauntered in, sporting the Steam Constabulary uniform, but in a striking crimson red.

The Strange Case of Private Ornshaw and the Martian Detective
David Turnbull

Prologue

Private Charlie Ornshaw waited at the end of the row of infantrymen, rifle to his shoulder, eye aligned to the sight, finger fidgeting nervously on the trigger. His heart was thumping a merry dance in his chest. The unit was stationed in formation halfway up a verdant Surrey hillside, blessed with an abundance of flowering green gorse. A bright morning sun beat pleasantly down. The lazy humming of bees whispered in the air. Butterflies flitted hither and yon. By the stone wall which bounded the lower slope of the hill a rabbit went snuffling through the grass. It was a day that in more peaceful times might have been perfect for an idyllic picnic.

But these were no longer peaceful times.

Beyond the hill a terrible enemy was approaching. A strange enemy, unlike anything mankind had ever encountered, or even imagined before. Ornshaw had yet to catch his first sight of this enemy, but if the rumours coming out of Horsell Common had a grain of truth to them, they were the stuff of nightmares. There came the dull boom of a mortar shell being fired. A plume of smoke rose skyward. A returning flash like a crack of lightning. The resonant echo of an eerie alien battle cry, so strange that it tingled down Ornshaw's spine. Sweat trickled down his brow from beneath his tin helmet. A cold shiver ran through him.

Then, like the stark manifestation of some terrible arachnid thing, the three-legged war machine loomed monstrously over the crest of the hill. It paused for a moment like a conquering giant, sunlight sparking from its metallic cockpit, mechanical arms writhing like serpents. Every man in the battalion drew breath as its distorted

171

shadow bled like an obsidian oil down the hillside. Bathed in the gloom of this soul-smothering shadow, Ornshaw bit down on his lip and felt his body tense and lock, awed by the gargantuan structure of the metallic foe they were about to engage with.

'F-fire at w-will!' came the stuttering, panic filled order from their captain.

Volleys went off. *Crack-crack-crack.* Chaotic and uncoordinated. A gunpowder-laden stench filled Ornshaw's nostrils. The war machine lurched down the hill, leaving deep muddy craters where its huge feet fell. Some of the men broke ranks and fled. Ornshaw pulled his trigger and felt the rifle butt kick against his shoulder. The astounding size of the war machine was enough to ensure that no one who fired missed their mark. But this didn't slow the lumbering incessancy of its menacing advance. Their bullets were like gnats trying to bite an elephant's hide.

A high-pitched howl ripped at his ears. An arcing beam, which brought with it a blinding flash of white light, traced the hillside. An intense eruption of fire knocked him from his feet and tossed his comrades like rag dolls left and right. The pain was gut-wrenching as his uniform burst into flames. Rifle and helmet lost in the fiery eruption, he tried to stand up, but the agony brought him to his knees. He collapsed onto his side and found himself rolling wildly down the hill, flying sparks stabbing at his face and eyes. Then, with a bone shaking halt, he tumbled into a ditch and its chilly slime of mud doused the flames.

Semi-conscious, body jerking with fits of shock, he peered over the lip of the ditch through the staccato flutter of his badly singed eyelashes. Black smoke filled the air. The smell of burning flesh closed in on him and gagged at the back of his throat. One of the huge mechanical feet of the war machine crashed down only a yard away, flattening a clump of gorse bush, drawing a cry of terror from his raw throat.

He passed out for a moment, limp body slumping low in the mud.

When he opened his eyes, the air was clearing. The hillside was littered with charred corpses scattered across blackened soil. Coils of smoke rose from smoldering bushes and shattered trees. An unearthly silence all around. No bees. No butterflies. Not even a crow dared come near. In the distance rang out the thunderous boom of more artillery fire. The ground juddered, causing the mud to ooze and ripple around his scalds and burns. His last thought before consciousness escaped him once more was that he hoped to God the howitzers would do their job.

Chapter One

A strange passenger boarded the horse-drawn omnibus at Clapham Common. He was so tall he had to stoop as he made his way to the only empty seat. His frame was far too skinny for the long-tailed frock coat which seemed to weigh down his narrow shoulders. A pair of spectacles with tinted blue glass concealed his eyes. Leather gloves concealed his hands. His bowler hat was pulled low on his brow. A tautly tied silk scarf covered his mouth and nose.

Ornshaw could tell he was of Martian origin. An interloper. A refugee from the civil war that still raged far away on the red planet. But a Martian nonetheless. It offended him that the government was giving asylum to such beings. How could they be trusted after all that had happened? Even if they claimed to have attempted to prevent the invasion.

Ornshaw slipped his hand inside his threadbare jacket and his filthy fingers checked the hilt of the military issue bayonet that was sheathed inside the holster strapped to his chest. He decided that he would follow the stranger and—as soon as the opportunity presented itself—kill him—slice him like a kipper and slit his filthy alien throat for good measure. He'd leave him to rot in an alleyway.

It had become common knowledge that if you made eye contact with a Martian, he could easily worm his way inside your head and brazenly rifle through your thoughts like a cat burglar. Ornshaw turned and gazed out the window. The common had not yet been cleared of the pernicious creeping red weed—its jagged crimson incursions a gory reminder of the slaughter that had occurred. Clutching fronds still crawled like blood-caked claws over the shattered spire of the Holy Trinity Church.

Ornshaw winced as his mind flashed back to the terrible events of the Battle of Woking. The heat ray eviscerating his comrades. The sickening smell of the massacre. Rolling into that muddy ditch with his tunic ablaze was the only thing that had saved him.

He still bore the scars. Ugly mottled and molten flesh on his spine and shoulders. The scorched fragments of his uniform trapped forever in the rippled folds of those wounds. More scars afflicted his hips and belly from where his leather belt and brass buckle had shriveled like a rasher of bacon inside the loops of his combat trousers. Pain shot through him as he remembered the intensity of the agony he'd endured.

From the corner of his eye, he saw the Martian stiffen as if somehow sensing his distress.

Ornshaw chewed his lip and dug his fingernails into the hoary palm of his hand, forcing the pain back down. He needed a clear head and a calm countenance. Murder was a task that tolerated no distractions.

The omnibus came to a halt and the person who'd been sitting next to him alighted, leaving behind a newspaper. Ornshaw picked it up and refocused his thoughts, flicking through the pages, getting ink on his fingers, but remaining alert for any possible hint that his quarry might also be planning to disembark.

The contents of the newspaper dismayed him. It had been less than a year since war ended, but the plight of its veterans hardly warranted a byline these days. People were being quietly nudged to move on with their lives and put the traumas and bereavements of the past behind them, box them up like something stored in an attic.

He skimmed through an article about the American inventor Frank Reade, who—along with his son Frank Junior—had shortened the legs of two fallen Martian war machines and welded them to a railway carriage to create a wagon that resembled a six-legged insect. This wagon could transport passengers across the prairies from the east coast of America to the west coast at fantastic speeds. These days it was stories like this that the papers opted for. Stories that predicted a bright future in a brave new world.

It wasn't until the omnibus reached Waterloo station that the Martian stirred. Ornshaw followed him into the tunnels of the London Underground Railway. His uncommon height and bowler hat made him easy to spot. It was easy to maintain a reasonable distance. He boarded a carriage on the northbound track of the Bakerloo line. Ornshaw took the next carriage and remained standing so he could position himself at a spot where he could pretend to be engrossed in the newspaper while surreptitiously observing through the window of the door that adjoined the carriages.

Again, he was struck by how fast the population was getting back to normality. Not so long ago, huge numbers of Londoners had cowered on the underground platforms, trying to escape the Martian scourge. Even then they were not entirely safe. There had been instances where the toxic black gas that had been part of the invaders' arsenal had been released to snake though the tunnels, asphyxiating anyone unfortunate enough to inhale it. Due to the ongoing hostilities, their rotting corpses had not been recovered for weeks afterwards.

It wasn't yet rush hour, but the train was busy. Uniformed maids with wicker baskets of shopping or laundry were returning to the hastily-repaired townhouses of their wealthy employers. A group of cloth-capped navies were engaged in boisterous banter, work clothes covered in dust from clearing rubble as part of the recovery efforts. Here and there were gents with top hats and walking canes, grinning like the cats who got the cream, no doubt buoyed by the expectation of handsome returns for investments in post-war reconstruction and engineering projects.

The train pulled into a station and juddered to a halt. Ornshaw glanced over the top of the newspaper to see if the Martian was getting up from his seat. No movement. He sat there, overly tall amongst the rest of the commuters, head slightly bowed, almost as if he were asleep. No one paying him anything but a passing glance of attention.

The Martian didn't know it yet. But this would be the last journey he'd take. He'd never see his homeworld again. Ornshaw planned to make sure that he was caught for the murder. The hangman's noose would be a blessing, but the courtroom would serve as a platform from which to air his grievances. When the judge put on his black cap and asked him if he had anything to say before the sentence was passed, he'd have his speech prepared and rehearsed. He'd give them chapter and verse about the gross injustice of impoverished veterans left to fend for themselves on the streets while refugees from a distant civil war were clothed and housed and inoculated against the germs that had thwarted the invasion.

The Martian rose imposingly from his seat at Paddington. He hunched and alighted. Ornshaw folded the newspaper under his arm and followed him.

Back at street level, the Martian passed swiftly through the cobblestone alleyways that led toward the Grand Union Canal. Here there were dozens more impossibly tall men and women, all similarly dressed, all with blue tinted spectacles, mingling freely with the local populace, going about their business, strutting around like they owned the place. To Ornshaw it felt sickeningly like the way things might have been if the Martian invasion had succeeded in bringing humanity under their yoke.

A tight knot of anticipation twisted in his belly. His quarry was heading for Little Sirenum, the teeming Martian refugee enclave which had been established along the banks of the canal. Any minute now he'd be deep within a nest of vipers. But what better place for his act of vengeance to be enacted? It would be a gloriously symbolic gesture. It would cause a shockwave that would reverberate across the city and wake people up to the plight of the poor men who'd sacrificed everything in the war between the worlds.

The Martian turned a corner and Ornshaw picked up his pace, dropping the newspaper and reaching into his coat to grip his bayonet. He began sweating from the nervous tension coiled up in his belly—heart pounding, he was ready to strike—ready to make his grand gesture.

But when he turned the corner, he found himself in a seedy, litter strewn courtyard. His way was blocked by a sooty brick wall.

The Martian was nowhere to be seen.

He looked left and right, caught in momentary confusion.

'Release your weapon,' demanded the gruff voice that came from behind him.

Ornshaw stiffened. He'd been careless. His desire for an act of revenge had lured him into a trap.

'Raise your hands in the air,' instructed the Martian. 'Then turn around slowly.'

Chapter Two

Ornshaw complied with the instruction, tensing himself for the possibility of close-quarters combat. The Martian was holding a funnel-like instrument in his right hand. It was silver in colour and tapered at the end that was pointing toward Ornshaw, who had seen a sketch of one before, accompanied by a description, in the pages of The Illustrated London News. One little click of the Martian's long finger and a tiny air-driven piston would launch the sleek hunter wasp housed in the small chamber at its base. If the creature didn't get Ornshaw with its paralyzing stinger first time round, it would circle and dive for a second attempt.

The Martian reached up with his free hand and removed his spectacles. Ornshaw knew he had no chance of fighting back. The black orbs of the Martian's eyes looked oversized and distinctly marsupial. The hypnotic power of them fixed Ornshaw to the spot, caused his own irises to pop wide, and awed him with a powerful mesmerism. He felt an intense stabbing in his head as if his brain had been swiftly skewered.

'Ah,' said the Martian. 'I see that you intended to murder me.'

He spoke perfect English, but his oddly accented voice crackled like dry leaves and hissed like gas leaking from a faulty valve. His eyelids blinked vertically over the pronounced bulge of his eyes. Ornshaw felt himself slump a little as he was instantaneously released from the thrall. The pain in his head eased and was gone as soon as he drew breath.

'You shouldn't go intruding on people's private thoughts,' he said.

'I apologise,' said the Martian, slipping his tinted spectacles back on. 'But it was imperative for me to establish your intentions.'

'If I thought I might better you in a fair fight, I would still try,' warned Ornshaw.

'That would be ill advised,' said the Martian, head swaying from side to side beneath his bowler hat as he jutted the wide barrel of the wasp gun slightly forward.

Ornshaw didn't need to be convinced. His opponent was at least a foot taller than him, and the length of his spindly arms would give him a distinct advantage when it came to reach. An unexpected knife lunged swiftly into the back, severing the spinal cord in the manner the army had taught him, might have given him the advantage. But that was now lost to him.

'Your plan had no logic whatsoever,' said the Martian. 'Had there been a war between the British and Ottoman Empires. And had the Turks committed atrocities on English soil, would you seek out the nearest Chinaman on whom to exact your revenge?'

'No, I would not,' replied Ornshaw. 'But that is not the point.'

'It is precisely the point,' said the Martian. 'On Mars not only do we have different races and nationalities as you do on Earth, we also have entirely different species. Other than the fact that we originated on the same world, I share nothing whatsoever in common with the Masorobians who instigated the invasion of this world. Neither in physical appearance nor political outlook.'

Ornshaw had seen one of these Masorobian monstrosities for himself, preserved and displayed in a huge bell jar inside a display case at the Hunterian Museum near Lincoln's Inn Fields. It looked like a bloated octopus, tentacles like a nest of serpents, narrow beak for a mouth, owlish eyes. Nothing like the creature that stood before him.

'You are still a Martian,' he insisted.

When the Martian heaved a sigh, it stuttered from him like the rattle of a rattlesnake's tail. 'Killing me would have served no purpose.'

'It might have given me some satisfaction,' said Ornshaw.

'It wouldn't,' said the Martian. 'Murder solves nothing.'

'You've murdered people then?' asked Ornshaw. 'Hardly surprising.'

The Martian shook his bulbous head, his lower face still muffled by his silk scarf. 'I have known many murderers. I was a senior officer in the employ of the Basomoran Police Force,' he explained. 'No matter the killer's motive. The crime did not resolve whatever issue they had.'

'And now here you are on my world,' said Ornshaw. 'Draining resources that should by rights be going to veterans like me.'

'Terrible things have happened on Mars since their invasion failed,' said the Martian. 'The Masorob have taken the humiliation of their defeat out on us. Redoubled their efforts. Established death

178

camps and engaged in genocide.'

'You can all go ahead and kill each other with my blessing,' said Ornshaw. 'Leave us in peace. The way we were before we even suspected there might be life on Mars.'

'You were hardly at peace,' countered the Martian. 'You too were forever fighting each other. Even now, in the aftermath of the invasion, there are still conflicts breaking out all over the globe.'

Ornshaw had to concede that this was true. Had he not been given a medical discharge he would likely be shipping out this very minute to fight the Boers in Southern Africa. 'So, what happens now?' he asked. 'I suppose you're going to turn me in to the coppers?'

'On the contrary,' replied the Martian. 'I am considering offering you a job.'

'A job?' Ornshaw almost choked on the word.

The Martian was unfazed. 'I am not an enemy of Earth. I am an ally. Your government recognises the particular skill set I acquired as a policeman. They keep me on a handsome stipend. I gather intelligence for them on the machinations of the Masorob and the potential risks of a second invasion. I report directly to Whitehall. Meanwhile, I supplement my income by acting as a private detective. Mainly for the community here in Little Sirenium. Occasionally for human clients.'

'What has any of this to do with me?' asked Ornshaw.

'I am in need of an assistant,' came the reply. 'A human. Someone who can help me negotiate the intricacies and mores of human society. Also, a bodyguard of sorts. Someone with a military background. I believe I may well be on the hit list of a somewhat xenophobic human organisation, which goes by the name of Britannia Foremost.'

Ornshaw had been to a few BF rallies in the East End. Lots of veterans were becoming members. They were vehemently opposed to the refugee program and believed it could only be ended by a coup against the current government. He'd toyed with the idea of joining himself, but had quickly realised their structure and outlook was based on the same class-based hierarchy that allowed educated idiots from Oxford and Eton to become officers in the army. Ornshaw had had his fill of being cannon fodder for toffs. He wasn't

179

ready to play a part in helping them to wrest power from the emergency government.

'If you agreed to work for me,' the Martian continued. 'You would be working against our common enemy.'

'It would be an affront to my principles to work for a Martian,' said Ornshaw, unshaven chin jutting defiantly forward.

The Martian lowered his weapon and slipped it into the pocket of his coat. 'I can see you are obviously down on your luck. I am offering you a job that pays well. It comes with board and lodgings. I would hazard a guess that my allocated apartment has more basic comforts than whatever room you currently rent. You can work for an employer and still despise them, you know.'

'I'd have to live under the same roof as you, here in Little Sirenium?' The very thought of it was making Ornshaw sick to the stomach.

'You still have your doubts,' said the Martian. 'Understandable. There's a little canal-side hostelry nearby. Let me treat you to your first taste of scented Martian ferment. See if that might mellow you a little. They also serve English breakfast if you fancy it. I have to confess I've developed quite a penchant for the humble Cumberland sausage.'

The thought of a hot meal and a stiff drink were very tempting propositions. Despite his reservations, Ornshaw found himself following when the Martian turned and beckoned.

'My name is Yil Axo,' he said over his narrow shoulders. 'You may call me Yil. What should I call you?'

'I go by the name of Ornshaw.'

'And do you have a given name?' asked Yil.

'I do,' said Ornshaw. 'But I prefer not to give it.' He'd made himself a promise that he would no longer refer to himself as Charlie. Charlie was long gone. He died in that muddy ditch at the foot of a hillside near Woking.

Chapter Three

Their visitor this morning looked spritely for a man who claimed to be in his eighties. He entered Yil's study with a bow-legged

180

swagger. He was far too short to have ever been a prize fighter, but he was clearly a seasoned street brawler. From the awkward crook on the bridge of his nose and the crisscross scars on his unshaven chin, it was obvious he'd seen more than his share of fisticuffs.

Yil's office and residence was on the third floor of a former tenement block. The block was three stories high. It had originally been built as artisan dwellings by the Peabody Foundation and had sturdily survived the invasion with little more than a slight charring of its brickwork. The first floor was used as premises for businesses. The top two as refugee accommodation.

From its rooftop, Martian engineers had constructed a jumbled network of rope and timber bridges that led to various other buildings. Below, at ground level, the foundations of dozens of destroyed houses had been filled with canvas yurts, constructed from reclaimed timbers, which were home to those Martians not fortunate enough to be housed in the main tenement. Through the middle of all this ran the canal, filled with ornate mechanical craft of Martian design.

At first Ornshaw's bigotry had caused him to view the enclave as an infestation, spreading out from Paddington Basin and the Grand Union to encroach on parts of Regent's Canal. To him the dense population of bug-eyed, angular refugees seemed like swarms of voracious locusts. It had given him terrible nightmares, in which he appeared as a pink maggoty grub, blind and legless, writhing in the filthy effluence of a ditch, looming over him a grotesque three-legged predator ready to roast him alive with its fiery breath before plucking him up and swallowing him whole.

It had been seven weeks now since he'd reluctantly accepted Yil's offer of employment. The nightmares were becoming less frequent. His initial intention had been to stay for a month. This would have given him a chance to get back on his feet. Earn some cash. Squirrel some away for a rainy day. Get three square meals a day into his belly to stop from wasting away. He'd thought that a month would be as much as he could stomach as the guest of a Martian. For a good while, he still toyed with the notion of murdering Yil before he departed.

Yet here he was, still working for the detective, still living under his roof, still eating at his table. His views had mellowed in that time. Yil liked to fire questions at him after dinner, and Ornshaw, half dozing by the fire, would reply, grudgingly at first, but then, as time passed, with genuine enthusiasm.

Yil was fascinated by Earth and the history of humanity. His study was lined with leather-bound volumes of numerous encyclopedias, which he devoured at an alarming pace, eyelids blinking rapidly over the bulge of his eyes. Often the questions he asked were far beyond Ornshaw's limited knowledge and experience of world history and geography. One night he decided to turn the tables and dig for some information of his own. 'How do there come be two different Martian species?' he asked.

Yil blinked and regarded him through the glassy blackness of his eyes.

'Evolution,' came the reply. 'My people, the Basomor, can trace their origins back to a simian ancestor that inhabited the ancient forests of Mars. Very similar to the ancestors of humanity. Our tentacled cousins, the Masorob, are descended from an amphibian lifeform, which gives them an entirely different physiognomy.'

Ornshaw blew air through his teeth. 'Old Chuck Darwin would have had a field day with that notion.'

Yil sighed, cradling his long fingers to his chest. 'I should have loved to engage in discourse with Mr Darwin. Such a pity he perished.'

'And thousands like him,' agreed Ornshaw.

'Long ago, while dinosaurs still roamed your world, the Basomor and the Masorob lived in harmony and mutual cooperation. The Basomor occupied the fertile continents. The Masorob the oceanic depths. There was trade between our two species, the fruits of the land in exchange for the fruits of the sea.'

'I'm guessing it all went pear-shaped at some point then,' said Ornshaw.

Yil gave a nod of his bulbous head. 'Our climate began to change. Oceans began to recede. Swathes of land were reduced to red deserts. The Basomor constructed thousands of miles of canals in our efforts to keep the land fertile. The Masorob developed machines which burrowed beneath the surface, allowing them to commence a subterranean existence by colonising the vast lakes they encountered in the depths beneath.'

'So, you were above, and they were below?' said Ornshaw.

'But it wasn't enough for them. Soon they came back to the surface encased within the prototypes of the war machines you have recently encountered. They seized one of our provinces on the remote outer reaches of the canal network. Basomoran refugees told of a gigantic observatory being built there. They were studying the Earth, coveting its oceans, planning their invasion. Diplomatic efforts were made to try and dissuade them, but these were met by acts of aggression. Those were the roots of our civil war.'

Yil shook his head and heaved a rattling sigh. 'We tried our best to save you. But ultimately, we failed to save ourselves.'

Slowly, through conversations such as this, Ornshaw's opinions changed. His room in Yil's apartment was claustrophobic. Not much bigger than an airing cupboard. But, having progressed from orphanage to poorhouse and then from army barracks to filthy doss house, the privacy was a luxury he had never experienced before. The more he became accustomed to the pleasures of sleeping alone behind a closed door without the snores and groans and flatulence of others all around him, the harder it became to muster the will to leave.

The work itself proved to be not too onerous. The types of cases that were brought to Yil Axo were not that different from those which might arise in a human community. Little Sirenum was a bubbling cauldron of infidelity, embezzlement, petty crimes, and wanton vandalism. Yil was good at his job, pernicious and persistent, proficient at joining dots and making connections that may not be immediately obvious to those who lacked his sharpness of mental clarity.

With his first week's wage, Ornshaw had taken steps to ensure he looked the part of a detective's assistant. He'd found a tweed suit and matching cap in reasonably good condition in a secondhand shop on Westbourne Terrace. In another shop, he'd acquired a pair of brogues which still had good wear left on their soles and were not so scuffed that a bit of polish and elbow grease couldn't fix them. He hadn't been able yet to afford a new shirt. But that was next on his list.

Through his somewhat clandestine government contacts Yil had procured him a pistol. A Webley MK IV revolver. The type

183

normally reserved for army officers. It had now replaced the bayonet in the holster inside his newly acquired tweed jacket. The bayonet slept under his mattress, within easy reach if he needed it in the night. In his seven weeks in Little Sirenum, he had not once had any occasion to reach for the bayonet. Nor had he drawn the pistol from the holster. In addition, despite what Yil had told him, that day in the alleyway, there had not been a single human client who had arrived at the office to seek his services.

This, however, was the day that changed.

The old man didn't wait to be asked to be seated. With a flip of his grimy coattails, he simply slumped down somewhat arrogantly into an armchair and regarded Yil and Ornshaw through rheumy eyes that barely disguised the cockiness that lurked behind them. Ornshaw watched Yil taking mental note of the little spots of blood on the man's shirt collar. This isn't his blood, thought Ornshaw, attempting to emulate his alien mentor's deductive reasoning. His face hasn't seen a shaving razor in days, and there's bruising on his knuckles.

'Name's Dawkins,' said the man, by way of introduction. 'Jack Dawkins. You may have heard of me.'

'Jack Dawkins?' blurted Ornshaw. 'You are this so-called King of Thieves?'

Dawkins grinned over his discoloured teeth. 'I've gone by many names in my time. Lummy Jack. Five Finger Freddie. Back when I ran with Fagin, I was known as the Artful Dodger.'

'Fagin?' asked Yil, blinking his eyes vertically.

'Notorious case,' explained Ornshaw. 'Sixty odd years ago. Fagin and his gang kidnapped an orphan boy.'

'Oliver,' nodded Dawkins in agreement. 'Scrawny little runt. Tried to take him under my wing so I did. But he'd never have made a cutpurse in a month of bleedin' Sundays.'

'He made quite something of himself once he was rescued, I hear,' said Ornshaw.

'Whereas I got transported to Australia on account of a measly snuff box,' complained Dawkins.

'How exactly can I help you?' interrupted Yil, hands clasped, long fingers interwoven.

Dawkins drummed his own dirty fingers on the armrests of the chair. 'You're that detective geezer, ain't ya?' he said. 'On our side, so I'm told. Good at solving mysteries.'

'I relish the challenge of a mystery,' said Yil, a grin spreading on the thin slash of his mouth.

'Well, I've got me a little mystery that requires solving,' said Dawkins. He cracked his bruised knuckles. 'The coppers won't have nothing to do with me on account of my reputation. And that jumped-up posh git on Baker Street 'ad me turfed out on my ear. So, I've been making my own enquiries. But I ain't getting nowhere fast.'

'Carry on,' said Yil, with a wave of his spidery fingers.

'There's some cowardly lowlife going around, see,' said Dawkins 'He's been stealing my nippers, so he has.'

Ornshaw tutted and shook his head. 'No honour amongst thieves then?'

'Nippers?' interjected Yil. 'I don't think I've come across the term before.'

'He means children,' said Ornshaw. 'He's clearly followed in Fagin's footsteps. He's taking advantage of destitute children. Teaching them to be pickpockets and house breakers. Drawing them into a seedy life of crime.'

Dawkins straightened his shoulders defiantly. 'I'm as entitled to make a living as any man. I'll 'ave you know my nippers are well treated. Hot meals and shelter. A farthing a job. A penny if they do a good job. Thruppence if the bring me something of exceptional value.'

'By *stealing*, I assume you mean someone is taking them away from you?' asked Yil.

'Someone with a good conscience, I'd say,' interjected Ornshaw. 'Offering them shelter and education in a children's home, like the one I grew up in.'

'If it was that,' said Dawkins, 'I wouldn't be making such a fuss. I'd be a bit peeved. But good luck to 'em, I'd say. This is different.'

'Different in what way?' asked Yil.

'Them what gets stolen gets brought back,' replied Dawkins. 'But they're changed. Not themselves. Glassy-eyed. Stone-faced. Like they've been hypnotised or somefing.'

'They get brought back to you?' asked Yil.

Dawkins shook his head. 'They get cleaned up and scrubbed. Hair all washed and combed. Dressed up fancy. Given to well-to-do folks up west whose own children died in the invasion. Again, I wouldn't mind so much. It's more or less what happened to my old mucker Oliver, all them years back. But there's something awfully wrong with these nippers when they come back. The vim and vigour has gone from them. They're like husks. Ghosts of their old selves.'

'And how do you know this if it's all such a mystery?' challenged Ornshaw.

Dawkins tapped his forehead. 'Got me a bit more up 'ere than old Fagin had back in the day. I have some businesses up west that let me invest some of my hard-earned income for a decent return. It was an associate of mine who makes the cash deliveries what first saw some of them kiddies with their new families and told me about how queer they looked.'

He coughed and cleared his throat.

'So, I went for a little gander myself. Went to the house near Regent's Park where my associate had seen one of 'em. A little firecracker of a girl we used to call Sassy Sal. She was out front of one of them posh townhouses. The ones that got repaired pretty pronto after the invasion. She had a little China dolly in her arms and she was just standing there staring into the distance. 'Sal,' I says. 'It's me, Dawkins. You've done well for yourself.' And when she looks at me, her eyes look like the soul has been sucked right out of her. 'Don't talk to me,' she goes. And it's not the voice of little Sassy Sal that comes out of her mouth. It's the voice of something cold and dark and terrible.'

The colour drained from his face. Ornshaw could see that he was visibly shaken by what he just recounted. Yil's bulbous head cocked slightly leftwards as he observed the man. 'You say your associate saw others in the same condition?'

Dawkins gave a nod of his head. 'McGregor, my accountant. Four of 'em he's seen now. And all afflicted in the same way.'

'I should like to interview this McGregor fellow,' said Yil.

'You're not actually thinking of taking on the case, are you?' said Ornshaw. 'You have your special arrangement to consider. I don't think your paymasters in Whitehall would be too pleased if you were to take a commission from the King of Thieves, of all people.

There could be consequences.'

Yil held up his hand, silencing him before he could say more. 'Where might we find McGregor?' he asked.

'I could take you to him if you like,' replied Dawkins.

'No time to waste then,' said Yil. 'Have you ever ridden in a Basomoran steam skiff, Mr Dawkins?'

'Bloody hell, Yil!' cried Ornshaw. 'This isn't a good idea.'

But it was too late. Yil was already bounding out of the office and heading down the tenement stairwell. In no time at all, the three of them were squashed up inside the glass cockpit of Yil's skiff.

Yil pulled back on the solitary brass lever. Pistons hushed as canal water was churned into the cylindrical innards of its engine and converted into gushes of steam. The propeller fan to the rear of the craft began to rotate. The blue sail above the cockpit unfurled, billowed, and filled with air. The cockpit lurched a little. Ornshaw felt his stomach lurch with it. Yil pressed his foot onto a peddle on the floor and released the brakes. The skiff went skimming swiftly along the surface of the canal, hissing as it sent up a spray of oily water in its wake.

Ornshaw saw a huge gas-filled dirigible ascending from the new air terminus at St Pancras. The livery on its cigar-shaped balloon read; Smallways and Butterage Airborne Logistics Company. Many of the roads leading to and from London were still impassable. For a good while to come, transportation by airship was going to be the main means of transporting goods and produce. Men like Bert Smallways and his partner Mr Butterage were moving quickly to cash in, overseen by the recently established and self-appointed Aerial Board of Control.

Chapter Four

They left the skiff tethered on the canal bank near Bethnal Green, cocooned in a protective shield which would apparently emit a painful electrical jolt should anyone unauthorized attempt to tamper with it. Squat, bow-legged Dawkins led them through the narrow warren backstreets that wound their way toward the docks. Yil kept his collar turned up and his bowler hat low over his brows, blue tinted spectacles concealing his eyes.

The area around the docks had its fair share of Britannia Foremost fanatics. Any one of whom would garrote and murder a Martian no sooner than blink. As they walked, Ornshaw kept a diligent watch for any hint of movement in the doorways of the warehouses they passed. A few weeks ago, he might have been the one lurking there, awaiting his chance. The irony wasn't lost on him.

Unlike more salubrious areas of Central London, where rebuilding was progressing at a rapid pace, the East End still bore the untended scars of the failed invasion. The streets were littered with the rubble, piled up in huge potholes caused by the death rays. Outcroppings of crimson weed still clung to brickwork. Random belongings dropped by people fleeing the advance of the war machines slowly moldering in the dirt. Here a rusting stew pot, there the broken remains of a washboard, near a gloomy doorway an infant's perambulator, wheels missing.

At the dock, they passed along the quay to a large warehouse complex. Its high walls were severely pockmarked by blast damage, not a window left intact, signs of a fire that had ravaged the upper floors. Part of the roof had collapsed. The downpipe from the guttering had come away from the brickwork, leaning forward at a precarious angle

Dawkins gripped the scruffy lapels of his jacket and puffed out his chest. 'Welcome to my castle, gentlemen. Be it ever so humble.'

'You own this building?' asked Ornshaw.

Dawkins tapped the side of his nose and gave him another wink. 'Let's just say I acquired it. On account of its previous owner meeting an unfortunate and untimely demise during the invasion.'

Yil was pacing impatiently back and forth. 'And McGregor is within?' he asked.

'He most certainly is,' said Dawkins.

'Can we go inside and talk to him?' asked Yil.

'I'd rather you didn't,' said Dawkins. 'There are things of a confidential and delicate nature in there. But give me half a mo' and I'll fetch him out to you.'

With that he entered the building, returning a few moments later with a bespectacled, slightly hunched, dark-skinned gentleman, dressed in a plain white shirt and black trousers.

'This here is McGregor,' said Dawkins. 'He's my right-hand man. His father was a slave in the Indies. Took the family name of the sugar plantation owner. McGregor here is a bleedin' mathematical genius. He was the best damned tally man ever seen on Tilbury Dock. But he got the boot on account of his tendency toward sticky fingers. He keeps a meticulous track of all my incomings and outgoings. Does my accounts. Makes sure there ain't too much pilfering going down amongst my nippers. Tell these gentlemen what you saw up west.'

McGregor spoke with a mild West Indian accent. 'The last one I saw was Sassy Sal. Mr Dawkins went and saw her for himself. But before her, I saw others. All taken in by well-to-do folk. Dressed up like little lords and ladies. Like they'd never known the streets, nor slept in a shop doorway.'

'And their demeanor?' asked Yil.

McGregor loosened his collar. 'Unsettling. No life in them. Blank looks in their eyes. Like some voodoo priest had found them dead and reanimated their corpses. Gave me the shivers down the spine. And I saw others too. Not ones I recognised. Not ones that Mr Dawkins had under his wing. But just as equally afflicted. It's like a plague or an infestation has taken hold up west.'

'A mystery what wants resolving pronto,' said Dawkins. He turned to Ornshaw. 'Whatever you might think of me, I care for my nippers. And this ain't right. It most certainly ain't bleedin' right at all.'

'It doesn't sound right,' conceded Ornshaw

'It's extremely worrying,' said Yil with a slow blink. 'A terrible theory is forming in my mind. I sincerely hope I am wrong.'

Just then there came a huge commotion as a gang of half a dozen filthy street kids came pelting around the side of the warehouse, yelling and screaming and waving their scrawny arms. 'Dawky! Dawky!' yelled the raggedy girl in the lead. 'Come quick. Some monkeys is trying to 'ave it away with Lambeth Sid.'

Chapter Five

The kids ran back the way they'd come, yelling for them to follow.

Before they even reached the courtyard, they could hear the screams and screeches echoing up the side alley. At first Ornshaw wasn't sure what it was he was seeing. A wildly tumbling ball of dirty brown fur. At its centre a small child, skinny limbs flailing as he tried to make his escape from two vicious creatures that were trying to overpower him.

'Ger out of it!' yelled Dawkins, picking up half a brick and lobbing it at the melee.

The brick hit one of the creatures on its mangy back. It untangled itself and turned to face him, crouching low and hissing aggressively through bared teeth. Ornshaw realised that it was some sort of monkey, just as the kids had said. But it wore an item of clothing, which looked for all the world like an embroidered waistcoat. Dawkins picked up a piece of broken timber and swooshed it through the air.

'Come on then,' he challenged. 'You want some?'

McGregor meanwhile was skirting round the edge of the courtyard to where the other monkey was still wrestling with the poor little boy, trying to drag him into the warren of backstreets. Following Dawkin's lead, he picked up a handful of stones and hurled them through the air.

Several of them hit the second monkey on the back of the head. It released the boy, turned and snarled. This one had a pearl necklace around its neck. The boy sat upright, wailing in distress, his face covered in snot and tears, blood dripping from scratches that had been clawed across his check.

Dawkins swung at the first monkey with his stick. It easily scurried away from his reach. McGregor threw more stones at the second one. It snarled again and bounded straight for him. The group of kids let out a unified scream of terror. With seconds to spare, McGregor dived to the ground. The monkey had gained such forward momentum that it was unable to stop itself from crashing awkwardly into a wall.

Both monkeys quickly regained themselves and faced their respective assailants. Dawkins and McGregor were taller and now both armed with sticks. But Ornshaw could tell from the physiques of the would be simian kidnappers that they possessed considerable strength. From the murderous looks in their eyes and threatening manner in which they proffered their sharp teeth and raised their leathery paws to reveal lacquered claws, it was clear their intention was to do maximum damage. No matter how seasoned these two elderly men had become on the rough streets of east London, this wasn't going to be a fair fight.

Ornshaw reached into his jacket and withdrew his revolver. Fearing that one of the children might get injured, or worse, should a stray bullet ricochet from one of the walls, he fired into the air. The sound of the shot echoed like thunder. The monkeys froze. Then with a duet of inharmonious screeches, they leapt to the wall, and scrambled in rapid ascent. They moved with amazing agility from window ledge to window ledge of a nearby building until they reached the rooftop.

'Quick,' cried Yil, breaking into a lolloping trot. 'Follow them. No more gunshots. We need to see where they go.'

As Ornshaw turned, he saw Dawkins run to poor little Lambeth Sid and in a gesture of what appeared to be genuine concern and affection lift him up and wrap him in a huge hug. 'There. There,' he crooned. 'What have they done to you, me old mucker? What have they done to you?'

Chapter Six

Ornshaw followed Yil on a wild dash through the alleyways as the monkeys scrambled across rooftops and soared over the gaps between buildings. It was difficult to keep up while dodging round sharp corners and traversing narrow passageways. Above them the monkeys bounded noisily over roof tiles and wove between bricked chimney stacks. Each time they leapt from one building to the next, they seemed to instinctively find handholds and footholds where none might obviously exist. Faced with their astounding agility, Ornshaw was seized by a strange feeling that he had witnessed something like this before.

Whatever it was, the pair of them were far too fast and fleeting for either Yil or Ornshaw to take aim with their weapons. Had they been human quarry, there might have been a chance of bringing one of them down so they could be interrogated. But even that would have been a futile exercise. They were monkeys, and monkeys didn't talk. Yil was right, they had to follow them. Someone had trained them to steal children off the streets. They would be fleeing straight to their master.

Suddenly they were out of the maze of alleys and onto a main thoroughfare, where a huge procession was taking place. It looked to Ornshaw as if it had been organised by Britannia Foremost. Several hundred people, many brandishing Union Jacks, tightly huddled together, groups of them wearing the distinctive black-buttoned grey overcoat which passed as the uniform of sorts adopted by the Loyal Patriots, a gang of ruffians who'd attached themselves to Britannia Foremost. Amongst them was a column of teenage boys beating a rhythmic tattoo on snare drums. At their head the stony-faced gents in their Saville Row suits who were the organisation's ruling cabal.

There were police officers to each side of the march, keeping order with helmets strapped under their chins and wooden truncheons drawn. The crowd was so dense there was no way of crossing the road until it had passed. Above them the monkeys immediately recognised the advantage this gave them. Crouching low they used the combined force of legs and arms to launch themselves into a high leap, the one in the waistcoat slightly ahead of the one with the necklace. They soared unnoticed over the heads of the marchers, and with bounding gaits they were gone over the camber of the opposite rooftop. Ornshaw and Yil could only stand helplessly in the mouth of the alley and watch their escape.

The march continued to flow past them. It may have been organised by Britannia Foremost, but it had attracted a chaotic array of supporters of disparate causes. All keen to give voice to their concerns through an assortment of placards bearing scrawled slogans. Here, a group of veterans calling for the provision of work and housing for the war wounded, some with missing arms and some on crutches dragging hobbled legs. There blind men led by nerve-shattered men who still trembled from the trauma of the Martian heat ray. Behind them a cluster of sullen women dressed in mourning black calling for a decent widows' pension.

Then a group of religious zealots who were clearly followers of the fanatical teachings of Father Nathaniel, a former priest who had risen to prominence in the aftermath of the invasion. All seemingly convinced that the invaders had been demons sent by God to herald the coming of Armageddon. They bore placards proclaiming that the end was nigh and that everyone should repent.

Ornshaw saw a group of burly dockers marching beneath a gold embroidered trade union banner. There was growing anger directed at the Port of London for the number of men being thrown out of work because of the growing trend to utilise re-engineered Martian war machines as cranes to unload cargo ships.

Then the distinctive skirl of a bagpipe. And there, next to the piper, resplendent in kilt and sporran, the pretender to the throne himself, Horatio Campbell-Stewart, a man who virulently disputed Victoria's right to regency. Claiming to be directly descended from Bonnie Prince Charlie, he wanted to seize the throne back from the House of Hanover and restore it to the Stewart line. A handful of soldiers from his New Jacobite Army marched in two columns behind him, dressed in tartan trousers, and Tam O'Shanter bonnets, rifles slung over their shoulders. Rosettes pinned to their breasts bore the stylised New Jacobite symbol, a fist clenched around the stem of a thorny thistle bearing the motto; I Shall Not Flinch.

All of these groups no doubt had received promises of a favourable outcome for their causes should they align themselves with Britannia Foremost. 'Fools,' thought Ornshaw. 'Cannon fodder is cannon fodder, whatever the cause. The officer class expects you to follow like sheep. And follow like sheep you do.'

He turned to Yil and was shocked to realise that he was not wearing his tinted glasses. With his uncommon height, narrow frame, and eyelids blinking rhythmically over the bulge of his eyes, he stood out like the proverbial sore thumb.

'We need to head back to the dock,' said Ornshaw.

But it was too late. Yil had been noticed.

'Would you look at that?' cried a voice in the crowd. 'A filthy Martian. Right here on our streets. Bleedin' cheek of it.'

Orshaw took Yil's arm and began to draw him back into the gloom of the alley. Yil reached inside his morning coat, retrieved the tinted spectacles, and slipped them back on. Ornshaw noticed two of the grey-coated Loyal Patriots weaving their way through the procession. Big men. Brawlers like Dawkins, but with the muscles to deliver rather than just boast. The type of men the hierarchy of Britannia Foremost used to do their dirty work. One of the police officers made a half-hearted attempt at stopping them from leaving the march, but stepped to the side when they began to barge past him.

Ornshaw saw one of the men draw a bayonet much like his own. During the invasion, the bayonet had been the least potent weapon in an infantryman's arsenal. The prospect of close-quarters combat with a Martian was as improbable as it was impractical. It wasn't just soldiers who had pilfered them in the aftermath of the war. Scavengers had stolen them from the charred rifles that lay next to eviscerated corpses. They were now the weapon of choice of all sorts of cutthroats and hooligans.

For a fleeting moment, Ornshaw was seized by the notion of walking away. It would be easy to just step into the crowd. Disappear. Leave Yil Axo alone to face whatever violent end fate had in store for him. But there was a bigger picture to consider now. A common enemy. Besides, the Martian had proved himself to be a benevolent employer.

'Run,' he cried, tugging at Yil's sleeve.

Yil turned and followed as Ornshaw fled once more into the narrow-walled labyrinth. Behind them the two men yelled curses and threats as the thud of their boots echoed from the cobbles. Ornshaw pulled out his revolver. If the worst came to the worst, he would turn and fire over the heads of their pursuers. It would be a huge risk. A gunshot might draw more of the grey coats. The march could easily descend into a riotous lynch mob.

To the left of the next alley, they ran into a darkened mews. Ornshaw made out the vague shape of a handcart that had been parked there. He hauled Yil to where they could both conceal themselves behind it. Seconds later, the two thugs appeared at the end of the mews. They paused there. Ornshaw grasped the revolver, thinking they'd been seen.

'Which way did they go?' asked one of the men.

'I didn'ae see,' replied the other, in a guttural Scottish accent.

'Sod it,' said the other. 'Let's get back to the march. There'll be plenty of time to sort out his lot when we take over.'

'Oh, aye,' agreed the Scotsman. 'We'll have them strung from gas lamps like baubles on a fuckin' Christmas tree.'

Their laughter receded as they departed.

Ornshaw waited a few minutes before he felt it was safe to holster his revolver once more. When they both stood up, Yil looked down at him, removed his spectacles and blinked. 'I do believe you saved my life.'

'Well,' said Ornshaw, 'you did engage me partly to be your bodyguard.'

'Indeed,' agreed Yil.

They made their way back to the front of the warehouse where McGregor was tending to the scratches on poor little Lambeth Sid's cheeks with a handkerchief doused liberally in iodine. The other children were assembled in front of Dawkins, listening solemnly to what he was telling them. 'Get the word out, you hear?' he said. 'All the nippers are to get back here sharpish. No matter if they ain't nicked nothing today. Everyone back here, and safe inside till we find out what's going on.'

Ornshaw found his opinions of Dawkins mellowing a tad. The man was clearly a product of his own upbringing. He might be repeating the errors of the past by drawing children into a life of street crime, but he seemed to have a genuine concern for their welfare, and in the grander shape of things, picking a few pockets may well be a more dignified option than begging in shop doorways.

'Did you get 'em?' asked Dawkins, turning sharply as they approached.

Ornshaw shook his head. 'They were too fast.'

'Them 'airy brutes wants putting down for what they done to my little mucker,' said Dawkins. He sent the children off to find their fellow gang members and wrapped his arm around Lambeth Sid. 'Go find yourself a comfy pallet and have a nice little kip while I talk business.' Sid nodded cheeks red and angry, eyes swollen from his tears, nose still caked in snot.

This time Dawkins let the two of them come inside the building. The interior was ill lit and gloomy. Despite his curiosity, Ornshaw couldn't see what it was that Dawkins had wanted to avoid them seeing earlier. They were led to a small office where Dawkins sat with his scuffed boots resting on the tabletop. Leaning back in the chair, he uncorked a bottle of beer. His Adam's apple rose and fell as he glugged down a mouthful. He wiped his lips with the back of his sleeve, let out a loud belch and proffered the bottle to Ornshaw. 'Fancy a swig, me old mucker?'

'I'll pass,' declined Ornshaw.

'Damn sight better than the drinking water round these parts,' said Dawkins, taking another slug. 'You ask McGregor, here. Ain't that the truth, Mr McGregor?'

McGregor was standing beside a tall, slightly rusted filing cabinet. 'I wouldn't drink the water round here if you paid me my weight in gold.'

'Do you know anyone in this part of London who keeps monkeys as pets?' asked Yil.

'People keep all sorts of things round 'ere,' said Dawkins. He glugged from the beer bottle and wiped his lips on his sleeve. 'There was once a fella what used to 'ave a bleedin' rhinoceros. He'd parade it around the pubs for paying punters.'

'I've remembered something.' said Ornshaw. 'It began to click when we saw the monkeys leaping over the rooftops.'

The others looked at him expectantly.

'Back when I was about eleven or twelve, we were taken on an outing by the superintendent of the orphanage. Some wealthy benefactor had bought us all tickets to go to the circus. The tent was set up where the old Vauxhall Pleasure Gardens used to be. There was an act that left a great impression on me. Madame Macaque and her Barbary Band of Acrobatic Apes.'

Dawkins repeated the name under his breath as if it was a curse. 'Madam Macaque.'

'She'd trained these apes to do all sorts of stunts on the high wire and trapeze,' continued Dawkins. 'When the ring master introduced her, he relayed some cock and bull story about how her parents had been studying a troop of apes in the Atlas Mountains on the northernmost coast of Africa. Their camp had been set upon by bandits who had murdered everyone and stolen everything. But somehow she had survived and was adopted and raised by the apes. At the time, being young and gullible, I lapped it all up.'

'And you think this Madam Macaque is behind the kidnapping of these children?' asked Yil.

'One of those monkeys wore a waistcoat,' said Ornshaw. 'The

196

other had on a string of pearls. In the act I saw all of the monkeys were dressed in costumes.'

Dawkins turned to McGregor. 'Get the word out on the street. I want to know if any circus folk are holed up in a squat somewhere. And I want the address, sharpish.'

'No taking the law into your own hands though,' cautioned Yil. 'You hired me to get to the bottom of this.'

A hardness fell over Dawkins' face. 'You jumped in with both feet. But we didn't agree on a price, nor did we sign nothing, nor shake on it, nor spit on it.'

'There's the real face of the crook,' thought Dawkins.

'I would caution you not to do anything reckless,' said Yil, stepping closer to loom over the table. 'I have a theory that there is something deeper and more insidious going on here. Like Ornshaw, something has triggered a memory and set off a train of thought. It was what Mr McGregor said about how the abducted children he encountered no longer seemed to be themselves. If you go blundering in, we may never uncover the truth.'

'Which is?' challenged Dawkins.

'I hope I am wrong,' replied Yil. 'But I suspect we may be on the verge of exposing a grotesque Masorobian plot.'

'Masorobians?' asked Dawkins. 'Them's the slimy beasts what were the pilots inside the three-legged contraptions what fired the heat rays?'

Yil's huge head bobbed a nod.

''Nuff said,' acknowledged the King of Thieves, placing the beer bottle on the table. 'I'm not going one-to-one with any of those ugly buggers. If I find an address, I'll get it to you, and I won't do nothin' without your say so. In turn, you can pass an invoice on to McGregor for settlement once the job is done.'

Chapter Seven

Ornshaw and Yil rode the skiff back along the canal and tethered it near the St Pancras Airship Terminal, where a huge cargo dirigible returning from the continent was being flagged in to dock. Like the route from Clapham to Waterloo, the roads from the Euston Road to

197

the Strand had been cleared of rubble and debris. They were able to hire a horse-drawn cab to take them toward Trafalgar Square where Ornshaw was to wait while Yil sought an urgent meeting with his Whitehall sponsors.

Inside the carriage, Yil was so tall he had to remove his bowler hat, and although he crouched low, the smooth crown of his hairless head still pressed against the roof. Compared to the speed and efficiency of the skiff, their progress down Southampton Row seemed achingly ponderous. Out of the window Ornshaw watched a group of industrious navies scurrying like ants up and down the scaffolding erected to the front of one of the damaged buildings, wooden hods filled with bricks. It struck him, not for the first time, how primitive humanity was—even in this so-called age of invention—compared to the technological and scientific advances that had been made on Mars.

They passed a billboard erected by the nearby British Museum which promised handsome rewards for any citizen who donated Martian artifacts uncovered during the cleanup. Yil had been broodingly silent since they left Dawkins' warehouse. Ornshaw turned to him now and asked the question he'd been aching to ask.

'What is it you think the Masorobians are up to?'

Yil sighed, breath rattling unsettlingly in his narrow throat. His eyelids blinked. 'At the start of a civil war, reports of an alleged highly unethical experiment was uncovered. Before steps could be taken to verify their legitimacy, the plot to invade the Earth was also exposed, so it was set aside in our efforts to thwart the attack.'

Ornshaw shivered as an eerie tingle passed over him. 'What kind of experiment?'

'According to these reports, the Masorobians had developed a procedure by which their high command could render themselves virtually immortal,' replied Yil. 'By means of an infernal device, not unlike that which on Earth is used to make recordings onto a phonographic record. This device creates a small brass disc about the size of a coin onto which brainwaves can be etched. Once this disc is embedded by surgeons within the brain of another being, it was said to act like a mechanical parasite, gradually ousting all the thoughts and memories of the host and essentially transplanting the brain of the elderly general in the cranium of the younger host.'

198

Ornshaw's mouth fell open. 'They would have full control of the younger host? The way their pilots effectively become the brains of their war machines.'

'More than that,' said Yil. 'They would become the host. Refreshed. Rejuvenated. Continuity of the Masorobian command ensured. Knowledge intact. A huge tactical advantage. One which could be repeated over and over whenever the new host became elderly and frail.'

'You think they've been experimenting on the kids they abducted?'

'I fear it is possible,' said Yil. 'The Masorob are relentlessly ingenious and inventive when it comes to advancing their nefarious cause.'

'It means some of them are here,' said Ornshaw. 'Survivors of the invasion. They must have gotten their hands on a supply of the vaccine.'

'Or developed their own version,' said Yil. 'So you see why it is vital that I make my report.'

It was Ornshaw's turn to fall silent, pondering the multiple layers of what was being uncovered. The carriage reached the foot of Waterloo Bridge and turned into the Strand. Just beyond Aldwych a huge contingent of police, accompanied by a mounted battalion of cavalry hussars, had been assembled. Clearly the authorities were taking no chances of the Britannia Foremost march getting anywhere near Whitehall or Parliament.

At Trafalgar Square, Yil paid the cab driver and asked Ornshaw to wait while he went to make his report. The lions and fountains in the square had been shattered to smithereens by heat rays during the onslaught into central London. But, by some miracle, Nelson's column had not been toppled. It was scarred and severely marked from flying bits of shattered stone, and badly scorched. High on the plinth, Admiral Nelson's stone head had been decapitated. Nevertheless, it continued to tower defiantly over the skyline.

Ornshaw found a spot on the broken remains of the square's ornamental perimeter wall and perched down. For a while, he watched a dozen or so dust-covered labourers shooing pigeons as they shoveled rubble into barrows that were then wheeled out to the road and tipped into horse-drawn carts. From the direction of St

James Park he could see gas filled balloons ascending and descending at regular intervals. Many Members of Parliament from the Home Counties had purchased their own dirigibles and had hired experienced aeronauts to ferry them between their constituencies and Westminster.

His thoughts turned to Yil and who it might be he was going to meet in the shored-up corridors of Whitehall. During their conversation he had never named any of the people he had dealings with at the Government Offices. These were the faceless men—the ones who pulled strings and in turn had their own strings pulled by others higher up the chain of command. The ones who played war games behind closed doors. Those who never saw front line action themselves. Who never had to pull a trigger. Who never had to see the corpses of their comrades scattered and twisted on the field of battle. But who could condemn millions to their death on the flourish of an ink pen.

Ornshaw had read a few optimistic articles in the Evening Star which suggested the aftermath of the war was a chance to reassess and rebuild a brighter, more equitable future. Provide work for the destitute and jobless. Clear the slums. Use the advanced captured Martian technology for the benefit of all.

He'd been tempted to fall for that aspirational notion for a while. Full of cautious hope. But he'd been as naïve as the authors of those articles. It was the same old same old. Those on the top stayed on the top. Those below sank even deeper. Faceless men made convenient alliances with unfortunates like Yil because it suited their purpose and maintained the status quo. And the alternative, Britannia Foremost and their ilk, would be ten times worse.

Ornshaw began to brood. The bitter young man who'd boarded that omnibus on Clapham Common all those weeks ago crept back. His wounds and scalds started to twinge and ache in solidarity. Painful memories of that hillside near Woking, with its burning heather and burning flesh, flashed in his mind.

Deep within the sullen depths of these thoughts, he began to get the distinct impression that he was being stared at in the most intense and hostile manner. When he raised his head, he saw, not far from where he was seated, a well-dressed little girl with ringlets and pink ribbons in her blond, curly hair. She was holding hands with an equally well-dressed woman who was vigorously waving at a man in naval uniform, striding towards them from the direction of Whitehall.

The girl was looking back at Ornshaw. Blue eyes wide and filled with a burning fury that terrified him with its intensity. When their eyes met, Ornshaw felt that same dreadful stabbing pain he'd felt in the alleyway when Yil invaded his thoughts. The headache that swelled in his skull was so intense he almost keeled over. His thoughts were being exposed and stolen.

Ornshaw felt a fury rise within him at this intrusion. 'If I had my bayonet, I would slice open your skull and carve that demonic little coin right out of your brain,' screamed the angry thought that came rushing into his head. The little girl's jaw went slack. Her mouth fell open. She let out at gasp, unable to fathom how Ornshaw knew what he apparently knew.

The connection was broken as quickly as it had been made as the naval officer arrived on the scene, kissed the woman gently on the cheek, and crouched down to hug the little girl. He took her other hand, and the three of them set off along the Strand. Ornshaw groaned and rubbed his eyes with the heels of his hands. When he lowered his arms, the little girl looked back over her shoulder, wicked grin spread on her supposedly innocent lips. And Ornshaw knew without the shadow of a doubt that he had just encountered a surrogate possessed by the cold and calculating intellect of a transplanted Masorobian brain.

Chapter Eight

'Why did you do that?' scolded Yil. 'You may have alerted the Masorob to the fact that we are on to them.'

'The thought just jumped into my head,' said Ornshaw. 'I didn't have any control over it.'

'Who knows what else she was able to retrieve from that brief incursion,' said Yil.

They were back at the apartment in Little Sirenium. They'd journeyed back via cab to St Pancras and then along the canal in the steam-driven skiff in relative silence, each contemplating their

201

recent encounters. Now Yil wanted to know the full details of what Ornshaw had witnessed in Trafalgar Square.

'I never doubted your word,' Ornshaw assured him. 'But now I have experienced the hard facts first hand. There was a monster nestled within the husk of that innocent little girl.'

Yil blinked. 'Indeed. But I dearly wish that the representatives of your government had the same outlook.'

'They didn't believe you?' asked Ornshaw.

'Said it all sounded farfetched,' replied Yil.

'Farfetched?" blurted Ornshaw. 'A year ago the notion of Martians launching canisters through which to invade the Earth would have sounded farfetched.'

Yil nodded. 'But they said they would need evidence.'

'*I'm* evidence,' Ornshaw pointed out. 'I can tell them what I saw. What I experienced. Dawkins and McGregor too.'

'I doubt it would wash,' said Yil. 'They know you work for me. Your revolver was issued by them. They'd never accept Dawkins' word. And because of McGregor's association with him, they would never take him at his word either. They told me quite forcefully that they would not be minded to allocate valuable resources to an investigation into abducted street urchins.'

'It's down to us then,' said Ornshaw.

'That it is,' agreed Yil. He began to pace the room on his spindly legs, big head slightly bowed between narrow shoulders. 'What are they up to?' he muttered in unsettlingly hissing tones. 'What are they up to?'

'We know what they're up to,' said Ornshaw. 'They're using children to experiment with brain transplants. The very notion sickens me to the stomach.'

'But to what end?' said Yil. 'The Masorobian high command never does anything without a specific purpose in mind. And that purpose is always to advance their objectives through conflict and war.'

'Would they use children as weapons?' asked Ornshaw.

'They would,' said Yil. 'If it was to their advantage. But if they were creating a clandestine army, they would have used adult hosts. There's something else. I'm sure of it.'

With a sudden click of his long neck, he stood upright.

'Cooking!' he exclaimed. 'A bit of cooking always helps focus my thoughts. I recently acquired a recipe for something called faggots. Have you tried them before?'

'I have,' said Ornshaw. 'But I'm not sure they'll be to your taste.'

'We shall see,' said Yil.

As he clattered around in the kitchen, Ornshaw's thoughts turned to Madam Macaque and his visit to the circus on Clapham Common all those years ago. He recalled the knot of anticipation that had twisted in his belly when the ringmaster spun his tall tale of the orphan child raised by Barbary apes on the remote clifftops of the Atlas Mountains. And then the electrical buzz of excitement when Madam Macaque came swaggering into the sawdust ring with her troupe, all dressed up in assorted gaily embroidered costumes, scurrying behind her.

Madame Macaque, in her red jacket and black boots, startling flame coloured hair braided to a long ponytail, took an exaggerated bow. Ornshaw's own voice was carried on the wave of enthusiastic youthful cheering which rose from the stalls. Everyone gasped as one by one she scooped up her performing monkeys and tossed them skyward toward the swings and wires high above the heads of the crowd.

Ornshaw craned his neck and watched in awe as Madame Macaque cracked her whip and barked out orders in a strange gobbledygook language that had the monkeys leaping and somersaulting from swing to swing and wire to wire. At one point there must have been at least a dozen monkeys tumbling through the air. It was as if they could truly fly. More of a flock than a troupe.

Ornshaw had loved every single minute of the act, holding his breath so long he almost forgot to breathe, cheering until his throat was raw, clapping until his palms went purple and felt like they'd been stung by a thousand nettles. In the ring, Madam Macaque spread her arms wide, huge grin on her face, acknowledging the applause, lapping up the adulation.

He hoped he was wrong in suggesting her as a possible suspect. But the two monkeys that had tried to kidnap that poor child in the alleyway looked very much like the ones from the act, especially the one dressed in the waistcoat. How could she be in league with the Masorob? What possible motivation could she have for such a betrayal?

His thoughts were rudely interrupted by a loud and urgent knocking on the apartment door. 'I'll get it,' he said, rising to his feet.

When he opened the door, a gangling youth of around sixteen was standing there, red-faced and breathing heavily from the climb up the steep stairs. He was dressed in the mock Georgian clothing that seamstresses in the East End had been creating with off-cuts of cloth since the end of the invasion. It had become such a craze with young aspiring criminals that people had christened those who dressed in the manner "Georgie Boys". The quarter-length breeches and white stockings he wore beneath his narrow smock coat and cravat made his skinny legs seem even longer than they actually were.

'Dawkins says to come,' wheezed the Georgie Boy. 'He's found out where the circus lady is hiding.'

Chapter Nine

'I'm coming with yer,' insisted Dawkins once they'd arrived back at the warehouse.

'I don't think that would be a good idea,' said Yil with a studied blink. 'You are too emotionally involved.'

'Emotionally involved, my arse,' blustered Dawkins. 'They've been pinching my nippers. Doing terrible things to them. Look what them monkeys did to poor little Lambeth Sid.'

'That's exactly Yil's point,' said Ornshaw.

Dawkins jutted out his unshaven chin. 'I have every right.'

'They do have a point,' interjected McGregor. 'You might end up doing something you'd regret. The coppers would jump at the chance to arrest you. Even if the charges didn't stick, and anything you'd done was for the good of the country. The last thing you need is the coppers poking around in your business.'

At that moment, they were interrupted by the raucously breathless arrival of the somewhat bedraggled Georgie Boy. He'd refused point-blank to accompany them in the steam skiff, saying hell would freeze over before he'd ever set foot inside such a Martian contraption. Somehow though he'd made his way back only ten minutes or so behind them.

'Lanky, my old mucker,' said Dawkins. 'I want you to escort these two gents to where the circus lady is holed up. But hang back when you get there. I don't want you getting involved.'

'Bloody hell, Dawkins,' said Lanky, doubling over and rubbing the stitch in his side. 'I only just got here.'

They followed Lanky back through the maze of alleyways, Yil easily keeping pace with the Georgie Boy's lolloping pace, but Ornshaw having to break into a trot which uncomfortably agitated his wounds and scalds. It was dark now, and in the gloom, the two of them, with the forward motion of their respective skinny-legged gaits, gave him the unsettling impression that he was on the trail of a pair of Martian war machines.

They reached the main thoroughfare. With the gas lamps out of commission, it felt as if they had entered the London of a bygone era where the streets were illuminated by flaming torches and tribes of homeless people were huddled around wood fired braziers. The swirling smoke made Ornshaw's eyes sting. He coughed and shielded his mouth with his sleeve. The Britannia Foremost march had long since dispersed, but in the windowless hollows of what still passed for taverns and ale houses, the night was filled with the aggressively boisterous banter of the hard men who hunched in the flicker of candle-lit tables, guzzling beer and boasting of the coming insurrection.

Luckily, Lanky passed swiftly over the road, taking them through another warren of side alleys and out into a quieter, much darker street. He led them to the front of a tall, gaudy building whose shattered frontage had been partially boarded up. A girl stepped from the shadows. She was half the size of Lanky, but dressed similarly in jacket and cravat, quarter-length breeches and white stockings.

'This is my gal, Mol,' said Lanky by way of introduction.

Mol pushed her dark, wavy hair behind her ears and gave them a curt nod.

'Any movement?' asked Lanky.

'No one nor nothing 'as come out,' replied Mol. 'But them monkeys 'as been screeching up a right old racket, so they 'ave.'

'What is this place?' asked Ornshaw.

'It was a music hall,' said Lanky. 'Me and Mol once snuck in the back way to see Dan Leno. He was a right hoot.'

Yil blinked. 'Ah, music halls. Places of mirth and variety, and occasional debauchery. I have been reading up on the subject in one of the encyclopedias I acquired. Fascinating cultural history.'

It made sense to Ornshaw that Madam Macaque would hide out in such a place. 'Is there a way in?' he asked.

'Door's blocked by fallen masonry,' said Mol. 'But you can get in through this window. That's 'ow the circus lady gets in and out.' She pushed aside one of the boards to reveal a gaping, glassless hole.

Yil immediately crouched low and passed into the interior of the building.

'You two stay here,' said Ornshaw, gripping the splintered remains of the window frame.

'For sure,' said Lanky with an enthusiastic nod. 'I 'eard tell them monkeys has got sharp claws.'

Ornshaw passed through the window and followed Yil through the ruined area that had once been the foyer and ticket office. Through a gap in the roof, a beam of moonlight shined a spotlight on a tattered bill poster, still clinging doggedly to the wall. It advertised what had been an upcoming appearance by George Robey, billed as the Prime Minister of Mirth.

They ascended a wide stairway whose once plush carpet now lay thick with a gritty layer of dust. Near the top, they began to hear the chittering of the monkeys drifting down from the auditorium. A few more steps and they began to hear a woman's voice. When he saw Yil withdrawing his wasp gun, Ornshaw reached inside his jacket for his revolver.

At the top of the stairs, a shredded velvet drape hung where the door to the auditorium had once stood. Another set of stairs led up to where the balcony would have been. Yil nodded toward the drape and pulled it to one side with his narrow fingers. Ornshaw followed him through.

Most of the roof had collapsed onto the stalls. The moon was full, and when Ornshaw looked up at the starry sky, he could make out the bright speck of light that was Mars. There was a momentary flash. A canister had been launched. Ornshaw hoped it contained another group of Basomor refugees, rather than being the portent of a new invasion by the Masorob.

His attention turned to the stage. A plume of smoke rose from a little campfire that had been lit there. In its wavering glow, he could make out the two monkeys crouched down on their haunches beside a figure he assumed to be Madam Macaque seated on an upturned crate. Before her stood another small figure that may well have also been a monkey. The whole scene had an unsettlingly supernatural feel to it. Madam Macaque like a witch consorting with her familiar, as the monkeys, like a pair of chittering demons summoned from hell, looked on.

'If we are to have any chance at apprehending her, we need to get closer,' whispered Yil, making him jump.

'We should try to go backstage and come at them from behind,' agreed Ornshaw.

Back in the foyer, they found a door that led down a stone stairwell to the basement. Other than the large fissure in the ceiling through which the moonlight penetrated, the explosion that had damaged the upper floors had not afflicted too much damage this far down. Doors to half a dozen dressing rooms stood closed. Assorted stage props lined the wall of a narrow corridor. To one end, a stack of chairs, to the other, a pile of empty beer crates.

They found a cast-iron spiral stairway. From above, they could hear Madam Macaque.

'Best I can do by way of clothes,' she was saying. 'You're a handsome little tyke though. I think the lady and gent will be pleased when I hand you over in the morning.'

The reply was cold, emotionless and monotone. 'The effort is acceptable. Your reward will be forthcoming.'

Yil began to climb the stairs. Slowly, careful to place each foot gently on each step so as not to make any noise. Ornshaw followed, revolver in one hand, the other gripping the spiral stair rail to steady himself, breathing as quietly as possible through his nostrils. At the top, they found themselves looking onto the stage from the wings. They could see now a diminutive child of slight build stood before Madam Macaque. She had dressed him in a blue sailor's outfit with a white cap that sat jauntily atop his curly blond head of hair.

'Who shall I be residing with?' he asked in droll tones.

'I have found a scientist who is involved in the study of the

207

canisters used in the invasion,' replied Madam Macaque. 'He and his wife lost their only son when a war machine strafed Hampstead with its heat ray.'

'Excellent,' said the boy, gleefully rubbing his little pink hands together. 'The loss of a scientist will be a great setback to their cause. Even the Basomor agree that humans should never be allowed to acquire the technology that would allow them to launch canisters beyond their atmosphere.' He let out a high-pitched chuckle that sent a shiver of dread down Ornshaw's spine.

Without further hesitation, Yil stepped onto the stage, pointing his wasp gun directly at Madam Macaque. The Barbary apes rose to their full height, hissing with marked aggression and scurrying protectively to their mistress's side.

Ornshaw stepped forward too, revolver outstretched.

'Surrender,' said Yil. 'You are outnumbered and outgunned.'

Madam Macaque rose slowly from the packing crate with her hands raised above her head. She looked as if she had fallen on hard times, dirty and ragged, not even a quarter as glamorous and mysterious as she had appeared all those years ago beneath the big top on Clapham Common. Her monkeys looked destitute too, bald patches on their fur, gaps in their teeth when they bared them.

'I am on the official business of Her Majesty's Government,' announced Yil. 'You will come with us and I will hand you over as a traitor. Whatever plot was being hatched here is at an end.'

The little boy, who had dropped back into shadows when they'd appeared, now came closer to the flicker of the fire. He looked innocent and angelic. Ornshaw had to remind himself that he had been rendered no more than an animated husk that hosted a demon inside. He turned his revolver in the boy's direction, not trusting him for a moment.

'You are the traitor,' he said, pointing an accusatory finger at Yil. 'You could have acceded to the superiority of the Masorob, worked with us for the glory of Mars. Instead, you are in league with this human in a pathetic attempt to thwart our road to glory. Were it not for the constraints placed upon me by the ill-formed vocal cords of the vessel I am housed in, I would curse you in my own tongue.'

Yil replied in what Ornshaw assumed was the Masorob mother tongue. If there were actual words amongst the rapid succession of clicks and ticks and clacks that emerged from deep in Yil's throat, Ornshaw couldn't make them out.

The boy grinned demonically. 'You think firing questions at me in my own language will get you anywhere? It matters not in any case. Our plan is too far advanced now to be sabotaged.'

He nodded toward Madame Macaque, still with her hands up and the wasp gun trained on her. 'With the aid of our confederate here, suitable surrogate parents have been sought out for operatives such as myself. Each family has at its head someone who is of vital importance to the future defense of the Earth. When the time is right, the little assassins that they have unwittingly been housed under their own roofs will act swiftly and mercilessly to eliminate them.'

'You could have negotiated,' said Yil. 'Had you made contact with humanity, offered to share your technological advances, I am sure they would have given you a home. Their oceans are vast.'

'Hah!' scoffed the boy. 'Why ask when we can take? Why compromise when we can dominate? Why seek an alliance with creatures who contain all the protein we need to survive.'

And there it was. The one thing about the invasion that everyone avoided talking about. The red line that no one could face crossing. The fact that the Masorob had engorged themselves on the blood of those they slaughtered. The indignation tightened in Ornshaw's chest.

'Are you hearing this?' he challenged Madam Macaque. 'Do you realise what you've gotten yourself involved in? These creatures feasted on the blood of thousands upon thousands of humans.'

Madam Macaque jutted her chin forward. 'I care not,' she said defiantly. 'When I needed assistance. After the invasion, when most of my troupe was murdered and these two were on the verge of dying from disease and malnutrition, not a single soul would lift a finger to help me. As far as I am concerned, the entire human race can go to hell in a handcart.'

With that, she kicked violently at her campfire. Sparks and cinders flew in every direction. The monkeys screeched, and through the confusion Ornshaw became aware of the blurred outline of one of them leaping up toward the music hall's exposed rafters. A cinder had burned his cheek, his eyes were streaming from the billowing smoke from the half-doused fire. He staggered away, blinking and clutching his revolver.

'Look out!' cried Yil.

Ornshaw glanced up and saw the monkey hurtling down at him from above, hirsute limbs outstretched, vicious teeth bared, string of pearls rattling. He was too disorientated to take aim. But to his left there came a whirring noise, followed by a loud clicking and an urgent whizz. The falling monkey jerked and stiffened in midair as the wasp launched form Yil's weapon hit home and delivered its debilitating sting. The monkey stiffened and crashed onto the stage mere inches from Ornshaw.

Madam Macaque let out a strangled scream and ran to the fallen creature. 'Salome! You've killed her.' Behind her, the monkey in an embroidered waistcoat howled in anxiety and slapped the flat palms of his leathery hands onto the floorboards.

'Not dead,' Yil assured her, as his wasp came weaving its way back to the sanctity of the chamber in his gun. 'The venom stuns and paralyses. But she will recover.'

As the smoke began to disperse, Ornshaw saw that the little possessed boy in his sailor's outfit was gone.

'Find him,' said Yil, training the wasp gun on Madam Macaque. 'He mustn't leave the building.'

Ornshaw rushed backstage and hurtled down the spiral staircase. He progressed cautiously along the narrow corridor holding the revolver with both hands to steady his aim. Half way along, he noticed that one of the dressing room doors now stood slightly ajar.

'Come out,' he said. 'I know you're in there. Come out and surrender yourself.'

There was a scuffling noise.

'You can't hide,' warned Ornshaw. 'I'm coming in. If you force my hand, I will shoot to wound. I don't pretend to understand how the brain of one being can be transplanted into the body of another. But if you are connected to that poor child, then I feel certain you would experience the excruciating pain of a bullet fired from close range.'

Using his foot to push the door wide, he stepped into the dressing room. Part of the exterior wall had collapsed, allowing the moonlight to slant into the gloom. Immediately before him was a dressing table with a cracked mirror—its array of grease paints and brushes covered in dust and fragments of brick. To his left, theatrical costumes hung on a small rail were swaying as if recently disturbed.

'Come out,' said Ornshaw. 'Raise your hands above your head and step out where I can see you.'

The costumes parted and the little boy stepped into the beam of moonlight. He looked so innocent in his sailor's costume. No hint of the monster which lurked within. Ornshaw gripped his revolver and felt his shoulders tense. The boy didn't have his hands raised as instructed. Instead, he raised his head and stared intently at Ornshaw, baby blue eyes wide as saucers.

'Look me in the eye,' he commanded.

'No,' said Ornshaw, knowing his intent. He tried to turn his head, but the power of the command was compelling and the eerie draw of the eyes magnetic. Despite his best efforts, their eyes met. He felt an intense stabbing in his head, as if his brain had been swiftly skewered. But this was far worse than his previous experiences. Yil had been holding back, gently probing for the answer to why he had been followed. The girl in Trafalgar Square had been toying with him. This Masorob was applying his telepathic skills to full force—occupying Ornshaw's thoughts, seizing the vast territories of his brain.

'No!' he yelled. 'Get out of my head!'

Somehow, he mustered the wherewithal to pull back on the trigger. The shot went wide, shattering the mirror, showering the little sailor boy with sharp crystals of glass. Blood rolled down his rosy red cheeks. But the Masorob held his gaze, and in doing so fixed Ornshaw with his debilitating hypnosis.

Around the revolver, Ornshaw's fingers became fat and numb. He felt them unfurl like hunks of rubber. The weapon clattered to the floor. His arms flopped limply to his side and hung there like useless dead weights. Inside his head, the Masorob was an image, grotesque and multi-limbed, with tentacles writhing in all directions as it searched for something to use against him.

Ornshaw tried once more to think about his bayonet and how he might gouge at the engraved disc that had been supplanted inside the little boy's head. The Masorob easily deflected these thoughts and left Ornshaw floundering to grasp them once more.

Then it found what it was searching for. And seized it. And dragged it out. A dreadful memory that drew a strained whimper from deep in Ornshaw's throat. And he was there again on that Surrey hillside. On that summer morning. Standing in a row of infantrymen. Rifles shouldered and ready. A high-pitched howl ripped at his ears. An arcing beam which brought with it a blinding flash of white light. An intense eruption of fire knocked him from his feet and tossed his comrades like rag dolls left and right. Pain. Searing, gut-wrenching pain, as his uniform burst into flames. Rifle and helmet lost in the fiery eruption, he tried to stand up, but the agony brought him to his knees.

Instead of rolling down the hill and into the ditch, he found himself upright once again, holding his rifle, trembling at the sight of the three-legged war machine as it crested the hill. Then the sound of his comrades firing as it advanced. Once more, a high-pitched howl, an arcing beam, a sear of white light. Once more, brought to his knees. Once more, raised back to his feet. Over and over, the scene repeated in a rapid and dizzying sequence.

The Masorob was coldly and deftly weaving a re-occurring nightmare from the raw material of his trauma. He was trapped within it. Unable to regain his senses and escape. Cursed to relive and repeat the dreadful events of that day, the pain of his wounds intensifying until they equaled the agony he'd endured when they'd first been inflicted. Soon he would lose his mind completely. And, with it, Charlie Ornshaw would be lost forever.

Then a voice—distant at first, but growing incrementally louder. Yil's voice. Somehow Yil had gotten into his head too. 'Listen,' he urged. 'He has you trapped in a psychological fugue. But all is not lost. I can free you. But you must listen and follow. Try to find me.'

Ornshaw found himself on his feet once more on the summer hillside. As he waited for the war machine to appear, he heard Yil calling to him. 'Follow my voice.' It seemed to come from the left. Down the slope of the hill to where there was a small copse of birch trees. Before he could react, there came the high-pitched howl, the arcing beam, the sear of white light, and the scalding heat which felled him.

Back on his feet again, rifle in his grasp. 'Follow my voice,' urged Yil.

Knowing he had not a second to spare, he turned and began rapidly down the hill toward the trees. But he was not nearly fast enough. The heat blast exploding behind him knocked him flat on his face.

Up once more. Gazing up the hill. The men of his unit with their rifles ready. Yil calling out from the birch copse. 'Follow my voice'. Ornshaw turned and ran as fast as his legs would carry him, hurtling himself down the hillside. He heard the howl behind and saw how the countryside lit up from the white flash of the heat ray. He was sufficiently out of range that the blast that thumped at his back served to propel him onwards rather than knock him from his feet.

He ran for the trees, yellow gorse snagging at his boots.

The voice of the Masorobian roared inside his head. 'Turn around. I command you. Turn back this instant.' A cold sensation washed over him. He knew that if he looked back, he would see a set of grotesque tentacles crawling rapidly down the hill, ready to grab him and haul him back into the fugue.

'Almost there,' encouraged Yil.

Forcing himself to ignore the powerful beseeching of the Masorobian, Ornshaw went bounding down the last yards of the slope and found himself almost instantly amongst the trees. They seemed somehow to create some sort of protective barrier. The voice of the Masorobian sounded distant and far less compelling.

'Keep going,' urged Yil. 'Break free.'

Ornshaw ran to the other side of the copse of trees and found himself miraculously back in the dressing room of the music hall. The little boy in the sailor costume was no longer staring at him but at Yil, who was stood in the open doorway with his wasp gun trained on him.

'Surrender!' said Yil.

'Never!' squealed the boy defiantly.

With that, he launched himself into a dive and scurried between Yil's legs. Ornshaw heard his tiny feet slapping along the corridor floor. But his little legs were far from fast enough.

Yil turned and launched another wasp. The sound of it humming through the air was followed by a yelp and a dull thump as the boy hit the ground.

Ornshaw was almost overcome with nausea. His head felt as if it had been whacked by an axe and split in two. He leaned against the dressing room table to stop himself from fainting. 'What about Madame Macaque?'

'Long gone, I would think,' replied Yil. 'When you cried out and I heard the gunshot, I knew what was happening. I knew I had to make a choice.'

'I reckon you saved me from a fate worse than death,' said Ornshaw, the headache blurring his vision.

'You saved me from those thugs in that courtyard,' said Yil. 'We are even now. But this may not be the last time we rely on one another for our lives.'

'So, what now?' asked Ornshaw.

'We must deliver our prisoner to Whitehall with utmost urgency. Before the wasp venom wears off,' said Yil, with a blink. 'I intend to participate fully in his interrogation. As you know, he is not the only one who can rummage around inside someone's head looking for their deepest secrets. This will convince them that the plot is real. And that the device the Masorob has created is a genuine theat.'

Chapter Ten

It wasn't until late the following morning that Yil, looking drawn and drained, arrived back the tenement in Little Sirenium. He told of a long night battling to break down the Masorob's mental defenses. Finally, he discovered that the Masorob base was within the hull of the wreck of a merchant ship sunk in the Pool of London during the invasion.

'Did you get any information on which couples have unwittingly taken cuckoo assassins into their nests?' asked Ornshaw.

Yil shook his head. 'It seems the elusive Madam Macaque may be the only one with the full details.'

'Still, it's good that the location of the Masorob base has been identified,' said Ornshaw.

'I'm not so sure,' said Yil. 'The Admiralty had duly dispatched an ironclad to drop depth charges at the location.'

Ornshaw gave a shrug of his shoulders. 'Why would that not be a good thing?'

'It's a sledgehammer to crack a nut, to coin a human phrase,' said Yil. 'The Masorob hiding in that wreck will perish, or worse, they will escape with the etching device. The chance for more intelligence will be lost. But it seems the favoured human option to such problems is to blow them up.'

'At least the device will be destroyed,' Ornshaw pointed out.

Yil sighed. 'When the Masorobian told Madam Macaque that even the Basomor agree that humans should never be allowed to acquire the ability to launch a canister into space, he was correct.'

'He was?' said Ornshaw, looking flummoxed.

'Imagine if you were able to send canisters to Mars,' said Yil. 'It wouldn't be long before you were blowing things up in the name of conquest and empire. Humans may be similar in physical appearance to the Basomor but in attitude and outlook you have much more in common with the Masorob.'

Ornshaw didn't know quite how to digest that. In his heart of hearts, he knew Yil was probably right. Instead of attempting to challenge him, he changed the subject. 'You weren't able to draw out any clue as to the whereabouts of Madam Macaque?'

Yil shook his large head. 'Unfortunately, no. As we speak, images of her likeness taken from an old circus handbill are being distributed to police stations throughout the city. But I fear the worst. If she isn't apprehended soon, the assassinations will commence.'

'She can't hide forever,' said Ornshaw.

Yil rose to his feet, towering over him. 'I have found a recipe for something called Mulligatawny soup. Would you care to try some?'

'I've no idea what Mulligatawny soup is,' said Ornshaw. 'But I am famished.'

Yil clattered around in the kitchen and Ornshaw began flicking through the newspaper his employer had brought back with him. As the room filled with a pungent spicy aroma, a byline referring to "strange goings on in the ruins of Regent Park Zoo" caught his eye.

The zoo had been virtually destroyed during the invasion. Most of the surviving livestock had been housed in private menageries. A decision was yet to be made on what was to happen to the site. But its owners were having difficulties keeping hold of night watchmen. Each one they engaged would resign after the first or second night, complaining of ghostly goings-on and strange noises emanating from the ruins of the former monkey house.

Ornshaw gasped and folded the paper once more onto his lap.

'Yil!' he cried. 'I think I know where Madam Macaque has set up another hideout.

Chapter Eleven

'Rouse the messenger,' said Yil, once Ornshaw had shown him the article.

'Don't you want to send a message to Whitehall rather than Dawkins?' asked Ornshaw.

'I learned in my previous career that it pays to continually consolidate one's position,' said Yil, with a slow blink. 'If we can bring in Madam Macaque without seeking official assistance, we'll engender the idea that we might be indispensable. Before the alternative idea that we might be surplus to requirements begins to creep in.'

'One step ahead,' said Ornshaw. 'Smart move. But aren't there other Basomor here in Little Sirenium who might help us?'

Yil shook his bulbous head. 'I'm afraid not. My peers are happy for me to sort out infidelities and embezzlements, but given their recent experiences on our homeworld, they're more than reluctant to become embroiled in another conflict.'

He stepped toward the cabinet where his colony of wasps slumbered in their labyrinth of honeycomb chambers. 'Ask the messenger to tell Dawkins to raise a posse and meet us by the canal behind the zoo,' he said.

The messenger was one of Dawkins' dirty-faced urchins. He had been tasked with being the link between Yil and the King of Thieves. On his own insistence, he was asleep in the corridor beneath a blanket that Yil had provided. 'I ain't never slept in no bed,' he said when Ornshaw had attempted to entice him inside. 'And I ain't planning on doing so. An 'ard floor's what I finds comfy.'

When Ornshaw roused him and gave him his instructions, he blinked, rubbed his eyes, and unravelled himself from the knot of the blanket. Ornshaw handed him a small flask containing a portion of Yil's Mulligatawny soup.

'Thanks guv,' he said, snatching it with a grimy hand. 'This'll set me up good and proper, once I get back to Dawky's place.' With that, he leapt to his feet, instantly alert, and scuttled down the stairs on the first leg of his chore.

Chapter Twelve

The moon's bright image reflected from the canal waters as Ornshaw and Yil waited by the tethered skiff. Mars was a red poker dot in the star-filled sky. No evidence tonight of any canisters being launched toward Earth. He reflected on what Yil had said earlier. His assessment was probably correct, if humanity acquired the skills to launch its own canisters into space, it wouldn't be long at all before someone became gripped by the fever dream of colonisation.

Yil stood tall, dressed in his bowler hat and overcoat, casting a long shadow along the canal path. Arms hanging at his side, fingers of his right hand gripping his wasp gun, he blinked as he gazed expectantly along the canal to the east. Not long ago, Ornshaw might have been considering this as a suitably secluded spot to stab him with his bayonet and push him into the canal to drown.

A barge came into view, motor humming. A dark stream of smoke billowed from its funnel. It was steered toward the tow path, lapping oily water against the edge. The bargeman stepped to the path and tethered his craft. Its passengers began to disembark. Dawkins, elbow supported by McGregor as he stepped onto dry land. Lanky and Mol, accompanied by four other Georgie Boys and Girls. A gaggle of scruffy kids, one of them with a snarling bulldog, straining on its leash. Ornshaw could make out an assortment of weapons. Coshes and cudgels and the like. Dawkins had a battered cricket bat slung over his shoulder.

'Whotcher?' he said, swaggering merrily along the path with his bow-legged gait. 'I'm looking forward to this. I ain't had a good rumble in donkey's years.'

As he drew nearer, Ornshaw could smell the beer on his breath.

'I'm hoping Madam Macaque will surrender once she sees how outnumbered she is,' said Yil.

'And I'm hoping otherwise,' quipped Dawkins with a wink of his eye. 'I wouldn't hit a woman. But them 'airy brutes of 'ers 'as got it coming.' He swung his bat to demonstrate.

Ornshaw led them up the embankment to the tumbled down perimeter wall of the zoo. They entered near a burnt-out crater that had once been the elephant enclosure. Ornshaw seemed to remember that in the latter part of the invasion a canister had fallen here, from which a three-legged war machine had emerged to strafe the battalion of armed police sent to deal with it. Many animals had died in the process. Some had escaped to cause further havoc amidst the chaos of the invasion.

Once they'd assembled themselves, Dawkins addressed his unruly band of urchins. 'You young 'uns hang back, you hear?' he told them. 'Me and McGregor, and Lanky and his lads and lasses, will be up front. None of you are to get stuck in unless it's absolutely bleedin' necessary.'

When this was met with a bleating chorus of complaints and disapproval, he thumped his cricket bat down hard on the ground. 'You mark my words well,' he warned them. 'I don't want none of you getting hurt for no good reason.'

The former Artful Dodger might be a thoroughly corrupting influence on the morals of these street kids, but he was once again demonstrating a genuine concern for their welfare.

'My words must also be marked,' said Yil, blinking as he adjusted his bowler. 'Myself and Mr Ornshaw will go in first and try and negotiate a surrender before things escalate.'

'Fair enough,' agreed Dawkins, resting the bat on his shoulder once more. 'I just hope I get a good swing at one of them monkeys, that's all.'

They proceeded in that manner through the ruins of the zoo, Yil and Ornshaw in the lead, Dawkins and McGregor behind them, Lanky and his gang in the middle, the street kids at the rear. The former monkey house was still standing, brickwork blackened from blast damage. Strange noises were echoing out from its interior. Ornshaw could see why the night watchmen had been spooked.

He pushed open the door. Inside, the darkness was impenetrable. He could hear scuffling and low huffing noises. His pulse quickened a little. 'Fetch a lamp up here,' barked Dawkins from behind him. One of the kids struck a match and lit an oil lamp. It was passed from the back to the front from one hand to the next. Dawkins handed it to Ornshaw.

As soon as the interior was illuminated, there came an ear-piercing cacophony of screeching. The cages, supposed to be empty and evacuated, were inhabited by all sorts of primates, from chimpanzees and baboons to marmosets and tamarins. They threw themselves at the bars of the cages, baring their teeth, tossing up heaps of straw, slapping their hands on the stone floors.

'You found me then,' came a woman's voice from deeper in the gloom. 'A lot sooner than I had anticipated.'

'Step into the light and surrender yourself,' demanded Yil.

A set of slow, deliberate footsteps was followed by the appearance of Madam Macaque, dressed in her worn-out costume and flanked by her Barbary apes—the one in the embroidered waistcoat to her left and the one with the string of pearls to her right. Both were on all fours and snarling.

'Hush,' said Madam Macaque.

An obedient stillness ensued as all the monkeys fell silent.

'These would have become my personal guard,' said Madam Macaque. 'I found them in parks and on heaths and brought them back here. The Masorob promised to make me Governess of London. I would have made Buckingham Palace my own. The gardens would have been the domain of my troupe.'

'How could you collaborate with Earth's enemies?' challenged Ornshaw once more. 'After all they did.'

'How can *you* collaborate with *him*?' she countered, pointing at Yil.

'He's on our side,' said Ornshaw.

Madam Macaque tossed her head back and laughed. 'What side is that? The side who panicked and slaughtered most of my troupe because they were so ignorant they thought they were Martians? The side who almost let these two starve to death and wouldn't even spare so much as a crust of bread no matter how I begged and pleaded?'

'So, you're prepared to see humanity come under the yolk of the Masorob?' said Ornshaw.

'Look around you,' came the response. 'This place. This zoo. This is how humanity treats its fellow creatures. Caged and

219

incarcerated. But had I been given the time, I would have trained each one of them and they would have been free.'

'And in the service of you and your Masorob masters,' said Ornshaw, feeling the ire rise within him.

'Enough,' interjected Yil. 'Whatever your plan, whatever the Masorob offered you, it's over now. I am taking you into custody.'

A smug grin curved on Madam Macaque's lips. 'Believe it is over if you wish.' With that she took each of her monkeys by the hand, stepped to one side and cried. 'Conga, come forth!'

A low growl sounded from the shadows, followed by a series of thunderous thumps on the ground, as if something huge and heavy was progressing toward them.

A mighty gorilla appeared, silver hairs on his back, powerful knuckles to the ground. The chaotic screeching commenced in the cages once more.

The gorilla rose to his full height and beat his barrel chest with his massive fists. Yil held out his long arm and took aim with his wasp gun. The gorilla lumbered forward, snatched it from his hand and tossed it to one side.

'Let me at 'im!' Dawkins ran at the beast, swinging his cricket bat. The gorilla swatted him like a fly, sending him crashing against the bars of one of the cages.

Ornshaw pulled the trigger on his revolver. The shot winged the gorilla on the shoulder. It staggered back, dark blood oozing down the wiry hairs on its bulging biceps. It rose again, roaring and beating its chest, furious eyes focused on Ornshaw. Luckily, Yil had retrieved his weapon. From low on the ground, he fired. The wasp zipped rapidly through air and felled the beast with a single sting. It hit the floor with the force of an oak falling in a forest. But it was too late. Madam Macaque had once more used the distraction as an opportunity to escape.

'Is there a back way out?' asked Yil.

'The monkey house was designed so you could walk through from one end to the other,' said McGregor, who was tending the semi-conscious Dawkins.

'Split up,' said Yil. 'Comb every inch of the zoo. Madam Macaque must be apprehended!'

A few minutes later, Ornshaw found himself alone near the sea lion enclosure. A dark moat surrounded a grey rocky islet. He leaned close to the railing. The rocks would make a good place to hide. It was the type of environment Madam Macaque's monkeys would be familiar with. The moon was causing the rocks to cast shadows across one another, making it more difficult to see what might be over there. He leaned closer to the railing.

Without warning, something came whipping out of the water and wound itself tightly around his wrist, causing him to drop his revolver into the moat with a loud splash. He pulled back, feeling the grip tighten. A hideous shape rose before him. A multi-limbed monstrosity, green in colour, mottled flesh, grotesque beak for a mouth, huge burning eyes. A Masorob had been lurking beneath the waters of the moat.

Still clutching his arm, it flopped over the railings. A second tentacle snaked around his waist, crushing in on his wounds and scars. Ornshaw screamed in pain and struggled to free himself. The monstrosity drew him close, trying force eye contact so it could invade his mind. He turned his head to the side and kicked frantically at its flaccid torso with his heels.

He saw Lanky and Mol come running to his aid along the path. Another tentacle lashed out and grabbed Lanky by the ankle, rising to dangle him in the air. Yet another wound around Mol's neck, taking her in a strangulation hold. Ornshaw saw her face darken to a deathly purple hue as her eyes rolled back in their sockets. If he didn't act quickly, she'd be asphyxiated.

It came to him in an instant, the additional precaution he'd taken by sheathing his bayonet next to the revolver. The Masorob had him by the right hand, so he had to feel clumsily inside his tweed jacket with his left, which was pressed tightly against his chest by the tentacle wrapped around his waist. He managed to touch the hilt of the bayonet with the tips of his fingers and inch his way along it enough to get a grip.

Mol was dangling limply now. Lanky was still struggling, but less vigorously, and clearly wearing himself out. One thought, Ornshaw told himself. Keep one thought foremost in your mind. The bayonet and what you intend to do with it.

He turned his head and gazed straight into the huge alien eyes. A sharp pain shot through his head, telling him his thoughts had been penetrated. The Masorob saw what he planned and immediately recoiled, dropping Lanky and Mol in the process. The tentacle around his right wrist slackened. But the one around his waist tightened to an unbearable pressure.

Ornshaw groaned, struggling for breath. It took all the strength he had to raise his left arm high. With a guttural grunt, he plunged his bayonet down hard into one of the huge unblinking eyes. Dark glops of viscous blood splattered against his face. The Masorob's beak went wide as it issued a piercing howl of pain. Ornshaw screamed too, feeling that same pain through the forced medium of their telepathic connection. The tentacle around his waist unravelled as the connection was severed. The creature fell back into the dark waters of the moat.

Ornshaw dropped heavily onto the path. Before consciousness escaped him, he saw Dawkins' gang of kids come swaggering toward him, cheering triumphantly, leading Madam Macaque and her duo of monkeys. All of them bound and hog-tied. They'd done what the adults had failed to do.

Epilogue

Deep beneath the Thames Estuary, within the sunken wreck of the ironclad *The Thunderchild*, the acting commander of the Masorob Earth Forces was receiving a telepathically transmitted report from her wounded soldier. From an air pocket in the hull echoed agonised groans and cries for help from the captive crew of a fishing vessel who were being drained of their blood to nourish the survivors of the attack on the previous Masorob base at the Pool of London.

'All of our clandestine operatives have been captured?' she asked, limbs weaving and winding above her warty torso.

The one-eyed soldier floated before her. 'Once Yil Axo got into the monkey lady's thoughts, he had all the information necessary for the human authorities to round them up,' he relayed back.

'Have they been executed?' asked the commander.

The soldier expelled a flurry of bubbles from his open beak. 'Using children as hosts was a wise decision. The humans had no stomach to eliminate them. They have been incarcerated. We have

222

yet to discover the location.'

'And the human who took your eye?'

'Alive, and still in the service of Yil Axo.'

'Fear not,' relayed the commander. 'The war goes well on Mars. The Basomor are all but defeated. Our troops have been inoculated. Upgraded war machines are being loaded into canisters. The second invasion will commence any day now. Our orders are to prepare.'

'And what will my role be?' transmitted the one-eyed soldier.

The commander revealed the small brass disc she had coiled within the wormish tip of one of her tentacles. 'I am going to select the strongest of the fishermen we hold captive. Your brainwaves will be harvested from you and etched onto this coin. It will be inserted into his brain by our surgeons. You will become him. And in doing so, you will become the assassin who puts an end to the interference by Yil Axo and his human cohort.'

The soldier's solitary eye blinked. His bloated body trembled as he spewed out a gush of bubbles on a guttural wave of deranged laughter. 'Revenge will be mine!'

'And this world will finally be ours,' joined the commander.

AUTHOR BIOGRAPHIES

S. B. Watson lives in Keizer, Oregon, with his wife, five children, three cats, and one dog. His stories have appeared in *Mystery Tribune*, *Punk Noir*, *Spinetingler*, and *Mystery Magazine*, as well as various anthologies including *The Black Beacon Book of Pirates* and Murderous Ink Press' *Crimeucopia – Through the Past Darkly*. For more information visit SBWatson.com, or find him on Twitter/X at https://sbwatsonmysteries.wixsite.com/my-site

Karen Bayly began writing as a child when she wrote soap operas for her dolls to perform under her creative direction. These days it's her biology PhD, research background, and general dismay at the way the world is going that informs her writing, a fusion of science fiction, horror, and fantasy. She lives in the outer suburbs of Sydney, Australia, with two cats, a guitar, and a ukulele. https://karenbayly.com

Cameron Trost is an author of mystery, suspense, horror, and post-apocalyptic fiction best known for his puzzles featuring Oscar Tremont, Investigator of the Strange and Inexplicable. He has written three novels, *Flicker*, *Letterbox*, and *The Tunnel Runner*, and three collections, *Oscar Tremont, Investigator of the Strange and Inexplicable*, *The Animal Inside*, and *Hoffman's Creeper and Other Disturbing Tales*. Originally from Brisbane, Australia, Cameron lives with his wife and two sons near Guérande in southern Brittany, between the rugged coast and treacherous marshlands. He is a registered heritage tour guide (guide-conférencier) and runs the independent publishing house, Black Beacon Books. He is also a lifetime member of the Australian Crime Writers Association. https://camerontrost.com

Diana Parrilla, born on March 17, 1994, in Barcelona, Spain, is a keen reader, using writing as a means to explore her imagination. With her degree in economics and masters in Japanese, she is always learning new languages. She shares her passion for anime and games on her YouTube channel through reviews, translations, and language learning tips. She is a passionate writer with a diverse range of interests. Her publications span various horror and speculative fiction genres, driven by her limitless imagination.
https://linktr.ee/buffyta17

David Turnbull is a member of the Clockhouse London group of genre writers. He writes mainly short fiction and has had numerous short stories published in magazines and anthologies. He has had stories read at live events such as Solstice Shorts, Liars League and Virtual Futures. He is the author of *HUSks, Maggie's House* and *The Dragon Breath Chronicles* as well the flash fiction anthology *Once Hundred Predictions*.
https://www.tumsh.co.uk

Below is a heartfelt message from all five authors:

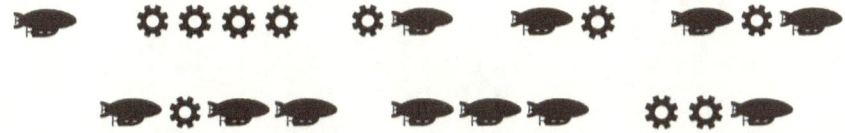

Also Available from Black Beacon Books

An edge-of-your-seat anthology of new fiction inspired by the classic films of Alfred Hitchcock, the Master of Suspense!

For news, reviews, competitions, author interviews, and exclusive excerpts

Visit our website
blackbeaconbooks.com

Like us on Facebook
facebook.com/BlackBeaconBooks

Join us on Twitter
@BlackBeacons

Find us on Instagram
instagram.com/blackbeaconbooks

Subscribe on Patreon
patreon.com/blackbeaconbooks

Discover all our Social Media Links
https://linktr.ee/blackbeaconbooks

www.ingramcontent.com/pod-product-compliance
Lightning Source LLC
Chambersburg PA
CBHW032116170626
46808CB00006B/1965